A Measure of Revenge

A Detective Pete Nazareth Novel

Hampton, Westbrook Publishing
2016

First Edition

Hampton, Westbrook Publishing
Princeton Junction, New Jersey

For all those who built America
one brick and one dream at a time.

A Measure of Revenge

A Detective Pete Nazareth Novel

R.H. Johnson

Here on my knee I vow to God above,

I'll never pause again, never stand still,

Till either death hath closed these eyes of mine

Or fortune given me measure of revenge.

William Shakespeare
Henry VI, Part III, Act 2, Scene 3

New York City . . . land of the free

Oh, please, let's just call it what it is: land of the freeloaders!

And you can spare me that Liberty Island nonsense about the world's wretched refuse yearning to be free. The filth now slithering onto America's shores yearns only to GET IT for free. **Gimme! Mine! More!** *Those are the first three words our newest refugees learn when they step onto our sacred soil, and those are the only words most of them will ever bother to learn, no matter how long they park their asses in America. They are content to speak their mumbo jumbo in homicidal ethnic neighborhoods where life is the same as it was back in the old country -- whatever desert, jungle, or shantytown that might have been -- only better. Here they get it all for free. Free food. Free medical. Free housing. Even free defense attorneys when they murder someone. Free, free, free! And they wouldn't know how to say "thank you" even if they wanted to.*

I am an expert on this subject. I watch them arrive day by day from every putrid alley and disease-ridden rainforest of every godforsaken Third World hellhole you can name. I see where they come from. I see what they do when they get here. I see them flushing my country down the toilet.

My grandparents came here as immigrants, true enough. But they worked for whatever they got. Yes, they worked until they were bent and broken by their quest for the American dream. They kept their kids in school and out of jail. They blended in, went to church, paid their taxes. They asked for no handouts and sure as hell got none.

And now the American dream is free for the asking. Slink off a ship in New York Harbor or crawl under a fence in Texas, and you win the lottery. Can you say **gimme**, **mine**, *and* **more**? *Ah, but someone pays for every handout. I am that someone. I work so that I can pay more taxes . . . so that my country can provide more handouts . . . so that another wave of Third World wretched refuse will want to join us.*

Enough! It must stop. It **will** *stop. This I swear.*

1.

At 4:23 a.m. on a chilly late-September morning, Ruthie Carlson walked alone on 44th Street in Times Square. She had spent the last ten hours tending bar at Otis B's, a hot after-hours club where the drinks were always top-shelf and the tips generous. A long but satisfying night in every way. She had cleared over $500, all of it off the books, and had set the hook in Bobby Timmons, the young stud who visited at least three times each week. Timmons had finally deciphered the message in her eyes, and they now planned to spend next weekend at his place in the Hamptons. But at the moment all she cared about was catching the 3 train at 42nd Street and collapsing in bed at her Brooklyn apartment.

She passed the old Paramount Building, a 33-story landmark built in 1927, and turned onto 7th Avenue. Ruthie hated the darkness and the lonely walk. In this city, she knew, the question was when, not whether, you confronted a really bad dude. When that happened, would someone come to her rescue . . . or just cut and run? Count on no help, she advised herself. Keep your eyes open, girl, and your thumb on the pepper spray canister.

After taking a dozen steps on 7th Avenue she spotted the homeless guy lying half on and half off the curb 20 feet ahead. A loud brain alarm sounded. She couldn't see exactly what he was up to in the dark, but he definitely wasn't sleeping. Maybe he was crouching, waiting for her to come within striking distance. She edged closer to the building, gripping the pepper spray in her right hand.

The guy was motionless, but something was off about his body position. Was he getting ready to lunge at her? Or was he throwing up in the gutter after a hard night with his Thunderbird wine? Either way, Ruthie wanted no part of him. She picked up her pace and prayed for a cop to come along. But, no, it was just the two of them -- a skittish, overtired bartender and a street guy up to no good.

She held her breath as she passed him and looked over her left shoulder to make sure he kept his distance. That's when she noticed the traffic light's bright red glow reflecting over the entire length of the guy's body. What the hell? She stopped at what she considered a safe distance and turned for a better view. At that moment a taxi drove past, and in its headlights she saw the figure for what it really was: a misshapen, lifeless heap that had been tossed against the curb. As she dialed 911 on her cell Ruthie realized that the entire body had been bound tightly in clear stretch wrap, a shining mummy. Whoever did this had added one final, brutal touch: a heavy plastic bag taped securely over the man's head.

Ten minutes later Officers John Donaghue and Mike D'Antoni took an even closer look at the victim. Olive skin. Twenty-five years or thirty years old. About six feet tall and rather thin. But two things stood out from the rest. With a red marker the killer had scrawled the letters DR on the dead man's forehead before suffocating him, then with a rubber stamp had applied the words RETURN TO SENDER all over the stretch wrap covering the body.

The two officers had no way of knowing that by the end of the year the RTS Killer would become one of the most feared criminals in New York City history.

2.

L.E.S. Pawn and Loan had stood in the shadow of the Manhattan Bridge since 1922, when Padraig and Aileen Driscoll founded the business after leaving Kinsale, Ireland, and settling in New York City. Paddy worked with the customers while Aileen managed the books, kept the shop looking neat, and raised two enormously energetic boys, Patrick and Liam. The "L.E.S." in the store's name was a tribute to its Lower East Side home, and in time L.E.S. Pawn and Loan became a valued neighborhood institution. When you fell on hard times, you went to see Paddy, not some bloated, cigar-smoking banker in fancy clothes. You were treated like family at L.E.S., whether you went in to sell your goods or, as was usually the case, simply to arrange a short-term loan when you needed cash. This was business as it had been done back in County Cork.

Eldest son Patrick was killed by German machine gun fire on June 6th, 1944 at Omaha Beach in Normandy, France. So it fell to Liam, the younger brother, to help his parents run the pawn shop as they grew old. After Padraig and Aileen died, Liam took over the L.E.S. reins with his young bride, Colleen. Together they made ends meet, but doing business grew more difficult year by year. They faced increased competition, much of it from pawn shops whose owners were more than happy to make a buck off dirty business. At the same time, the clientele grew rougher around the edges. After two beatings and three robberies, Liam began keeping a loaded shotgun behind the counter. Showing the weapon was usually enough to run troublemakers out the door, but one rainy March afternoon Liam blew the face off a knife-wielding robber who had spent more time in jail than out. Although the police ruled the shooting self-defense, Liam was never the same. Within a few years Liam and Colleen's son Ryan became the new proprietor of L.E.S. Pawn and Loan. Nearly 30 years later, Ryan Driscoll still managed to keep the place afloat -- and still ran a clean business, the way his parents and grandparents had taught him to do.

"Ryan, good morning to you." Jed Butler loped into the shop with his blue U.S. Postal Service satchel slung over his shoulder. "I've got some USDA Prime bills for you this morning, my man."

"You wait right there, J.B.," Driscoll smiled. "Let me get my gun from behind the counter."

"Oh, hell, in that case I'll take the bills over to your competition up on Pitt Street."

"Now you're talking. But if you have any checks in there, I'll gladly take them off your hands."

"Nope. I already deposited those in my retirement account. Gotta take care of number one, you know."

"I hear you, J.B. Just remember me when you buy that 200-foot yacht."

"I absolutely will, Ryan. I'll have the captain blow the whistle for you as we sail out of the harbor for France."

"Ah, a true friend."

"Go team!"

As Butler headed off to continue his morning rounds, Driscoll remembered when the two of them had first met. Scary long time ago it was. They had been freshmen together at Xaverian High School in Brooklyn, both busting their butts to earn a spot on the basketball team. Butler ended up starting at center, a 6-4, sky-walking star who averaged 23 points per game over his four-year career. The 5-10 Driscoll, on the other hand, had been a modest talent who played only well enough to ride the bench for four years. But during that time he had become good friends with Butler, the team's only black player, and they remained friends to this day. Friends or acquaintances? he wondered as he stirred a packet of sugar into his coffee. They didn't hang out together, since Driscoll was single and Butler now had a wife and four kids. And they no longer met in the schoolyard to shoot hoops the way they once had. Heck, they didn't even talk much anymore -- maybe a few words when Butler came by with the mail each day.

Still, J.B. was a keeper as far as Driscoll was concerned. A solid citizen who earned an honest living and did his best to keep his kids out of trouble in a city that was infected with trouble. So, yeah, they were friends . . . or at least something more than acquaintances.

Driscoll told himself they should get together again for a beer sometime. Good idea. You can't put these things off forever, he thought as he stared into the large two-way mirror behind the counter. He wasn't entirely pleased with what he saw: a 52-year-old guy with a thick middle, sagging jowls, and shoulders more rounded than they should be on a man his age. Thinning gray hair and a flushed complexion made him look 10 years older than he was, and his weight had ballooned to 193, up from 181 a year ago. Damn, 181 had been too much! J.B., meanwhile, looked as though he could still throw down a mean tomahawk dunk on the hardwood. Nah, J.B. looks better than he really is, Driscoll decided. All that walking with a satchel on his shoulder has probably screwed up his back and worn out his knees. Appearances can be deceiving.

A single door chime announced the arrival of a customer. Thirty-something business type in a suit, moving quickly and working hard to look important as he entered. Another Rolex Man, thought Driscoll. Looking to buy or sell? These guys never looked for short-term collateral loans. They considered such transactions beneath them. But they had no problem trying to unload something for more than it was worth, and they were always ready to fight for another 10 cents off the asking price.

"Good morning," Driscoll said as he walked out from behind the counter. "How can I help you today?"

"Yes, hi, I'm interested in selling a watch," the guy answered, "and a friend of mine told me this is a reputable store."

"Well, I'm glad to hear that. We get quite a few referrals," said Driscoll, who virtually never got referrals. "What kind of watch are you looking to sell?"

"A Rolex Submariner," he said as he raised the cuff of the left sleeve. "Great condition, paid about $15,000 for it." The guy didn't offer to remove the watch, and Driscoll didn't bother to ask. A three-second look told him that this was a complete waste of his time.

"How much are you hoping to get?"

"I know that Submariners can actually increase in value," the guy said as though he knew what he was talking about, "but I'd be satisfied to get something close to what I paid."

Driscoll had two styles: the let-'em-down-easy approach for nice folks who were really desperate for money, and the kiss-my-royal-ass approach for clowns who thought that a navy blue suit and button-down shirt magically transformed an asshole into a Wall Street deal-doer.

"This particular model -- two-tone stainless steel and 18k gold -- was manufactured in the early nineties," Driscoll began. "I don't know what they sold for back then, but today they're widely available for about $7,500 in good condition."

"No way in hell," the guy barked. "I've looked online, and I know that a watch like this sells for well over $10,000."

"Actually I was talking about a genuine Submariner of this vintage," Driscoll replied. "And the $7,500 is right on the money. That's the current market. For your watch, probably $85 since it's a knockoff."

The guy's face turned red, and his eyes bulged. Driscoll thought he might be having a heart attack.

"Knockoff my ass!" he screamed. "Where do you come off telling me shit like that?"

"Hey, if you're satisfied with the watch, I'm happy for you. But check this out. First, your second hand ticks. On a genuine Rolex the second hand glides -- it never, ever ticks. Second, some of the gold has flaked off your band, which means it's gold-plated. A genuine Rolex is never gold-plated. Never. And third, your watch has a skeleton dial, meaning you can see the watch's inner workings. How many Rolex watches have skeleton dials? Answer, none. So," Driscoll concluded, "either you're trying to rip me off with a fake watch or someone ripped you off big-time. Either way, I'm not interested. But thanks for stopping in."

Driscoll picked his opponents carefully, and he figured that he was safe pushing this one harder than usual. He outweighed him by about 40 pounds and could still handle himself if necessary. Besides, all he usually had to do with surly customers was mention the live video feed to his nonexistent security company. That always ended the unpleasantness.

"When I get back to my office," the guy told him, "the first call I make is to the City's consumer affairs office. Scam artists like you shouldn't be in business."

"And as soon as you get your ass out of my shop," Driscoll said as he pointed to the video camera mounted on the wall above the front door, "I'll send the police a copy of the video that you and I just made. Why don't you hold your watch up so they can see it?"

The guy took one look at the camera and headed for the sidewalk. Score one for the good guys, Driscoll thought.

3.

The last step in becoming a full member of the UT Blades was to hospitalize someone -- anyone at all -- in Downtown Manhattan during daylight. Whatever brain-dead gang elder had conceived of this requirement was probably serving life at Riker's Island now, but the younger punks honored the tradition. Members of the UT Blades -- UT as in Uptown -- devoted most of their time to dealing drugs, and a majority of the members had been arrested for multiple crimes ranging from pimping underage girls to armed robbery. But all of them would have been arrested for felony assault if they had been caught during their final initiation ritual: beating or stabbing a Downtown victim so badly that he or she needed to be taken away by ambulance. The gang's initiates rarely failed to deliver, and they almost never got caught.

All they needed was 15 seconds with a length of pipe or a knife before disappearing into the subway system like roaches skittering under a refrigerator. Would-be members were not allowed to use guns during "the Downtown," or DT, as this final test was known, because the assault was supposed to demonstrate the recruit's in-your-face manliness.

On a blustery early October afternoon two senior UT members, O.Z. and RexMan -- both of them grade-A bits of garbage by anyone's standards -- accompanied Kofi "Kool Fang" Rosario to the cemetery alongside Trinity Church on Broadway near Pine Street. The churchyard, a peaceful oasis of tended graves and lush trees that had just begun taking on some fall color, was an excellent spot for what the gang members had in mind. Throughout the day, but especially on pleasant afternoons, many Wall Street types in pinstriped suits and designer dresses strolled leisurely along the cemetery's walks on their way to or from lunch. So this was a perfect spot for targeting someone who would soon be in a hospital bed, ideally on life support. Kofi

Rosario figured he would improve his chances of joining the gang if he took out a captain of industry rather than some pizza delivery guy.

O.Z. and RexMan hung back by the cemetery's Broadway gate while Rosario positioned himself along the main churchyard walkway that connected Broadway and Trinity Place. He tried to look nonchalant for the two senior gang members, but his eyes hinted at the wild rush that came with being on the hunt in this exceedingly public place. His right hand was in the pocket of his loose NFL hoodie, closed tightly around the black epoxy handle of an Emerson combat knife with its stainless steel blade. The blade was open and ready for the young couple that approached from the Trinity side of the cemetery. Rosario knew that two swipes at each victim -- one at the neck, another at the midsection -- would leave them somewhere between dead and dying. Then he, O.Z., and RexMan would slip onto the 4 train right outside the cemetery and be on their way home.

Rosario stole a quick look at the couple. Well-dressed guy in his thirties, light hair, light skin, slender but not skinny. Nicely shaped young woman in a blue pant suit, deli bag in her right hand. Both jabbering away, clueless. Ready to go back to the office and make some more big bucks by screwing the little man, Rosario mused. Dicing these two rich assholes would be a pleasure. He looked over at his mentors, smiled, pulled his knife, and swung the blade as the couple came alongside of him.

A half second before the razor-edged steel reached his throat, NYPD Detective Pete Nazareth grabbed the attacker's wrist with his powerful left hand and twisted so viciously that O.Z. and RexMan heard the elbow snap from 10 paces away. As the knife fell to the ground, Nazareth drove his right palm into the punk's upper arm with lightning speed, breaking the humerus and ripping the shoulder out of its socket. Nazareth's counter-attack had lasted less than two seconds, but the agony was something the howling Rosario would remember for the rest of his life.

"Motherfucker," screamed O.Z. as he and RexMan raced toward their crippled friend. Both had serrated hunting knives out and ready for business. When O.Z. lunged for Detective Tara Gimble, she sidestepped the thrust, locked one hand onto his attacking arm, the other onto the front of his shirt, and used his momentum to swing him over her head and down onto the paved walk. His broken back and dislocated shoulder immediately took him out of play. RexMan, meanwhile, tried to drive his blade up and into Nazareth's gut. Long before the knife reached its target Nazareth had planted a ferocious sidekick on the guy's chest, stopping his heart, while blocking the attacking arm with both hands. By the time NYPD back-up and the EMT folks arrived, Nazareth had been able to get RexMan's heart beating again with nicely executed CPR. But all three gang members had to be carried out of Trinity Churchyard, and they would all endure long hospital stays before facing charges.

When the detectives got back to One Police Plaza they found that their two hot paninis were cold. But they inhaled them anyway. The exercise had made them powerfully hungry.

4.

Detective Pete Nazareth and his partner Detective Tara Gimble had spent most of the spring and summer trying to reel in a serial killer who had been targeting aged widows in the Metro New York area. After that they were immediately handed a high-profile case involving the CEO of one of the City's most prestigious investment firms. The guy's 53-year-old wife had been stabbed to death by his 28-year-old mistress, who apparently wanted to become the latest trophy wife for the 71-year-old businessman. Nazareth noticed some curious inconsistencies in the CEO's story, and after two weeks of digging he and Gimble successfully closed the case. The CEO had killed his wife, then staged the crime to implicate his mistress, thereby ridding himself of both women so he could take up with the 21-year-old of his dreams. "You can't make this stuff up," Nazareth remarked at the time.

The young detective was widely recognized as a rising star within the NYPD ranks. A 33-year-old Staten Island native, he earned a bachelor's degree in political science from Fordham University, where he was also a sub-four-minute miler and a standout black-belt competitor for the school's Taekwondo club. After college he served as a Marine Special Ops officer and won a Silver Star for combat action in Eastern Afghanistan. When not chasing down bad guys he spent much of his time training, either in his well-equipped home gym or at the Taekwondo training hall. Nazareth's Taekwondo workouts were almost exclusively three-on-one, heavy contact sparring with other black belts. He figured that if he could handle three highly trained fighters -- and he could -- he should be able to take on at least that many street punks. At 165 pounds and with body fat under 5%, he was a walking, talking secret weapon.

His partner, 31-year-old Tara Gimble, had similar glowing credentials. A soccer all-American at Stanford, where she majored in psychology, she was an expert marksman, a superb 5K competitor, and a judo black belt. After nine years on the force she had proved herself in a host of dangerous assignments, all of them handled beautifully. As the gang members at Trinity Church had learned, the 120 pounds that she carried on her 5-7 frame were street-ready at all times. No warm-up required.

Although they had worked together for only a few months following the shooting death of Nazareth's former partner, the two detectives were an impressive team. They both wanted the toughest cases. They both were willing to work around the clock when that's what the job required. And they both were ready to put their lives on the line if that's what it took to clean up New York City. Their passion to succeed was genetic -- something you either had or you didn't. Nazareth and Gimble had it in spades.

"Do you know you lost a button on your sport coat?" Gimble asked him after downing the last bite of her veggie panini.

He took a quick look at the blue blazer that hung on the back of his chair.

"Damn. Has that been missing all day?" he asked.

"No, just since it was sliced off by young Mr. Rosario's combat knife."

"No way."

"Yeah, way." She put her right fist on the table, opened it slowly, and showed Nazareth his button. "As you can see, the threads have been cleanly sliced by a stainless-steel blade."

Nazareth looked off into the distance while he replayed the attack in slow motion. He shook his head.

"Nope, the guy went for my throat. He never got near that button."

"He didn't, but the knife did." She flashed her cover-girl smile. "While you were snapping his arm in half, his knife was falling to the ground. It sliced the button off when it passed your large gut."

"Oh, wait a second," he said in mock outrage. "That's two counts of felonious verbal harassment. First you say the guy cut me, and then you accuse me of having a fat gut."

"No," she corrected him, "I didn't say he cut you. I said he cut your button off. And logic dictates that's because your gut was in the way."

Nazareth prepared to launch a verbal counterattack when Deputy Chief Ed Crawford walked into the conference room with his customary soggy, well-chewed cigar in one hand and a cup of rancid coffee in the other. The coffee, the two detectives assumed, had come from the vile electric pot that Crawford kept behind his desk. If you had suicide on your mind, Crawford's coffee was among the surest methods to be considered.

"Well, if it isn't my very own police brutalists," Crawford growled. It was his amiable growl, not the ferocious one. Only officers who had worked with him for a year or so could tell the difference.

"What's with the *brutal*, Chief?" Gimble asked him.

"Three minutes ago a buddy of mine at the *Daily News* called to tell me that the punk whose heart your partner stopped is claiming police brutality."

"You can't be serious," Nazareth said.

"When was the last time I walked all the way down here to make a joke?" Crawford asked.

"Right, never. So let me rephrase: there's no way in hell it was police brutality. It was plain old self-defense."

"Of course it was," said the chief, "and the Rev. Dr. Timothy Mellon has already given a statement to that effect. He's the rector at Trinity, and he caught the entire episode from his office window."

"Ah," said Nazareth. "In that case you came to see us for a different reason."

The chief gave Nazareth the cop stare and pointed his cigar at him.

"You must be a detective," he said soberly.

"Careful, chief," said Gimble. "That's awfully close to being a joke, and you don't want to ruin your reputation."

"Right, thank you. Let's keep that quiet, okay?"

"Sure thing, chief."

"But there's something on your mind," said Nazareth.

"Yep, the usual. Midtown South has gotten nowhere with a body that was dumped on 7th Avenue right near 42nd Street, and a very wealthy old lady called the mayor about it."

"She's related to the victim?" Gimble asked.

"Not at all," the chief replied. "She's a pain-in-the-ass old biddy who has nothing better to do than throw bricks at the NYPD, in this case complaining that she no longer feels safe walking the streets because there's a madman on the loose."

"She's a street-walker?" Nazareth smiled.

"Don't bust my chops, Pete. I hate getting messages from the mayor."

"That's because you hate the mayor."

"What's to like? But still, we've got a problem."

"In other words, Tara and I have a problem," said Nazareth.

"You read my mind, Detective. Come on down to my office," the chief said, "and I'll fill you in. I'm also buying the coffee."

"Okay if I jump out the window instead, Chief?" Nazareth asked.

"No, but you can kiss my fat ass if you want."

Gimble reached into her small purse as they began walking to the chief's office.

"Let me get my cell phone out so I can take a picture of that," she taunted.

5.

Two days after her sixteenth birthday Meryl Connolly and three of her friends took the 2 train from Midtown Manhattan to Brooklyn's Prospect Park. Their plan was to meet up with some of their classmates at a free Friday evening concert featuring several hot new bands from the Metro NY area. The last thing her mother had yelled to the girls as they left the apartment was, "And for God's sake stay together while you're there!" What she got in return was the customary, "Oh, Mom, please give us some credit, will you?"

Janette Connolly vividly remembered being young once, 16 even, so she understood why Meryl and her friends couldn't resist the lure of an outdoor concert on a sultry August evening. But that didn't mean she couldn't worry. She still had trouble imagining her little girl as a young woman, and the tag that daughter Meryl and husband Bobby had stuck on her was *clingy*, as in, "God, Mom, stop being so clingy," or, "C'mon, Janette, no 16-year-old needs a clingy mother." She couldn't help it though. You invest 16 years of your life in an only child, and you can't let go even when you know you should. The only family member who really seemed to understand was her brother Ryan, whose Manhattan pawn shop had introduced him to the kinds of unsavory characters that roam the streets nowadays. "Keep Meryl on a short leash for as long as you can," Ryan had told her years earlier, "because she'll be a magnet for every lowlife in the City before you know it."

By the time the girls reached Prospect Park at 8:30, night was falling and the crowd was enormous, so they had no chance of finding their other high school buddies. Even worse, they were stuck watching from back by the trees, about as far from the stage as one could get. They were still deliriously happy, though, because they were surrounded by music, kids, and the buzz of a perfect summer evening on the loose. The first band was pretty good, Meryl thought, but she was waiting for the next group. Johnny Zaga, one of the coolest guys in her high school, was lead guitarist for the J Street Reapers, a group that had cut a record six months ago. Although no one had yet heard "Blood Apocalypse" on the airways, everyone was sure it was destined to be a breakout hit by the end of the summer.

"I need to use the bathroom before the next band starts," Meryl told her friend Katie at 9:20.

"What?" Katie screamed, trying to be heard over the 100-decibel noise that pounded through immense, skull-crushing speakers.

"I need to use the bathroom!"

"You'll never get near the bathroom! Look at this crowd," she yelled.

"But I've got to."

Katie turned and pointed to the woods behind them.

"Trees, Meryl. Go back by the trees."

Meryl warily eyed the darkened shapes of the trees. She didn't feel like using the woods when a real bathroom was within reach, but she also didn't want to miss the full J Street Reapers set.

"Come with me," she said to Katie.

"Oh, give me a break, Meryl. It's like 20 feet away."

"Yeah, and it's also dark as hell, Katie. Come with me, okay?"

"I want to hear this next song."

"You'll hear it from the woods," Meryl complained. "You can probably hear it on the moon it's so loud."

"I'm not going now, Meryl. Just hold it."

Like this is what friends are for, Meryl told herself as she stalked off toward the woods. How much do I do for Katie? Everything, basically. And she can't spare two minutes for me? That's bullshit. It really is. She reached the trees, found a large oak to provide cover -- not that she needed cover in this blackness -- and squatted. After she finished and began pulling up her expensive distressed skinny jeans, the voice in the night said, "You like it in the woods, sugar?" She could barely see the five members of the Khyber Kill U gang, known in their Pakistani neighborhood simply as KKU. Meryl screamed for her friends, but the only people who could hear her over the throbbing music were the KKU members. And they didn't plan to rescue her.

The tallest guy put a knife to her throat. "Next time you scream, bitch, I hack your head off and leave it for the raccoons." They pushed and dragged her to one of the most heavily wooded areas of the park, not far beyond the ball fields, and assaulted her for the next 45 minutes. When they finally swaggered off, they left her naked on the ground, her hands and feet tightly bound with strips of denim cut from her designer jeans.

The next morning two police officers found a young girl who would never fully recover. She was alive . . . but in some ways dead. Part of her was gone forever, stolen by the unspeakable viciousness that followed New York City's gangs wherever they went. Bobby and Janette Connolly got a daughter back, but it was Meryl in name only. When Janette told her brother, Ryan Driscoll, what had happened, he cried inconsolably for nearly 30 minutes. A beautiful life ripped apart, he told himself, by the trash that keeps floating into New York Harbor every day of every year.

This is going to stop.

6.

A half hour before closing L.E.S. Pawn and Loan on a cool mid-October evening, Ryan Driscoll spotted the guy on the sidewalk peering nervously into the shop window. One of two things, Driscoll told himself. He's either looking to unload whatever it is he just stole, or he's planning to rob the place. Driscoll stepped closer to the Mossberg 500 tactical shotgun that he kept under the counter. Being robbed wasn't in his business plan. As the man walked into the shop, Driscoll lowered his right hand to the gun's stock.

"Hi, there," he said mildly. "How can I help you today?"

Dark-skinned guy about 6-2, maybe 25, thin but fit. He wore a long-sleeved Ralph Lauren shirt and designer jeans along with $200 Nike LeBron basketball shoes. Didn't seem like much of a threat as he walked confidently up to the counter.

"Hello, my name is Saliou Ba," he said in heavily accented English.

"I'm Ryan Driscoll. How can I help you, Mr. Ba?"

Ba looked over his shoulder, then reached into the left pocket of his jeans. Driscoll was ready to grab the shotgun when the guy produced a glittering princess-cut diamond engagement ring. If that thing is real, Driscoll thought, it's at least two carats and could be worth $20,000.

"I want to sell this," said Ba. He held the ring out for inspection.

Driscoll was no gemologist, but he knew enough to determine whether a diamond was real. He studied the huge stone with a jeweler's loupe and satisfied himself that he was holding a ring worth tens of thousands.

"Very nice, and very expensive," he said to Ba.

Ba simply nodded and grinned. I wonder whose throat you cut for this, Driscoll thought.

"Do you have a receipt?" Driscoll asked. "To prove that the ring is yours?"

Not in a million years would L.E.S. Pawn and Loan buy a ring that obviously had been stolen. Driscoll would lose whatever he had paid for it when the real owner showed up and the police confiscated the property. But he kept the conversation going until in halting English Ba slowly revealed the following: he had come to the U.S. from Senegal; he claimed to have found the ring in a park; and he had not told any friends about the ring because . . . well, because those friends would probably slit his throat for it.

Driscoll took a piece of note paper from his desk and wrote down a name, an address, and a time.

"You have a cell phone?" Driscoll asked him.

Ba produced a new iPhone from his right pocket. Ah, thought Driscoll, something else Mr. Ba must have found in a park. He took down Ba's phone number.

"Okay, look, I can't buy this unless you have proof of ownership. That's the law," he said solemnly. "But I have a business associate who specializes in high-quality merchandise of this sort, and I'm sure he would love to give you top dollar for the ring."

"How much you think he'll pay?"

"I'm not a jeweler, so I can't say for sure," Driscoll said, "but I'd say at least 10 grand. Maybe more."

Ba's eyes lit up. "You think that much?"

"Let me put it this way. If I could buy the ring from you, I'd probably offer $10,000 to start. But I can't buy it because I'm required to file reports that show proof of ownership. My associate will love it, though, and he always has buyers for something as nice as this."

"And he will not need, uh, proof of ownership?"

"If you walk in with the ring," Driscoll winked, "you're the owner as far as he's concerned. He runs a very private business. But this is important. He only works with people who are referred to him by an associate like me. Do not try to bring anyone else to him, because if you do, he will not do business with either of you. You understand?"

"Yes, of course. No one knows I have this ring."

"That's great. Here's what you do. Stand on the sidewalk at this address on East 14th Street at 9:00 tomorrow night. When you are

R.H. Johnson

there, Mr. Adolphus Fleischer will call you on your cell phone and meet you a block or two away from this spot."

"This address, it is his store?"

"No. It's where you wait to hear from him. He needs to make sure there are no police around when he meets you. This is for your protection as well as his. If it's safe to do business, he'll know. If he sees police, he won't call you. So at 9:10 you can walk away and go home. But if everything is okay, he will call on your cell phone and tell you how to get to his shop. If he likes what he sees," Driscoll offered, "he'll pay cash, all fifties. You might want to bring a gym bag, because that's a lot of bills."

"I love lots of bills," Ba grinned.

"Well, Mr. Fleischer has the bills because he sells to very wealthy people who like bargains. You understand?" Ba nodded. "And here's the best part. Once you work with him, you're on his list. So you can keep bringing him things as long as it's high-quality stuff."

"So we become partners?"

"Exactly. And he's the best partner you can have in New York City."

"This is very good."

"This is very good for all of us, my friend. I'll call and let him know to meet you tomorrow night."

"I cannot wait."

7.

Nazareth thumbed through a folder of 8x10 crime-scene photos as he and Gimble stood at the corner of 44th Street and 7th Avenue, where Rafael Tejera's body had been dumped at the curb in late September. At this point they had little more than the victim's name, the address of his tiny studio apartment, and a few details about his job. And those facts had simply walked in the door when Tejera's girlfriend filed the missing-person report a few days earlier. Nazareth hated getting put on this case before the guys in Midtown South had been given a fair chance to solve it themselves, but things always went ass-backwards whenever the mayor's office got involved. So the young detective kept the grumbling inside his head. Focus on the police work, he told himself, and let the mayor focus on his reelection campaign.

"Are you picking up on anything, Pete?" Gimble asked him.

"Tough to say. This is the problem with getting pulled into a case that's acouple weeks old," he said. "Any evidence that might have been on the sidewalk or the street is probably long gone, so we're pretty much left with these photos and the statements by the two cops who wrote this up -- and possibly a couple of useful points from the ME. I like seeing everything with my own eyes right after it happened."

"The detectives who were taken off the case assumed it was gang retaliation. Is that not what you're thinking?"

He shook his head as he examined one of the more graphic photos of the victim's body. "I don't buy that at all," he told her. "The guy's girlfriend had been with him almost since the day he moved here from the Dominican Republic a year ago, and she's squeaky clean. No way the secretary to some big New York City banker is hooked up with a gangbanger. Plus she said the guy broke his butt at some Downtown printing shop. You don't put in 12-hour days if you're flying gang colors."

"He could have owed money to the wrong people," she offered.

"Yeah, that's always a possibility, but if the preliminary information is accurate, Tejera earned a pretty good salary, paid his rent on time, and had a little cash in the bank. Could he have had a big gambling debt? Sure. But that doesn't fit with everything else we have on him."

Something about the photo in his hand had grabbed Nazareth's full attention. He walked down 7th Avenue toward the spot where Tejera's body had lain, knelt at the curb, and studied both the pavement and the sidewalk.

"When's the last time we had rain?" he asked.

"Serious rain instead of a few drops? Mid-September, I guess. Why?"

"Could be nothing," he said as he stood up and examined the photo again. "But in this photo it looks as though some of the plastic that the guy was wrapped in had been worn down. See here? And if you get down and take a close look at the street you'll see there are tiny bits of plastic stuck to the rough cement right next to the curb."

"Same plastic?"

"Anyone's guess," he said. "But if we haven't had any heavy rain lately, this could be plastic from the vic's body. And if it is, I'd say the guy wasn't just dropped here. He was tossed from a car moving at relatively high speed. The body skidded along 7th Avenue, which explains how the plastic got worn down, and slammed into the curb. That fits with the ME's report of major post-mortem damage to the right shoulder and rib cage. If you hit the curb at 30 or 40 miles an hour, you get banged up. Even if you're already dead."

"Okay, so in that case the killer had an accomplice," Gimble reasoned. "One guy to drive, the other to dump the body from the back of the car."

"That's the likeliest explanation," Nazareth agreed, "but let's keep an open mind on that. When you stage a murder as odd as this one -- victim wrapped up like a damn mummy in plastic -- do you really want a partner? Ritualistic murders tend to be committed by loners, genuine sickos who aren't going to find very many like-minded buddies who are willing to kill people. Too risky to have an accomplice. Much safer to work alone."

"How do you toss a body from the back seat while you're driving?" she asked. "Even if the body was in the front seat, how does the driver lean over, open the door, shove the body out, and close the door? I have trouble seeing that."

"Agreed. It couldn't have happened like that, which is why I want to keep an open mind. It's probably what you said: two bad guys, one in front, one in back. But it still feels off to me."

"I'll tell you what feels off to me," Gimble said. "Even at 3:00 or 4:00 in the morning, this seems like a pretty stupid place to dump a body. Times Square, Broadway, blinking lights, you name it. Why not some side street off 11th Avenue?"

"Good question," Nazareth nodded. "The killer obviously wanted to make a statement. That's why he wrapped the body and stamped RETURN TO SENDER all over it. But if that was the only statement he wanted to make, he didn't need to leave the vic in one of the City's busiest areas. So my gut tells me there's something else he's trying to say."

"It's possible the killer was sending a message to one of the businesses along here," Gimble said. "Restaurants, theaters, banks, ABC TV, Hard Rock Cafe, whatever. Maybe Tejera was connected somehow."

"That would make sense. However he managed to get the body out of the car -- and I'm still not sure how that happened -- the killer wouldn't have been able to hit the spot with pinpoint accuracy. So if he was sending a message to someone along this strip, it could have been a business on either side of where the body was found." Nazareth stood quietly for a moment, lost in thought. "Actually we need to consider both sides of the street because 7th Avenue is one way south. So it's possible he was targeting someone or something on the opposite side of 7th."

"Of course, that assumes the killer was acting alone. A partner could have shoved the body out on the driver's side."

"I'm ready to scratch the idea of a partner," Nazareth told her. "I don't think anyone is dumb enough to bring someone else in on murder this bizarre. This guy has an axe to grind. There's something very personal about the way this was staged, and he invested a lot of time and effort into killing Tejera. We need to understand the message behind this RETURN TO SENDER business. Once we do that we can start making some real progress."

8.

At 8:54 p.m. Ba stood in a steady rain outside the closed deli on 14th Street where Ryan Driscoll had told him to wait for a phone call from Adolphus Fleischer. Driscoll seemed like an okay guy, Ba thought, but the proof would be in leaving Manhattan tonight with at least $10,000 in his Nike sports bag. Hey, probably more than $10,000. Driscoll had said "at least $10,000," hadn't he? That meant the ring could fetch an even higher price. Ba wondered how he could negotiate the best price when he didn't know what the ring was actually worth, so he decided that he would offer it at $15,000 and come down to $10,000 if necessary. Obviously Driscoll knew more about the value of hot merchandise than Ba did, so $10,000 sounded good for a ring stolen in a Midtown robbery. A few more $10,000 rings, Ba told himself, and he could live like a king back in Senegal.

He checked his cell for the time. As the numbers changed from 8:59 to 9:00, the phone began playing the funky African-drum ringtone that Ba considered one of the coolest sounds he'd ever heard. So much big music from such a little box.

"This is Ba," he said softly.

"Good evening, Mr. Ba," the voice responded confidently and clearly, the way a businessman of some stature should. "I'm Adolphus Fleischer, and I am very glad to meet you."

"I am glad to meet you too."

"I have been watching the street since 8:30. I know the faces of all the undercover officers who work around here, and I am pleased to say that none of them is here tonight. So you and I are free to do some big business."

Ba smiled as he tightened his grip on the gym bag. Pretty soon, he thought, this bag will be bulging with $50 bills.

"I look forward to doing big business with you." Ba looked around to see if he could spot the man speaking with him, but almost everyone on the street was talking on a cell phone. He had no way of knowing which one might be Fleischer.

"Good. I'm going to give you the address of the office where I do my private business. Do not write this down. Memorize it." After Ba had repeated the address twice, Fleischer said, "Now this is extremely important, Mr. Ba. As soon as we finish talking you must turn your phone off so that we can be absolutely sure no one is tracking you. It's always best to be extra careful, you know. So each time we do business together we will be as careful as possible."

"I agree completely," Ba grinned. But after tonight, he thought, you will be doing business only with the undertaker.

Ba's basketball shoes were soaked through by the time he had walked five blocks east and one down to 13th Street. As he reached the basement address a voice behind him said, "We meet again, my friend." Ba turned to find Ryan Driscoll smiling from under a large black golf umbrella.

"It is you!" Ba said, unable to mask his surprise.

"Yes it is. As you now can see, I have two businesses. One that operates according to police rules, and another that operates according to my rules."

"Yes, I understand. This is wonderful. I am pleased that you can buy my ring after all."

"Well, let's go do business." He politely allowed Ba to go down the stairs ahead of him. "The door is open," he said. "Let's get out of this rain."

As Ba entered he saw only the light from what appeared to be an office at the far end of a long, dark room. After taking only three steps he triggered the alarm on the walk-through metal detector that Driscoll had installed a few feet inside the front door.

"Carrying a weapon, are you, Mr. Ba?" Driscoll said.

Ba turned quickly and reached for his right pocket, but Driscoll had his Glock 20 pointed at Ba's chest.

"Put your right hand in the air," Driscoll ordered, "and then reach across with your left and remove the gun from your pocket. Very slowly. Yes. Perfect. Now throw it to the side. Excellent, Ba. Now I don't have to kill you."

"I brought the gun in case there was trouble," Ba lied. "Let's do business now."

"Yes, let's do business. Please, Ba, walk straight ahead to my office, have a seat, and we can do our business there."

Ba walked through the shadows and entered the small box of an office. He sat in the plastic folding chair alongside the cheap plastic table. On the table were a granola bar, a small plastic bottle of water, and a plastic bucket. A 100-watt ceiling light gave the room a stark, merciless feel. Driscoll remained at the doorway.

"So tell me," Driscoll said from the doorway, "what did you have planned for tonight? Were you going to kill me and leave with the ring as well as my money?"

"No, I . . ."

"If you lie to me," he grinned, "I will gouge your eyeballs out with a rusty spoon. Do I make myself clear?"

"Yes, I understand," Ba whimpered.

"So you came here to kill me, Ba?"

"No, I came only to do business with you. I brought the gun to protect myself on the way home."

Driscoll grinned. "Why don't I believe you? Is it because you're lying about the gun the same way you lied about finding the ring? Tell me, Ba, where did you get the ring? And if you tell me you found it in a park, I'll put a bullet in your head."

Ba hesitated, then decided not to risk having his head blown off. "I found it on a woman's hand," he said, his voice cracking.

"And this nice woman simply took it off and gave it to you as a gift?"

"No," he said in halting tones, "because I put the gun to her chest."

"The same gun you brought with you tonight?"

"Yes, the same one."

"And tell me, Ba. Did you shoot her anyway?"

"No, I did not."

"But you did something, didn't you?"

Ba wanted to lie and say he hadn't harmed the woman. But what if Driscoll already knew? Is that what this was all about? Was the woman Driscoll's wife or girlfriend?

"I hit her with the gun."

"Ah, of course you did. Good man for not lying to me. And where did you hit her, Ba?"

"In the face."

"And did you hit her only once?"

Ba was trembling. "No, more than once."

"How many times?"

"I didn't count."

"A lot, though?"

"Yes, a lot. Mr. Driscoll, please keep the ring. I give it to you."

"Okay, slide it to me on the floor." Ba did so immediately. "Thank you for this fine gift, Ba. Now tell me, when you were finished hitting the woman, was she able to walk?"

"I gave you the ring . . . ."

"Answer my question, Ba, or I will splash your brain all over the walls."

"No," he squealed. "She could not walk."

"So you hit her just for fun?"

"Not for fun," he stammered. "So that she wouldn't be able to call the police."

"Because she had seen your face, right? You were afraid she would be able to identify you."

"Yes."

"That was smart, Ba. Always get rid of victims who can identify you." Driscoll slammed the door, locking his quarry in a room that had been carefully and lovingly built for precisely this purpose. "Always get rid of them."

9.

Nazareth and Gimble sat across from each other at the long conference table where over the past several months they had spent what seemed like an eternity. Once again they confronted a tangle of 8x10 photos, police reports, and notes, this time in pursuit of Rafael Tejera's killer. For two days they had visited every business along 7th Avenue near the crime scene, hoping that someone would recognize Tejera. But after a few false IDs that had wasted valuable time, they were still essentially nowhere with the case.

Their luck began to change with a brief phone call from the ME's office. Tejera's toxicology results were finally complete, and the report showed a high concentration of flunitrazepam in his system. Nazareth was obviously excited by the news.

"Flunitrazepam?" Gimble said.

"Yeah, ME-speak for Rohypnol, aka America's favorite date-rape drug. About ten times more powerful than Valium," he said. "In this case it was used to put the victim out while the killer wrapped the poor guy in plastic. If Tejera woke up before the plastic bag was placed over his head, he had a really nasty ending. For his sake I hope he was already gone by the time that happened."

"Can't argue with that," she said. "But I'm not sure it really matters whether he was drugged or hit over the head. Either way he ends up dead in a gutter."

"Amen. But this gives us an extremely useful insight into the killer's mind. This is a guy who values process. If you whack someone in the head with a baseball bat or a tire iron, you put the guy down. Brutally effective and fast, right? Putting Tejera down with Rohypnol, on the other hand, tells me two things about the murderer. First, for some reason he didn't want a body that was battered and bloody. Second, he's a meticulous planner. We already suspected that from the way the body was prepped -- the wrapping plastic, the RETURN TO SENDER message, and possibly even the location. But now we know he went to the trouble of getting his hands on an illegal drug he could administer in what obviously was a highly effective manner."

"No spur-of-the-moment activity. Everything carefully planned. So once again we find ourselves tracking a guy who's smart as well as homicidal."

"Afraid so," he nodded. "Hey, where's the missing-person report that Tejera's girlfriend filed?"

They scoured the conference table and eventually found the report buried under several crime-scene photos. Nazareth read the entire report front to back, after which he reversed and examined the words backwards. This was a quirk of his. Claimed it helped him notice details that he might overlook in a quick reading. Toward the middle of his second reading the word *Dominican* popped out. He had breezed past the word earlier, but this time it caught his attention.

"Dominican." He repeated the words several times. "The building on the corner of 44th and 7th, where the body was dumped, that's a landmark, right? The Paramount Building."

"Sounds right."

"Okay, listen. This guy is into process. He's staging everything for a purpose. So I seriously doubt that he would pick either a random victim or location. Is your laptop turned on?"

"Did the sun come up this morning?"

"All right, what's the address for the Paramount Building?"

Gimble typed in the name, hit ENTER, and said, "1501 Broadway."

"Good. Search Google Maps for *1501 Broadway, NYC, Dominican*. See if anything comes up."

Twenty seconds later Gimble looked up from the screen, gave Nazareth a confused look, and said, "How the hell do you do that?"

"Do what?"

"You really don't know?" she asked.

"You've lost me, Tara."

"Consulado Dominicano en Nueva York."

"Are you serious? The Dominican consulate is in the Paramount Building?"

"Bingo. Are you suddenly psychic?"

"Hell, no. But I'm definitely excited. We now know we're after a hate killer. He giftwraps a Dominican victim, stamps the body RETURN TO SENDER, and dumps the body outside the Dominican Consulate."

"And the big DR he wrote on the guy's forehead was the address. Dominican Republic."

"So now we're racing the clock."

"Because?"

"Because I'd be willing to bet the Dominican Republic is only the first country that's going to get the same kind of package. We've got a really sick puppy on our hands."

10.

If Driscoll stood perfectly still, held his breath, and listened hard, he could hear Ba screaming. The safe room that he had built here in the basement on 13th Street was a masterpiece, he had to admit -- a hand-crafted work of art that justified the months he had devoted to its completion. His first step had been to rent a cheap first-floor apartment that came with its own mildew-ridden basement. He had no plans to use the apartment, but this way no one in the building would hear the noise from his basement construction zone.

First he had assembled the 8'x8' welded-wire security cage with its steel roof. The components had set him back $1,500, but his accountant would have no problem writing that off as a business expense for L.E.S. Pawn and Loan's "alternate storage facility." He needed nearly two weeks to construct the cage, partly because he worked alone but mainly because he restricted his time on 13th Street to evenings. After all, he didn't need any prying neighbors stopping by for meaningless chitchat.

Once he had the security cage in place he got serious about noise suppression. His careful plan to rid New York City of its undesirables would get nowhere, of course, if people on the sidewalk could hear captives screaming in his basement. So he enclosed the safe room's walls and ceiling in thick, top-of-the-line soundboard. After that came a layer of drywall, followed by one more layer of soundboard. Soundproofing didn't get much more serious than this.

Next he designed two small breaks in the safe room's heavy shell. The first was a six-inch-square bulletproof polycarbonate window so that he could observe his prisoners. The second was a four-inch diameter circle cut into the sliding steel door, enabling him to pass small objects into the room. After rigging the hole with electrified razor wire, he was certain that whoever was in the room would not be able to expand the opening in order to escape or call for help. As an added security measure, he bolted a small steel access door over the hole and secured it to the soundproofed shell. By the time the project was finished Driscoll believed that he could stage World War III in this room without bothering anyone in the building or on the street.

The room had fulfilled all of its potential when Rafael Tejera became its first resident.

Now it was Ba's turn.

11.

Alejandro Abreu, the Dominican Republic's Consul General in New York City, had never heard of Rafael Tejera until Nazareth and Gimble put the file on his desk at 1501 Broadway. After they briefed Abreu on the suspected hate crime, he called his secretary into his office and asked her to show Tejera's photo to every member of the consulate staff while the detectives waited.

"You think this madman is sending a message to all Dominicans in New York City?" he asked as he studied the crime-scene photo showing Tejera's body stamped all over with the words RETURN TO SENDER.

"It's either that or a remarkable coincidence," Nazareth answered. "We weren't sure what the RETURN TO SENDER message meant until we linked Mr. Tejera to your consulate. In that context it makes perfect sense. I believe we're dealing with someone who has a serious problem with Dominicans and possibly other immigrant populations in Manhattan."

"What kind of problem are you talking about?" Abreu asked.

Nazareth deferred to Gimble because of her psych degree from Stanford.

"It's possible the killer was actually harmed in some way by a Dominican immigrant," she explained. "He or a member of his family may have been robbed, let's say. That might be enough to set someone off. If his issue is specific to Dominicans, I'd say there's a good chance he'll go after another Dominican victim."

"And what can we possibly do to prevent that?" Abreu asked, obviously alarmed by the prospect. "Today there are nearly 800,000 Dominicans living in all of New York City. We cannot possibly know who this killer might go after next."

"I think you've touched on the second possibility," Gimble continued. "There are 800,000 Dominicans in the City, but there are millions of immigrants from all over the world living here. It's possible we've got a killer who hates immigrants in general. It wouldn't be at all unusual to find that we're dealing with a disturbed individual who blames his shortcomings or failures on everyone but himself. Lashing out at others is a lot more palatable for some people than accepting responsibility for their failures."

Abreu's secretary returned to the office with Tejera's photo. She had met with every member of the consulate's staff, and no one recognized the victim.

"So what would you like from me, detectives?" Abreu asked.

"For the moment," Nazareth answered, "it would be helpful if you asked members of your staff to stay alert for anything that might relate to this incident. For example, if someone remembers hearing about neighborhood disputes, or threats, or physical harm being done, please get word to me or Detective Gimble. I wish I could be more specific, but we're very early in this investigation. It's possible that we're reading the facts all wrong, Mr. Abreu, and that this really is nothing more than a coincidence. But I doubt that."

"I doubt that as well, Detective." He handed the crime-scene photo to Nazareth. "This is a terrible thing to do to another human being, and I fear he will do it again."

Nazareth nodded. "And I fear you're right."

As they stepped onto 44th Street Gimble said, "Abreu seemed like a pretty straight-up guy. Very polished, classy."

"You obviously like those $10,000 suits, Tara," he smiled.

"That too."

"Well, it's no surprise that Abreu is a quality individual. I can't imagine any country sending a guy here unless he's a star. The first team always plays in New York City, Tara."

"I suppose. Anyway, it was a real kick to meet my first Consul General."

Nazareth forced a half smile. "I doubt he was your last."

12.

The next night shortly after 10:00 Driscoll parked his white van outside the 13th Street apartment, locked the doors, and went in to check on Ba. When he looked through the safe room's small security window he found Ba sound asleep at the plastic table, head resting on his folded arms. The granola bar wrapper and empty water bottle had been tossed to the floor, and the plastic bucket was now in the room's far corner, a makeshift toilet. All good, thought Driscoll, as he flicked on a dim overhead basement light.

He walked over to the heavy duty hand truck and made sure the tires were adequately inflated. Perfect. Next he slipped the top off a large corrugated box that had once held a treadmill and removed his equipment: a hefty roll of 90-gauge stretch wrap measuring 18 inches by 1,500 yards; several rolls of clear two-mil industrial adhesive tape; a large plastic bag; a self-inking RETURN TO SENDER stamp; and a box of markers in assorted colors. Finally, from the pocket of his oversized sweatshirt he took another granola bar and a plastic bottle of iced tea in which he had dissolved enough Rohypnol to put Ba down for at least an hour or two.

He walked back to the safe room, opened the small access door, and shouted, "Time to rise and shine, Ba."

It took Ba a few moments to figure out where he was. Then he yelled, "Please let me out. I'm starving and thirsty, and I have done nothing wrong!"

"You've done nothing wrong?" Driscoll snarled through the access door. "How about destroying New York City? Doesn't that count? Three million of this City's residents were born in another country. Did you know that, Ba? Forty percent of the total! It makes me want to vomit. You all come here to rob, murder, and rape for a living. You take everything America has to offer but give nothing back. And even while you're sucking the place dry you jabber about how much you miss whatever cesspool you came from -- your so-called homeland. You hate America, but you take and take and take."

"No, I love America!" Ba cried. "Please let me go. I promise I will tell no one about you."

"I'll make you a deal, Ba. If you behave yourself tonight and do exactly as I say, I will set you free. But if you make trouble for me, I will shoot you between your eyes."

"I will do whatever you say," Ba said meekly.

"Good. Take these." He dropped the granola bar and the iced tea into the room. "I'll be back."

He watched from the security window as Ba sucked down the iced tea and devoured the granola bar. Then Driscoll prepared for the evening's work. He moved the hand truck and the empty treadmill box close to the front door, laid out the stretch wrap and adhesive tape, and tested the RETURN TO SENDER stamp on the inside of the box to make sure it was properly inked. After that he sat on the floor and rested his head against the cinder-block wall. Nothing to do but wait now.

A half hour later when he peered through the safe room's security window he was pleased to see Ba lying motionless on the floor. Gun drawn, he entered the room and applied a couple of hard kicks to Ba's legs. No reaction. It would be hours before the drug wore off, and by that time his prisoner would be long past caring. He dragged Ba over to the box by the front door and meticulously began tightly wrapping him in layer after layer of the heavy stretch tape from his neck to the soles of his feet. Finally he rolled Ba into the box and applied the RETURN TO SENDER stamp wherever he thought it might be readily noticed by whoever found the body.

"I wish you and I could have a final conversation, Ba," Driscoll said as he worked, "but I'd be wasting my breath anyway, wouldn't I? I can't trust anything you say. I, on the other hand, am a man of my word. I told you I'd set you free, and I will. You'll be free of everything, my African friend. You can trust me on that."

With a neon-red marker Driscoll printed the letters SN on Ba's forehead before applying the clear plastic bag and taping it securely around his neck. For the next few minutes, while the bag did its deadly work, he sat against the wall and enjoyed a buttered corn muffin and small thermos of black coffee that he had brought with him. He would need all of his energy for the next part of tonight's ritual. Ridding New York City of its vermin was hard work, but Driscoll felt up to it.

13.

As they drove away from the Dominican Consulate on Broadway, Nazareth was once again alone inside his head. His partner had learned early in their time together that it was best not to bother him when he got like this, because very often his silence led to a breakthrough idea. So Gimble wasn't surprised when he said, "Let's take a little side trip to The Heights."

"I'm guessing that would be Washington Heights, as in Little Dominican Republic?"

"Si, señorita bonita. Vamonos."

"Bonita am I?" she smiled.

"What, you speak Spanish now?"

"No, but I understand *bonita.*"

"It's a fish, sort of like a tuna," he grinned.

"No, that would be *bonito. Señorita bonita* most definitely means *pretty lady.*"

"Well, there's nothing wrong with having a pretty lady for a partner, is there?"

"Absolutely not, mi amigo guapo."

"Fat man?" he cried in mock anger.

"No, my handsome friend," she corrected, "but don't let it go to your head."

Twenty minutes later, at the corner of Broadway and 175th Street, the detectives found themselves in a country within a country. Little Dominican Republic was for the most part a cozy, well-kept neighborhood of ethnic shops, brick apartment buildings, and a lot more trees than Downtown. Almost all the first-story windows had either steel bars or cages over them, evidence that they were still in New York City. But the joyous beat of Latin music echoed from cars and open apartment windows, and the folks who sat on cement stairways passing time with each other were obviously delighted with the autumn afternoon. Many of the buildings had a glistening pearl-gray, freshly scrubbed look to them. Very little graffiti, the detectives noticed. Just a few elegant murals painted here and there, another clear sign of the great pride that residents of The Heights took in their neighborhood.

Nazareth double-parked in front of a red-brick apartment building where six young men in their late teens and early twenties sat on the steps nursing bottles of Presidente beer. As Nazareth and Gimble walked up to the group, the largest guy -- a handsome, 6-4 body builder with flowing dark hair -- smiled broadly and said, "Buy you a beer, detectives?"

Nazareth grinned and began patting down his chest with both hands. "Did I forget to take my nametag off?"

"You don't need no nametag, bro'. The car said it all. The way you two look confirmed it, that's all."

"Never heard of Presidente," Nazareth said as he eyed the beer bottles.

"Straight from the homeland, man. You drink this, you stop drinking Bud Light and all that other crap," the guy told him. "First one's on me."

"Let me make sure my partner won't report me," Nazareth said.

"Hey, I'd never stop a man from trying his first Presidente," Gimble said. "I'll be the designated driver."

"There you go, Detective," the guy said as he flicked the top off a bottle and handed it to Nazareth. "One taste of this, and you'll be buying a ticket for the Dominican Republic."

Nazareth took a long pull from the bottle, gave his new friend a thumbs-up, and cracked, "Now I can arrest you for bribing an officer."

"Hey, bro', these guys'll swear you pulled a gun on me and stole my beer."

"All right, in that case we'll call it even. Excellent beer. Thank you. Pete Nazareth," he said as he extended his hand, "and Detective Tara Gimble."

"Luis Castillo, detective. Nice to meet you both. But let me guess," he said. "You didn't come here because you wanted to taste your first Presidente, did you?"

"Actually he did," Gimble joked, "but I'm trying to find someone who recognizes this guy." She handed Castillo the photo. "His name is

Rafael Tejera. Anyone know him?" The guys on the steps took turns studying the photo, but no one had seen the face.

"He on your Most Wanted list?"

Gimble shook her head and explained how the guy had been dumped on 7th Avenue in Times Square. Without mentioning Nazareth's theory on the motive, she told the men that she and Nazareth were trying to locate anyone who had been involved in an altercation with Dominicans recently and might have mistaken Tejera as a combatant.

"If by *altercation* you mean someone got his ass kicked up here," Castillo said, "yeah, that happens every time someone comes to The Heights looking for trouble. If you hang at the clubs or restaurants, everything's cool. But if you look for trouble, you find it."

"Especially if you mess with CF," said one of the others. "That's Cuatro Fantasmas."

"Four ghosts," Gimble translated.

"You got it," said Castillo. "It's a very angry local gang named after the four dudes who started it. There's over a hundred of them now, and they do their own sort of policing in The Heights, you know? Somebody screws with them, these guys do the rest."

Nazareth set the bottle down with a little more than half the beer left in it. "If someone had a run-in with CF," he asked, "is there a particular neighborhood where that might happen?"

"Oh, yeah. Try six blocks north and three east. But if you go there, Detective, stay in the car, because those guys won't offer you a Presidente, believe me."

"I believe you, Luis, and I appreciate it. I also appreciate the beer. Can't finish it right now, but I owe you one." Nazareth and Castillo shook hands again before the detectives drove off into the late-afternoon sunshine.

"So those were the good guys," Gimble offered, "and now we visit the not-so-good guys."

"Might as well since we're here."

"And how did you really like the Presidente?"

"Compared to Brooklyn Lager?" he said. "Not great."

"How about we keep the results of your taste test secret until we leave here?"

"Si, señorita. Whatever you say."

The detectives knew that even a pristine neighborhood like Washington Heights, which happened to be rated as one of the safest communities in New York City, must have its war zone. And that's what they found after they drove six blocks north and three east.

"Oh, my God!" They said the same words at the same time, then laughed.

"Great minds think alike, Tara. And I guess we're thinking we've turned onto the road to hell."

"You've got that right. If this is what Cuatro Fantasmas is doing for Little Dominican Republic, I think Luis Castillo and his friends should come up here and clean house."

The first thing the detectives saw was the virtually uninterrupted scrawl of spray paint that ran from one end of the block to the other. This was menacing gang graffiti, quite unlike the charming murals they had admired only a few blocks away. The most common word seemed to be *muerte*, or death, which repeated in a variety of Spanish phrases that apparently encouraged strangers to stay far away from CF's turf.

On both sides of the street they noticed derelict late-model cars whose wheels had been removed. Each car's windows had been smashed, most likely with a sledgehammer or a serious length of steel pipe, and all but one had been covered with raging graffiti. The lone exception was a Honda Accord that had been set ablaze and was now a charred hulk.

Gimble seemed baffled by the trashed vehicles. "What the hell happened here? Gang war?"

"Doubtful," Nazareth replied. "The owners of these cars probably live on the block and made the regrettable mistake of calling the police on the CF assholes. This is how neighborhoods collapse, Tara. The good people learn that they better keep their mouths shut, or bad things happen to them."

"Like their cars get destroyed?"

"Or much worse, believe me."

The street was littered with broken glass and torn garbage bags whose contents now attracted flocks of hungry gulls. One of the flocks took to the sky as a beer bottle slammed onto the pavement a few feet ahead of the unmarked NYPD cruiser. Nazareth looked to his right and saw a group of five gangbangers lounging on the steps of a rundown apartment building and passing a joint among them. One of the punks was laughing hysterically and fist-bumping the Neanderthal to his left.

"Stay right here and call for backup if things get ugly," Nazareth said. "I may have to put my foot down Laughing Boy's throat."

"Let's make the call first, Pete, so that I can go out there with you," she argued.

"No, we can't call in backup just because some asshole tossed a bottle at us."

"Fine, then let it go, Pete. No harm, no foul."

"No, I came here to find out whether someone got roughed up by Dominicans and still holds a grudge. These are the kinds of guys who should know."

He slammed the door as he left the vehicle and held his ID up for the guys on the steps. "Which one of you nice young gentleman threw the bottle at my car?" he demanded.

"One of the birds dropped it," said the Neanderthal as he raised his 6-5 frame from the stairway. "So fuck off and get your ass back to your part of town, boy."

"Yo," said Laughing Man, "bad things can happen to that little ass of yours up here. Or is that what you come lookin' for, chickie?" The others howled and began grabbing their crotches. "We all got some for you, pretty boy," one of them yelled.

Nazareth walked confidently toward the group, hoping that when he showed no fear the crew would settle down and prove willing to talk. Although these weren't the nice young guys that he and Gimble had spent time with a few minutes ago, he believed in giving everyone the benefit of the doubt. As he drew closer, though, the Neanderthal drew a 10-inch chrome hunting knife outfitted with four holes in the handle for each of his huge fingers.

"Get back in your PO-LICE car while you still can, Mr. Downtown," he said.

When Nazareth kept coming, the guy charged him. As the punk's right foot touched the ground, the detective planted a devastating sidekick on the guy's right knee, driving the joint 90 degrees in a direction it wasn't supposed to move. It was the same kick Nazareth had frequently used in Taekwondo tournaments to crush ten one-inch pine boards. The Neanderthal passed out from the pain and landed on his hunting knife as he fell, driving the blade into the front of his left shoulder and out the back. Laughing Boy turned and ran up the stairs into the apartment hallway while one of the other gang members took off down the street. The remaining two came for Nazareth. Number one immediately found himself on the sidewalk choking on blood after a jumping front snap kick had destroyed his throat. Number two hesitated, reached for something in his pocket, then hit the ground screaming when his right collarbone snapped under the force of Nazareth's well-placed palm strike traveling at nearly 40 miles per hour.

As the detective admired his handiwork, Laughing Boy jumped out of the apartment hallway with a Bushmaster AR-15 semi-automatic rifle in his hands. Nazareth had no time to recover. Laughing Boy raised his weapon and slipped his finger onto the trigger as his head exploded in a mist of blood and brain. Gimble stood by the open door of the cruiser, her smoking Smith & Wesson 5946 in hand.

She looked over at Nazareth and calmly said, "Backup's on the way."

14.

Driscoll's homemade safe room was a work of art, but in some ways his Chevy cargo van was an even more impressive creation. With his native intelligence, a bit of common sense, and a few online videos he had transformed the $12,000 used van into the perfect victim-disposal unit. For less than $300 he had installed a pair of hydraulic actuators on the van's rear cargo doors, enabling him to open and close the doors from the driver's seat. Another $48 had outfitted the van's cargo bed with a six-foot-long section of steel gravity roller, the type normally used to move items along a factory assembly line.

He had affixed the roller bed at a 35-degree angle so that whatever was placed on it would slip quickly out the open doors. Finally, he had bolted lengths of heavy sheet metal to both sides of the conveyor so that its cargo wouldn't fall off while in transit. Total cost: under $12,500, all of it depreciable according to his accountant. The vehicle was, after all, a perfectly legitimate expense for a simple pawn shop owner who needed to deliver large objects from time to time.

Tonight's large object was Ba, the young Senegalese mugger who had chosen the wrong business partner. Driscoll checked the guy's neck for a pulse and was satisfied the plastic bag had done its job. He taped up the large treadmill box, but only well enough to keep the top closed until he had put it in the van. With the hand truck he hefted the package up the basement stairs to the back of his waiting vehicle. Five minutes later the treadmill box was empty on the side of the van's cargo hold, and Ba rested comfortably atop the roller bed that would soon deposit him at the proper doorstep.

As he pulled away from the curb Driscoll wasn't at all concerned about nosy neighbors. If someone had looked out the window shortly after midnight, he or she would have noticed a hard-working business owner preparing tomorrow's delivery for one of his customers. He made sure that everything in the 13th Street basement looked quite routine for storing and protecting retail items. Might make sense to store some inventory here, he thought, in case anyone should ever visit. Yeah, excellent idea. But hold that thought for later. Tonight is all about delivering the goods.

He took his time driving up 3rd Avenue. Traffic was light, and he could have reached his destination more quickly if he had wanted to. But he was in no hurry. Compared to the Rafael Tejera delivery, tonight's drop should be a piece of cake. The neighborhood was much quieter than Times Square, so he didn't need to wait until 3:00 or 4:00 in the morning. Something close to 1:00 a.m. would be fine.

Who the hell are these people? Driscoll asked himself. People on the sidewalks, people in restaurants, people in cars. Don't they sleep? Don't they have someplace better to go? He knew the answer. These were the foot soldiers of the immigrant swarm that was devouring New York City. These were the whores, the pimps, the drug dealers, the muggers, the rapists, and the murderers whose success in America had become the siren call of the Third World. "Come to New York City," they cried, "where you get everything for nothing." Well screw all of you, Driscoll mused. The times they are a-changin'. I am rewriting the script.

He hung a left on West 116th Street and casually drove along one of the main drags in Harlem. As he crossed Malcolm X Blvd. he began scanning addresses on the right, looking for #115. Damn. Even though he was rolling slowly, he missed #115 amid the jumble of storefronts. So he drove to Adam Clayton Powell Jr. Blvd. and hung a left, took another left on 114th Street, and worked his way back north via Malcolm X. This time when he turned onto 116th he was fully prepared to finish the night's work.

A few people walked the streets farther ahead, but no one was in the immediate vicinity of #115. He wasn't particularly concerned about observers anyway. White vans outnumber buses in the City, so who can tell one from the other? Besides, tonight his vehicle wore the plates he had stolen several weeks ago at a Home Depot parking lot in Brooklyn. So even if some do-gooder happened to catch his number, Driscoll would still be out of harm's way.

He pulled toward the curb on his right, slowed to 10 m.p.h. while throwing the switch for his homemade hydraulic "launch system," and quickly accelerated to 25 as Ba's heavily wrapped body began to roll between the open cargo doors. The doors were fully closed by the time he turned left on 7th Avenue and took off for Central Park. He glanced back toward the delivery point. No one had yet noticed the special delivery package he had left at the front door of the Consulate General of Senegal.

15.

Gimble's use of deadly force automatically triggered an NYPD investigation that, according to a shooting-incident manual that ran more than seventy pages, could take ninety days or longer. But after only four days of administrative duty she was back on the job. She testified to having fired only when her partner's life hung in the balance, and eight neighborhood residents were delighted to corroborate her testimony. These were good people who were sickened by what the CF gang had done to their neighborhood and seized the opportunity to set things back on the right path.

These residents also knew that the three punks Nazareth had crushed were among the original four founders of the gang. All three would spend at least 25 years in prison for the attempted murder of a police officer. The body of the fourth founder had already been cremated. Although Nazareth and Gimble hadn't gotten any leads on Rafael Tejera's murder, their actions had triggered a process that would eliminate a major threat to Little Dominican Republic's future.

"I'm sorry you had to go through that because of me, Tara," Nazareth said as the two headed toward their favorite hot dog cart around the corner from One Police Plaza. "If I had stayed in the car the way you told me to, you wouldn't have had to save my dumb ass."

"Listen, Pete, you followed your instincts," she said gently, "and I'll never second-guess you on that. You've got the best cop instincts of all time as far as I'm concerned. And the whole thing turned out right. The gang was a blight on the entire neighborhood, and now it's being eradicated. That's a huge win."

"But I'm sorry you had to shoot Laughing Boy. I should have expected him to come back with heavy artillery, and I should have been the one to take him out."

"Uh, Pete, you sort of had your hands full. Your feet, too, I believe. As for me, I bagged my first buck at 10 when my father took me hunting in Pennsylvania. A harmless deer is a lot tougher to shoot than a piece of garbage like Laughing Boy, I guarantee you. Don't give it a second thought."

Nazareth studied her eyes as they walked. "You're a first-class person, Tara, and I'm lucky to have you."

She looked surprised and was about to respond when they were greeted warmly by Sameer Khan, sole proprietor of the best hot dog cart in the City. "Good afternoon, detectives!" he called as they approached his famous section of sidewalk. "Two each today or three?" A few years earlier Khan had rigged a grill to his cart to separate himself from the vendors who sold hot dogs soaked in greasy water, and he was now a fixture in the neighborhood. Since most of his loyal customers were cops, Sameer Khan was not only one of the hardest working vendors in New York City but also the best protected. No one messed with Sameer Khan or his territory.

"I'll pretend to be ladylike today," Gimble said, "so let me have two with sauerkraut."

"And I'll pretend to be a pig, so let me have three with chili," said Nazareth.

They sat on their customary bench under a maple that had begun dropping its red and orange leaves. After eating her first hot dog, Gimble turned to her partner and said seriously, "You know, I'm a detective . . ."

Before she could go any further Nazareth jumped in with, "Ah, that's why we've been working these cases together. I was wondering how that happened."

"Right, wiseass, I'm a detective. Which means I'm paid to notice things. For example, a few minutes ago you said, and I quote, 'I'm lucky to have you.'"

"Absolutely. You're a terrific partner," he smiled.

"But, see, you didn't say you're lucky to have me as a partner." She casually brushed aside the blonde hair that the afternoon breeze had blown across her face. "All you said is you're lucky to have me. There's a difference."

He considered her words carefully. "Not really. Two ways of saying the same thing." His grin contradicted his words.

"And the other day you called me *pretty lady.*"

"No," he replied, "I called you *señorita bonita*. And as you said a few seconds ago, there's a difference."

"You're deliberately making this difficult."

"Nope, all I'm doing is eating."

She nodded, then began working on her second hot dog. When she was finished, she turned to Nazareth and said, "What's going on in that head of yours, Pete? I know that you never speak just to hear the sound of your own voice. If it doesn't mean something, you don't say it."

He looked off into the distance and considered what should or should not be said. Having arrived at this critical fork in the road, he weighed his options carefully.

"Let me put it this way, Tara. If you and I were not partners, I would ask you to have dinner with me."

"And I would say yes. By the way, we've eaten together many times before, Pete. That's what we're doing right now, as a matter of fact."

"Yeah, but . . . ."

"But it's never been a date." She studied his face and knew she had read the signals correctly. "And you'd like for it to be a date."

"I guess," he said quietly.

"So would I. But you're conflicted," she smiled, "because you've never dated a partner."

"I never date guys," he said solemnly.

"Always the wiseass."

"Hey, someone has to be. But seriously," he continued, "I don't think it's possible to mix the two -- being a partner and dating someone. We've got two extremely different worlds that probably need to be kept apart."

"And you're not just talking about cosmetics -- what people might think?" she said.

"Not at all," he shook his head. "I live my life and let people think whatever they think. No, I mean I'm not sure you can be romantically involved with someone who's standing alongside you facing down murderers day after day. At some point the two relationships could create a problem."

"Care to give me an example?"

He thought about that for a moment, hoping he couldn't actually come up with an example that made sense. But several immediately came to mind.

"Okay, here's a hypothetical. I have time for only one shot. I can either shoot the guy who's about to blow up a train loaded with commuters or shoot the guy who's about to kill my partner. One shot only. What do I do?"

"You shoot the guy who's after the train and let your partner take care of herself."

"Easier said than done, Tara. That might be the right decision, but could I really let someone kill the woman I love? Not likely."

She studied his eyes and liked everything she read in them. "Were you ever a Boy Scout, Pete?"

"Yeah, an Eagle Scout, actually."

"Why am I not surprised?"

16.

New York City's record cold temperature for the month was 27 degrees in 1988, so the 35 degrees that Jed Butler faced one morning during the last week of October wouldn't make history. Nevertheless, the chill had certainly gotten his attention as he lugged his USPS satchel from one Lower Manhattan address to the next. He considered himself lucky to have a high percentage of storefronts on his route, because every few minutes he was able to step inside a heated place and warm his aging bones.

Crazy weather, he thought. They keep talking about global warming, and next thing you know you get this. One day it's near 70, and the next day it's near freezing. The forecaster on channel 7 promised his viewers a return to warmer temperatures later in the week. In the meantime, though, Butler wished he had worn an extra pullover under his jacket. Rain, sleet, snow, and cold hadn't been a problem for him when he was a young man starting out on the job, but after nearly 30 years he felt it all: the cold, the heat, the aching back, the tired legs.

Most of all he felt the fear of growing old and not having enough time to do things that mattered. Like hanging with his two grandkids. Or helping his oldest son finish the basement of his new home. Or traveling America with his wife while they could still enjoy it. He had spent many hours dreaming about things he either didn't have time for or believed he couldn't afford. Yet the clock kept ticking. Stop procrastinating, he told himself.

Toward mid-morning he walked into Sung Ko's convenience store, set his satchel down next to the counter, and handed Mr. Ko his mail.

"How are you today, Mr. Ko?" he said.

"Too chilly, Mr. Butler. Too chilly for me," the 72-year-old Ko answered. "Please, today you have coffee, my treat. Stay warm."

"I believe I'll take you up on that," Butler smiled. "Thank you very much, Mr. Ko. It's really terrible out there. I should have worn another shirt."

As Butler filled his styrofoam cup from the decaf pot, three Jamaican teens, the oldest of them seventeen, boisterously entered the store. The first guy through the door yelled into his cell phone while the other two shouted insults at him. "Yo, bredda, tell that cheap ho she got no class," one of them yelled. The guy on the phone snarled "Kiss mi back side" at his girlfriend before hanging up. All three howled and fist-bumped each other as they brazenly began stuffing chips and candy bars into their jackets.

"Put it all back," Ko screamed as he hurried around the counter toward them. "You want, you pay." Ko stood only 5-5 and weighed no more than 140 pounds, but he had never been shy about defending his modest income.

"Yeah, and kiss this, old man," said the largest of the teens, a six-footer who had Ko by at least 40 pounds." He shoved the old guy in the chest, sending him backwards into a display rack filled with jars of salsa. The three punks laughed as Ko slid around on the floor amid the broken glass and spilled sauce. As he struggled to his feet, the youngest kid -- a 14-year-old not much larger than Ko -- kicked him in the face and put the old guy flat on his back.

The largest of the three turned toward Butler too late to stop the punch that was already streaking toward his right ear. When the kid flinched, he ended up turning his face into the blow so that he took its full force on the side of his nose. Butler had gotten all 6-4 of him behind the punch, and the young thug's nose collapsed with a sickening crack as he immediately began spraying blood wherever he turned. As Butler grabbed the next-largest kid by the front of his shirt, the smallest guy plunged a sharpened eight-inch screwdriver into the back of the postman's neck, piercing the spinal cord. Butler dropped his hands and began to topple, but not before his attacker stabbed him through the heart. The kid left the screwdriver in Butler's chest as he and his friends casually walked from the store eating chips.

For slightly more than 48 hours Dajuan Sobers bragged about the killing to his friends in Crown Heights, Brooklyn. He told them how he had created his own custom shank, his "cutlass" he called it, by working the tip of his screwdriver with a small sharpening stone he had stolen from Sears. When he was able to drop the weapon from his outstretched hand and have it stick in the linoleum floor of his mother's kitchen, he knew it was ready for action. He smirked when friends asked whether he was afraid of getting arrested.

"Ease up, mon," he grinned. "I be 14 and gettin' mi Y.O." Youth-offender status, he reminded them, would put him back on the street with nothing more than a wrist-slap if he ever got caught. After 49 hours at large, Sobers and his two friends were behind bars, and the D.A. decided that all three would be charged as adults. It was a welcome bit of justice, the newspapers all said, but it wouldn't bring Jed Butler back to his wife and four kids.

When Ryan Driscoll read about the murder, he put the CLOSED sign in his shop window, went into the back room, and cried. He remembered the good times he and J.B. had shared in high school. He would miss J.B.'s wit and joy each day when he delivered the mail. Above all, he would relish the opportunity to avenge J.B.'s death.

Ryan Driscoll had just declared war on Jamaicans.

17.

Nazareth and Gimble weren't especially in love with today's job: sorting through case files at One Police Plaza. But they were grateful to be indoors. New York City was riding a major cold snap from October into November, and the street was a place the detectives preferred not to be right now. Maybe they'd head out at lunchtime to throw Sameer Khan a little business. Must be tough making a buck on days like this, they agreed. But otherwise they planned to spend their time trying to connect the hidden dots between vic #1, Rafael Tejera, and vic #2, Saliou Ba.

The two detectives had been rousted out of bed at nearly 2:00 a.m. on the night of Ba's murder. By the time they each arrived at the crime scene, two uniformed officers had already put a name with the body. Three different neighborhood night owls had identified Ba within minutes, even though he still had a clear plastic bag over his head. Ba was apparently well known in the community as a charming but potentially vicious scam artist who did his business south of Harlem. As long as he didn't rob me, the logic went, I never cared how he got his money.

"I'm seriously flashing back to our Rosebud psycho," Gimble said. Earlier in the year she and Nazareth had helped take down the Rosebud Killer, whose self-appointed mission had been murdering widows. "One guy likes to kill old ladies, and this screwball likes to kill . . . what? Non-whites?"

Nazareth shook his head. "I don't think this is a white versus non-white thing, Tara. If that were the case he wouldn't be going to the trouble of dumping bodies outside foreign consulates. He's clearly delivering a highly specific message, and I think it's immigrants he's after. One guy from the Dominican Republic, one from Senegal. And all the nonsense about RETURN TO SENDER." He drummed the table with the fingers of his right hand while his left hand cradled his chin. "The next murder will confirm my theory."

"You think he's just getting started," she said.

"Most definitely. Somewhere in New York City this guy has set up a processing center, if you will, where he can gather, prepare, package, and ship victims. Think about what we've seen so far. Now ask yourself whether this could be the work of someone who snatches random victims off the street and kills them."

"He could certainly snatch and kill, but he wouldn't know that he was actually targeting an immigrant, would he?"

"Not very likely. And if through sheer luck he did abduct an immigrant, how could he be sure of knowing where the victim had come from? No, I just don't see this happening on the spur of the moment. This guy targets specific people and gets them someplace where he can work on them safely."

"Feel like running this by the FBI profiler you used for the Rosebud case?"

"Actually I'd rather leave the analysis to you this time, Tara. You've got a psych degree and you've got a whole lot more street experience than most profilers. I'd like you to think about who this guy is. Where does he come from, what makes him hate, and what enables him to target and abduct victims according to a highly sophisticated plan?"

"Uh, okay," she smiled. "Is that all?"

"Well, since you ask," he laughed, "is there any chance you could do it today?"

18.

The bloody riots of November 3rd began, as such things often do, with a peace rally. The Rev. Dr. Thaddeus G.W. Harrison, a long-in-the-tooth bastion of the civil-rights community, had urged New Yorkers of every color to gather at noon that day in front of the NYPD's 28th precinct at the corner of Frederick Douglass Blvd. and West 123rd Street. His goal, he told everyone who would listen -- most especially members of the press -- was to demand that the NYPD protect the City's non-white population from . . . well, from everyone, but especially from the sicko that the *Daily News* had branded the "RTS Killer." The rally attracted more reporters and TV crews than actual protesters, but that was fine with Harrison. A bit of on-camera bluster was worth more than 1,000 protesters, he knew, and some fresh press coverage might help get his declining career back on track.

Standing close to Harrison's makeshift podium on Nov. 3rd was Andrea Wilson of the *New York Times*. Wilson was a highly regarded Pulitzer-winning reporter universally admired for meticulously separating fact from opinion. She took careful notes at the time-wasting rally, then filed a brief article in which she accurately quoted Harrison as saying, "These murders must stop. I wonder what the NYPD would do if this should happen to whites." The next morning her article was buried deep in the *Times'* Metro section, where it attracted virtually no attention.

But also covering the protest was Max O'Malley, an upstart local TV reporter whose stoned cameraman didn't begin taping the event until the words "this should happen to whites" passed through Harrison's lips. The video clip that ran on the 5:00 o'clock evening news showed the angry preacher in front of what the tight camera shot portrayed as a huge crowd. The words *This should happen to whites* appeared under Harrison's image, and it was off to the races. Even before the video ran again that night at 6:00, 9:00, and 11:00, bad things had begun to happen. In Central Park several white people were dragged into the bushes and beaten. In Midtown a husband and wife visiting from Belgium were pushed from a subway platform and minced by an express train. And in Harlem looters of all ages emptied local stores of everything that wasn't bolted to the floor, then set half the places ablaze. The fact that the stores were owned by their non-white neighbors seemed quaintly irrelevant at the time.

A fury of finger-pointing began early the next morning. A TV news crew taped the police commissioner, Edward Sheppard, calling the Rev. Dr. Harrison "the #1 hate-monger in the history of New York City." Harrison, meanwhile, branded the police commissioner and his "uniformed thugs" the "worst blight on this planet since Hitler and the SS." Mayor Homer Bratwell -- known to every cop in the City as Gomer Bratwurst because of his anti-police sentiments -- fired Sheppard for slandering Harrison, whose supporters had helped get the mayor elected. Social scientists blamed the Harlem residents for exhibiting irrational pack behavior, and the ACLU argued that the social scientists were out of touch with street dynamics, "Meaning they're complete assholes," said a spokesman who chose to remain anonymous. At the end of the day Rafael Tejera and Saliou Ba were still dead, and detectives Nazareth and Gimble were no closer to finding the RTS Killer.

After the riots came a burst of RTS-like murders, none of which the NYPD attributed to the RTS Killer. For several days it became fashionable for the City's gangs to dispose of enemies -- meaning everyone who wasn't a member of their respective gangs -- by packaging them in stretch wrap and stamping RETURN TO SENDER all over the corpses. Unlike the RTS Killer's victims, however, these unfortunates had been shot, stabbed, beaten, or burned prior to being tossed in a dumpster in some dark alley. After viewing a few such bodies, Nazareth got the word out that he didn't want to be called unless someone in the chain of command actually thought the RTS Killer might be involved.

"Tara," Nazareth asked her one afternoon in the midst of all the insanity, "how did people get so screwed up? You majored in psychology, so please tell me you have an answer. It seems to me that everyone in this city, from the mayor on down, is completely nuts."

"Not everyone," she said. "The RTS Killer isn't at all nuts, and he's got to be loving this. It's an ideal backdrop for what he's doing."

"And you don't think he's nuts?"

"Well, that depends on your definition, I guess. He's certifiable, but he's not nuts."

"Crazy but not stupid?" he smiled.

"There you go."

The peak of craziness came at midnight five days after the riots, when someone drove a black SUV onto the sidewalk in front of the 28th precinct headquarters. The driver stopped the vehicle momentarily while an accomplice in the back seat dumped a body wrapped in plastic at the building's entrance, next to a huge cement column that bore a plaque reading, "The Harlem community thanks the men & women of the 28th Precinct for their outstanding service." Then the SUV sped off in the direction of the Hudson River. No one thought about chasing the vehicle once Officer Arnie Nugent saw the bomb that had been heavily taped to the dead guy's chest. Nugent alerted the desk sergeant, and within minutes the entire building had been evacuated.

Detective Ralph Ryan of the 28th had seen his share of roadside bombs during his two Army tours in Iraq, so he took a quick look at the device. In less than 30 seconds he knew the weapon contained eight blocks of C4 -- total weight 10 pounds -- outfitted with a detonator fashioned from a .38-caliber shell casing. That was the easy part. Knowing how to defuse the bomb was way beyond his capabilities. Whoever had built the thing had wrapped at least a dozen different wires around the plastic explosive and taped the ends under the alarm-clock timer. So guessing which wire to cut was a fool's game. Maybe just yanking the detonator from the C4 would work. On the other hand, maybe it wouldn't. Detective Ryan didn't plan to find out. That's why God created the Bomb Squad, he told himself. The device's timer flashed 38:58, 38:57, 38:56 . . . and time to get the experts.

Less than a minute after the Bomb Squad got the call, the red phone next to the mayor's bed rang. As he groped for it in the dark he accidentally knocked his secretary in the jaw with his elbow.

"Damn, that hurt," she yelped.

"Sorry," he said curtly as he put the phone to his ear. "Yeah, what?"

"Bomb Squad's heading to the 28th precinct headquarters," his chief of staff told him. "Possible terrorist attack with a homemade bomb. The thing's set to detonate in just under 35 minutes."

"Okay, have my car ready in five, then call the B List." He hung up and apologized again to Cynthia, who was still rubbing her sore chin. The young woman had been warming his bed while the mayor's wife was in Europe with some college friends.

"From now on you sleep near the phone, okay?" she whined.

"I promise," he said as he kissed her on top of her blonde head. "While I'm gone, turn on the news and watch me take charge of a terrorist attack."

"A terrorist attack?"

"Just a homemade bomb," he assured her, "planted by some nut jobs. But I need to be on the scene."

While the mayor was throwing on some manly clothes -- jeans, corduroy shirt, NYPD hoodie -- his chief of staff was furiously alerting the B List, a dozen carefully selected editors at the City's major news outlets. The mayor's standing order was to call him whenever there was even a hint of terrorist activity and then to notify the press. Nothing boosted a reelection campaign like a take-charge mayor riding shotgun over the Big Apple when bad guys were in town. Homer Bratwell was a marketing master who knew how to work a crowd.

By the time Bratwell arrived at the 28th precinct building, Detective Fernando Calderon of the Bomb Squad had studied the device on the dead man's body and decided to have it placed in a bomb containment chamber that his crew had towed to the scene. This was the ultimate in high-end chambers, and Calderon was completely confident that it would render the weapon harmless. Before the detective could have the chamber rolled into place, however, the mayor strode up to him under the glare of TV camera lights.

"How much time is left, Detective?" he barked.

Calderon was shocked to see the boss of all New York City bosses walking up to him in the middle of the night, and for a moment all he could think of saying was, "About 18 minutes, according to the timer."

"Good, we've got time," Bratwell announced. "Show me what you've got."

Calderon finally found the courage to say, "Mr. Mayor, you need to get the hell away from here. This thing is live!"

"So are the cameras, Detective. Keep your voice down, point to the bomb, and talk to me about it."

"Sir, we need time to get the device into the containment chamber."

"Point and talk for 30 seconds," Bratwell snarled, "and then stick the device wherever the hell you want it. Captain, come over here."

Captain Leona Hines wasn't happy about joining the mayor's entourage at that particular moment. She had been called at home about the attack on her headquarters, and she had dutifully presented herself at the scene. But she had no desire whatsoever to see the bomb better than she could from 100 feet away.

"Sir," she yelled back, "I don't think that's a good idea."

What she saw in Bratwell's face was the unmistakable image of her NYPD career swirling around and around in a large toilet bowl. She hated this guy more than ever right now, and that was saying a lot. But she valued the position she had spent 23 years attaining.

"Yes, sir. I'm coming," she said grudgingly.

A block away, sitting in a 2008 black Honda Accord, Rahman Aziz eagerly watched the scene through his compact binoculars. He had been no more than two seconds away from striking when to his utter shock the mayor of this heathen capital of the universe rolled up with his police escort. Now I must wait, he told himself. He watched as the mayor strutted about like a bantam rooster in the henhouse, then was stunned to see Bratwell walk over to the actual bomb. Now! he told himself. But wait. He held his breath as the police captain joined the mayor and the man from the Bomb Squad. This cannot be happening, Aziz thought. But there it was, right in front of his eyes. He wondered what he had done to deserve such a blessing.

As Capt. Hines cautiously approached the mayor and Detective Calderon, Bratwell snapped, "You're wasting everybody's time here.

The detective would like to get rid of this thing, wouldn't you, Detective?"

"Absolutely, sir. And the clock really is ticking. Fifteen minutes left, Mr. Mayor."

What Calderon did not know, because he could not see under all the tape that had been wrapped around the dead man's body, was that the alarm clock fastened to the homemade bomb was connected to a tangle of dead, meaningless wires. The bomb's actual triggering mechanism was an old cell phone that rested under the C4. A phone call to the device would activate the ringer, which in turn would close the gap in the detonation circuit.

"I'm so glad you could join us this evening, Captain," Bratwell said sarcastically. "Okay, Detective. Let's give the cameras something worth filming, shall we?"

As the mayor poked his face closer to the bomb, Rahman Aziz offered up a short prayer and pressed the SEND button on his phone. Detective Calderon heard only part of the first ring and in that fraction of a second knew he had been tricked. But it no longer mattered. The explosion vaporized the mayor, the detective, the captain, and Max O'Malley, the young reporter who had finally become a TV star. The hard way. Two police vehicles near the blast site exploded in huge fireballs as their gas tanks ruptured. Twenty-five people were injured, eight of them critically.

Back at Gracie Mansion lovely Cynthia nearly fainted when she saw the blast live on TV. By the time she had stuffed her things into the small overnight bag and opened the front door, a camera crew had begun rolling tape. It was difficult to judge who was more surprised: the mayor's mistress or the reporter who had come to the residence hoping for a reaction from the mayor's wife.

19.

Ryan Driscoll was nothing if not loyal. Throughout his life he had been loyal to his grandparents, his parents, his sister, and everyone else in his extended Irish-American family. He was also intensely loyal to his old friends, even though he rarely saw them anymore. Jed Butler had been the only friend he still spent time with every once in awhile, and J.B.'s ashes now floated somewhere in New York Harbor. The poor guy had broken his ass all his life, and in less than 10 seconds some Jamaican gangsta wannabe had stolen everything Butler had worked for.

Spilled blood demands spilled blood, Driscoll vowed. His next shipment would be bound for Jamaica. This marked a significant shift in strategy. He had taken his first two victims as they presented themselves. One simply had happened to be Dominican, the other Senegalese. Targeting foreigners as they walked into his pawn shop was relatively easy since they represented a large portion of his business. But to hold out specifically for a Jamaican could waste days, maybe even weeks.

He couldn't settle for just any Jamaican. He needed a victim who was desperate enough or greedy enough to meet secretly with Adolphus Fleischer alone, at night, in a strange location. Rafael Tejera had been the first ideal candidate, a young illegal who faced losing his girlfriend, his job, and his American dream if he wasn't able to pay off the official who could block his deportation. He had turned to Driscoll, then to Fleischer, in an effort to unload a small bag of uncut diamonds that he had stolen before leaving the Dominican Republic. And Ba, of course, had been the ultimate greedy thug who wanted both his stolen ring and the money he expected to find at Fleischer's private shop.

Yes, waiting for a Jamaican with the same impeccable credentials could take time, but his mind was made up. J.B. would be properly avenged.

Over the next 10 days Driscoll carefully scrutinized every customer who might be Jamaican and learned that he couldn't really tell the difference between one Caribbean expatriate and another. To his untrained ear everyone from what he termed "de islands" sounded the same, and he would have been glad to rid the City of them all. But when he gently inquired about nationality, he got surprising answers from his prospective victims: Haiti, the Bahamas, Barbados, Anguilla, Trinidad and Tobago, and several more he couldn't remember. So many who don't belong here! But J.B.'s soul cried for Jamaican blood.

Kevaughn Brown walked into L.E.S. Pawn and Loan just as Driscoll thought about locking up for the night. It was only 5:45, but he'd done okay for the day and figured he'd get an early start on the evening. Maybe stop for a draft at that new Irish pub on the walk home. But his plans turned on a dime when the smiling Brown said, "Closing soon, mon?"

"Not yet, my friend," Driscoll replied warmly as he rested his right hand on the shotgun behind the counter. Closing time was always a high-risk moment of the day, especially during those months when darkness fell early. This was when you faced the greatest chance of getting robbed because all some punk had to do was turn the CLOSED sign in your door and order you into the back room. To folks on the street nothing would seem out of order. "How can I help you this evening?"

"With all this crazy rioting," Brown said, "I need some protection, ya know?" In fact he didn't look like a guy who needed much protection at all. A bit over 6-2, well above 200 pounds, dreadlocks down to his shoulders, and a long scar on his left cheek. "Everybody kill everybody."

Driscoll was in fact quite pleased with the recent murders since he assumed that most of the bodies belonged to illegals. The more they killed each other, the better off America was.

"What sort of protection did you have in mind?" Driscoll asked.

"Not too wild," he said. "A .45 maybe."

"Let me ask you this. Will you be using the gun for home protection or street protection?"

"Street protection."

Yeah, right, Driscoll thought. Mostly blowing people's heads off as you rob them, you son of a bitch. "Well, in that case you need to consider how easy the gun is to carry and conceal."

Brown smiled broadly. Yes, he thought to himself, I definitely want a gun I can conceal. "What kind of gun you think?"

"The best gun on the market for street use is the Sig Sauer P290RS," Driscoll offered. "It's a polymer 9mm perfect for concealed carry. They don't make them any better than this."

"You have one here?"

"First things first, my friend. I need your name, and I need to see government ID -- a driver's license maybe."

"Kevaughn Brown is the name, mon," he said, "but I not drive, so I have no ID like that."

"Then unfortunately I can't help you, Mr. Brown. Pawn shops are governed by all sorts of regulations, so I have to see government-issued ID. And selling you a gun requires a full federal background check."

"I thought the pawn shop be faster than some gun store, ya know?" Brown's disappointment bordered on desperation. "I need protection. Things be very bad on the street. I can't wait for background checks and all that."

"Okay, look," Driscoll said, "I can't sell you a gun, but I may know someone who can."

The guy's face brightened. "And this someone, he don't worry about that ID shit?"

Driscoll shook his head knowingly. "Let me explain how he works." A few minutes later an extremely grateful Kevaughn Brown left the shop with instructions for meeting Adolphus Fleischer that same night at 10:00 p.m. Driscoll gladly took a raincheck on the new Irish pub. He suddenly had a meatier agenda.

At 10:00 sharp Brown's cell phone rang. "Brown here."

"You're an undercover cop, aren't you?" Driscoll growled.

"What, no, mon, I'm no cop!" he wailed.

"Then who were you just meeting with across the street?" Driscoll demanded.

"How do I know? I walk by, he ask me for a dollar, and I tell him to screw off. Just like that. Mr. Fleischer, I'm no cop."

"I'm not so sure," Driscoll said, "so I think maybe we're done for tonight."

"No, please! I need that gun, or I be dead."

Driscoll relished the dread in Brown's voice. "Why? Is someone after you? Tell me the truth, Mr. Brown, or we're finished here."

"Yes, some bitch's husband say he going to kill me."

"Because you did something to his wife, yeah?"

"We did something with each other. Now the husband, he want a bullet in my head. So I need to fix this."

"Okay, memorize this address." Driscoll passed along the usual directions and rules, then sent Brown on his way. While Brown walked toward the address he had been given, Driscoll followed in the dark from a safe distance, watching closely to make sure that the guy didn't use his cell or stop to talk with anyone. No problems whatsoever. Everything according to plan. A desperate man indeed. When his quarry turned right toward 13th Street, Driscoll stepped up his pace and went over one extra block, then down to 13th. He wanted to be walking toward Brown when they met.

When he was a few paces away from Brown, he raised the brim of his Mets cap with his left hand but kept the right in his jacket, tightly wrapped around the gun's handle. Then he removed the tinted night-driving glasses that had modified his appearance just enough to keep him anonymous. He smiled at the obviously confused Brown.

"Good evening, my friend," he whispered. "Very good to see you again." Before Brown could say a word Driscoll put a finger to his mouth. "Shh. Very quietly."

"You are Mr. Fleischer?" Brown said softly.

"At this shop I am," he grinned. "And I have exactly what you need. Let's go inside."

Driscoll pulled his gun as soon as Brown set off the metal detector.

"What are you carrying, Mr. Brown?"

"Just a knife for protection," he said.

"Well in this shop I'm the only person allowed to have a weapon for protection. You understand, right? So please leave your knife here on the floor." When Brown complied, Driscoll told him to walk straight ahead to the office and have a seat.

"Did you bring your $300, Mr. Brown?"

"Yes, absolutely." He placed three bills on the table. "Everything just the way you said," he smiled. "And you can put your gun away, Mr. Fleischer. Let's do business."

"How many women did you rape this week?" Driscoll asked him.

"What?"

"Do you have a hearing problem? I asked you how many women you've raped this week."

Brown began to stand but stopped when he saw the gun pointed at his face. "I rape no women this week," he said, clearly confused by what was happening.

"Ah, so you admit that you raped women in other weeks?"

"What, no, I rape no one."

"Where are you from?"

"I come from Jamaica. I told you. Kingston."

"Well, if you're from Jamaica, we both know you've been raping women. So tell me how many before I put a bullet in your head."

Brown couldn't win an argument with a madman, and he knew it. Better to confess to raping women he hadn't raped than getting his head blown off.

"Two," he said.

"Ah, I knew you were a rapist the minute you walked into my shop. I'm a very good judge of character, no?"

"Yes, very, very good."

"Now tell me about my good friend Jed Butler."

"I do not know Jed Butler," Brown protested. "Please, let's do business."

"This *is* the business, **mon**!" Driscoll screamed. "You and your Jamaican brothers killed my friend, and this is the price you must pay for your sins."

"You a crazy man!" Brown screamed. "I kill no one."

Driscoll smiled as he slammed the door to the safe room. He would allow Brown to contemplate his sins for 24 hours, then ship him out.

By 11:00 p.m. the next night Brown had been neatly wrapped in plastic and wore a large red JM on his forehead. In addition to stamping RETURN TO SENDER all over the body, Driscoll had scrawled 4JB on the plastic bag covering his victim's head. "I claim you for my old friend Jed Butler," he said somberly as he shifted Brown's body onto the rollers in the van. "You are the most special delivery of all so far."

Driscoll was jittery as he traveled up 3rd Avenue. The Jamaican Consulate on 48th Street was located in an upscale part of town that housed other consulates, some big-name restaurants, and the United Nations. Police presence could be an issue tonight, he told himself, so be patient. Doing the job right matters more than doing it quickly.

He turned right at the corner of 3rd and 48th, where the Jamaican Consulate was conveniently located, and was delighted to find the neighborhood rather quiet at 1:30 a.m. No police vehicles and no evidence that anyone was particularly alert, even though some strange things had happened in the City recently. Strange in Manhattan? he thought. How the hell would you know strange from normal? The whole place is haywire. We open our doors to the world's worst, then complain when things fall apart. Gimme a break.

He made two tours of the block before deciding he was good to go. He rolled slowly up 3rd toward 48th, waiting for the light to turn green, then quickly accelerated to 30 as he opened the rear cargo doors. The body was still sliding toward the intersection as Driscoll turned onto 48th. No one was on the street to see Kevaughn Brown slam into the curb and come to rest against the base of the traffic light. Driscoll calmly turned onto 2nd Avenue and drove toward home, listening to Frank Sinatra sing "My Way" from a well-used audio tape.

"This one was for you, J.B.," he said aloud. "I hope you're smiling up there."

Early the next morning Nazareth and Gimble learned their agenda now included vic #3.

20.

"Seventy-six degrees on November 13th," Nazareth said as he and Gimble strolled toward Sameer Khan's hot dog stand. "How often does that happen?"

"Basically never," she replied. "Perfect excuse for a couple of hot dogs."

"When's the last time you needed an excuse to eat a hot dog?" he laughed.

She thought hard about that. "You're right, never. But when the snow is flying next month, you probably won't get me out here."

"We'll see about that. My friends in Narcotics tell me that hot dog withdrawal can be pretty tough."

"What's even tougher," Gimble said casually, "is waiting for that dinner invitation."

"Dinner invitation?"

"Right. Actually it was the last time you and I came out here for hot dogs. You said that you'd like to ask me out to dinner, and I said I would accept. Sound familiar?"

"Actually I think what I said is that I'd love to ask you out if we weren't partners. And then, as I recall, you accused me of being a Boy Scout."

"Uh, uh. I didn't accuse. I asked. And you said you had been an Eagle Scout. Is this all coming back to you now?" she said sweetly.

"Tara, it doesn't really have to come back to me, because I think about it all the time."

"You do?"

"Sure. How could I not? I see you every day," he said gently, "and like being with you. But we're partners, and that complicates things."

She stopped walking and faced him. "Pete, maybe it's only a small complication." He began to speak, but she held up her hand. "No, wait. I know you think it's a big complication. I get that. But maybe it would only be a big complication if we were a serious couple, you know? And who knows whether that would ever happen? Maybe we're meant to be great detective partners but lousy dates. If that's the case, nothing lost."

"So you're thinking that first we see what happens and then decide what to do?"

"Sure, why not?"

"Because I don't want to lose you -- as a partner, as a friend, or as the woman I may be in love with. That's why."

Gimble's jaw dropped, but before she could respond he said, "Don't turn around."

"What's wrong?"

He looked over her shoulder and kept his eyes on Sameer Khan's hot dog cart half a block away. "Something's not right about Sameer's cart."

"And I can't look?"

"Not yet, Tara. Tell you what. Let's head back into the building for a minute." As he took Gimble's arm, he noticed that Sameer had waved to him.

"Hey, Sameer," he yelled as he waved back and smiled. "Be back in five minutes."

"What's going on, Pete?" she asked as they headed back inside One Police Plaza.

He glanced at his watch. "It's 12:40," he said. "What time is that rally today?"

"Starts at 1:00 o'clock." A coalition of the City's religious groups expected more than 20,000 people to converge on Washington Square Park at 1:00 to speak out against the recent terrorist attack that had killed Mayor Bratwell and the others. Today's event was especially important to the four participating Muslim groups because an organization calling itself ISIS New York had claimed responsibility for the bombing. Once again the City's residents had begun blaming all Muslims for the disgusting behavior of a few crazies who had twisted religious verses to serve their own criminal ends.

"And then everyone marches to One Police Plaza," he said.

"That's it. So what's going on?"

"Sameer's hot dog cart isn't in its usual spot," he began. "It's quite a bit closer to where the marchers will gather once they arrive here."

"He's probably thinking he'll sell more hot dogs today."

"The location is only part of it. His cart is riding really low on its tires today," Nazareth told her. "In all the time he's been here that cart has always looked exactly the same, but today it's loaded down with a hell of a lot more than hot dogs."

"How much more?" she asked.

"I'm not much of a mechanic," he said, "but I'm guessing hundreds of pounds."

"Then how could he even move it?"

"If the weight's mostly over the wheels he'd have no trouble lifting the tow bar. In any case something is way wrong."

"You're thinking he's got a weapon in the cart?"

"You saw what ten pounds of C4 did at the 2-8 Precinct. Now imagine what a few hundred pounds would do in the middle of a big rally."

Once inside the building they hurried toward a window facing Sameer Khan's cart. After watching Khan from the window for a minute or two, Nazareth ran off to borrow a pair of binoculars and returned with Matt D'Elicio, one of his friends from the Major Case unit.

"What, you're thinking our buddy Sameer has gone off the reservation, Pete?" said D'Elicio.

"That cart is carrying a couple hundred extra pounds today, Matt. And we've got a whole lot of people heading our way around 2:00. You never know, right?"

Nazareth trained the binoculars first on the cart, then on Khan. "From this angle I can't see anything different about the cart except how low it's sitting on the wheels. But Sameer looks as though he's got fleas. The guy can't stand still. You ever notice that before?" he asked.

"I've always thought he was amazingly calm for someone who gets as busy as he does," Gimble replied.

"I'm with her," D'Elicio added. "Sameer is usually Mr. Cool. What the hell's going on?"

"There's only one way to find out, Matt," Nazareth said.

"Damn, we're going to look awfully dumb taking down the hot dog vendor who practically owns the building, Pete," D'Elicio told him.

"True, but we'd look even dumber sitting up here eating hot dogs while he wastes a few hundred people. Tell you what, you stay here with the binoculars and stay on my cell line. I'll wear the earpiece. If you see anything that scares the hell out of you, let me know. Otherwise, listen in while Tara and I check out Sameer and possibly make asses of ourselves."

"Possibly?" D'Elicio said.

"Okay, probably," Nazareth grinned. "You with me, Tara?"

"As always, Pete," she said.

Together they left the building and walked once again toward the hot dog cart. They smiled at each other and pretended to talk about the weather . . . or whatever it is young couples like talking about on one of the 10 best days of the year. When Nazareth noticed they had Khan's attention, he waved and shouted, "Told you we'd be back, Sameer." He held up two fingers. "Two and two," which translated as two with chili, two with sauerkraut. Khan waved back, then disappeared behind the far end of his cart.

"He's had his right hand in his jacket pocket the whole time," D'Elicio said from the window above. "He just took it out to fix some hot dogs."

"As long as he's fixing hot dogs, we're okay, Matt. But if the hand goes back in the pocket as we're walking up to him," said Nazareth, "let me know loud and fast."

"Pete, if he's really got a bomb, how do we know he's also got the trigger?" Gimble asked nervously. "He may just be the delivery guy. The bomb at the 2-8 was detonated remotely."

"We've really got no options here. If he's got bad intentions, he sure as hell isn't going to let the Bomb Squad walk up to him. At least you and I can get close enough to take him down."

"Unless he takes us out completely."

"Well, yeah, that's true." He looked directly in her eyes. "If we survive lunch, dinner's on me."

"Dinner as in dinner date?" she smiled.

"Yeah, dinner date for sure."

"Talk to me, Matt," Nazareth said as they approached the cart.

"Still putting together your hot dogs, Pete. Nervous as hell, but he's just working on your lunch."

When the detectives got within three feet of him, Khan looked at them with wide eyes and said, "Praise God you came back," he said earnestly. "I am in great trouble, detectives."

They were both taken by surprise. Instead of a bad guy who wanted to blow them to pieces they found a terrified Khan who seemed on the verge of tears.

"What's going on, Sameer?" Gimble said gently, keeping her eye on Khan's right hand. If he reached for the right pocket, she might have to break his arm.

"Do not look around. A man is watching us, and he has sworn that he will kill my entire family if I do not do his evil work today."

"Let's all smile as though we're having our usual lunch, okay?" Nazareth said. "Good. Now tell me what he wants you to do, Sameer."

"He has filled my cart with explosives," Khan whimpered despite his fake smile. "When the people all march here later, I am to push my cart close to them, and the man will blow all of us up. He said I will be a holy martyr. But all I want is to be a husband and father. Please, detectives, please help me."

"Try to stay calm, Sameer," Nazareth urged him. "And keep smiling. Let's keep this looking like a normal conversation. Tara, why don't you start eating?"

"Since this might be my last meal," she said, "I'll be happy to."

"Sameer, do you know where the man is?" Nazareth asked.

"Yes, he is sitting in a black car about a block away. When the time is right, he told me, he will use his cell phone to set off the bomb. He has men at my home, and they will kill my family if I do not do as I am told."

"What's his name?"

"Rahman Aziz, a terrible man," Khan told him. "It is he and his followers who murdered the mayor. They want to kill everyone who does not believe as they do. This morning they put a gun to my head while they filled my cart with explosives. Then Aziz made me call my wife, and she told me that four men sat in front of our house in their car. These men will murder my family, detective."

"Not going to happen, Sameer," Nazareth assured him. "Listen, Detective Gimble and I are going to sit down and eat our hot dogs. You just stand here and work as usual. Nothing different, understood? Just be yourself for me."

"Yes, Detective. I will do whatever you say."

As the detectives sat on the bench and began eating, Nazareth said, "Did you catch all that, Matt?"

"Damn right I did. And I've got the guy in the black car. One block straight ahead of where you're sitting, opposite side of the street. Black late-model Accord, New York plates. I'm having those run as we speak."

"Excellent. What can you tell me about the guy, Matt?"

"I'm catching a lot of sunlight off the windshield, but I'd say he's 60 or so, heavy beard. No skull cap, but that doesn't mean a damn thing. If he's out doing bad things he'd want to blend in."

"Got it. Are the car windows open?"

"Driver's window, yes, definitely. I think the front passenger window is open," he said, "but I can't be sure."

"Okay, stay on the line. We're going back to the cart to buy a bag of chips, then take a little stroll. We'll pass the Accord on our side of the street, walk one more block, then cross over and disappear, just in case he's watching."

"Then what?" D'Elicio asked.

"Still deciding, Matt. But we'll come up with something."

"How about some Special Ops help, Pete?" he asked.

"No way, Matt. You know these fanatics. He's out to kill, and if he sees anything suspicious, people die. Tara and I are the best shot we've got."

Nazareth and Gimble walked over to Sameer, who smiled a bit even though he trembled badly.

"Bag of chips, Sameer," Nazareth said, "and say your home address out loud for my friend on the phone." When Khan had done so, the detectives told him to have a nice day and took off. They smiled at each other as they walked shoulder to shoulder, and they were careful not to look at the black Accord when they passed it. At the next traffic light they waited patiently, still jabbering and munching their chips, then crossed the street and walked out of sight behind the buildings.

"Here we go, Tara," he announced. "Costume change."

"Nazareth goes undercover, does he?"

"It's the only idea I've got at the moment, and we can't spend all day thinking about this."

They walked over to a young guy who was hawking caps, T-shirts, windbreakers, and cheap sunglasses for both home football teams. "Good afternoon, friends. Giants, Jets, whichever you love. Got it all right here."

Nazareth went with the Giants. Ball cap with a gaudy Giants logo, neon blue sunglasses, extra large T-shirt, and a dark blue windbreaker.

"Okay, that's, uh, $58 plus tax -- I always charge tax, by the way -- less an automatic 40% NYPD discount." The guy smiled at both of them. "Kinda obvious, you know? But send your buddies over. Got plenty of stuff here for them and their kids."

"I absolutely will do that," Nazareth assured him as he removed his sport coat and button-down, then pulled on the oversized Giants T-shirt. When he added the windbreaker, hat, and glasses, he looked like just another Sunday fan still celebrating last week's win. "How do I look?" he said to Gimble.

"The slacks are a little off with that outfit, but not enough to notice," she said, "But the shoes don't cut it. They stand out big time."

Nazareth eyed the vendor's beat-up basketball sneakers. "What size do you take?" he asked.

"About eleven, I guess. Why?" the guy asked.

"Any chance I could borrow them for about 15 minutes for some police business?"

"Seriously?"

"Very seriously," Nazareth nodded. "We've got something major going down right now."

The vendor slipped off his sneakers and stood on the pavement in his bare feet. "Go for it," he said. "But you autograph the shoes when you get back, right?"

"Deal," Nazareth smiled.

"You look okay now, Pete," Gimble told him. "Just don't walk like a cop when you go down there. Put your hands in your pockets and shuffle along. Too bad you don't have a beer to carry."

"Hey, I can fix that for you," the vendor said as he opened his small cooler. He pulled out a 16-ounce Bud Light whose glistening red and blue can bore the N.Y. Giants logo. "You never know when it's going to get warm out here, you know?"

Nazareth reached for his wallet, but the guy said, "Hey, it's on me. Go kick some ass."

"Will do. And thanks. Hey, Matt, what's our guy doing?"

"Still sitting in his car watching Sameer. Left elbow is hanging out the window, and it looks as though he's scratching his beard with his right hand."

"Both hands are empty?" Nazareth asked.

"Looks like, Pete. But I don't have a great view because of the glare off the windshield. And I definitely can't see whether the passenger window is open. But I can tell you we've already got the start of a crowd outside the building. I guess a lot of people are skipping the park and coming straight here."

"Okay, here's what we do, guys," Nazareth said. "I'll head down the sidewalk as though I've had one too many. I'll stick close to the buildings so I'm less obvious in case Aziz is watching for me. If the passenger window is closed, I'll stagger around the back of the car and grab him through the driver's side window. But if the passenger window is open, that's how I'll take him down."

"If he's got the doors locked," Gimble said, "he may have enough time to detonate the cart before you can get in."

When the vendor heard *detonate,* he uttered a low, "Oh, shit. Should I be leaving now?"

"You'll be fine right here," Gimble told him. "Just don't go around the corner until this is all over."

"And how will I know when that is?"

"You'll know it if you don't hear it," Nazareth answered cryptically. "You have a mirror, Tara?"

"On my cell phone," she nodded.

"Okay, give me about 30 seconds, then use the mirror to watch me. As soon as I'm in the vehicle, get down there as fast as you can. Go to the driver's side and do whatever needs doing. Don't worry about getting blood on me as long as it's his." He gave her his best wiseass smile, then popped the beer can. "Gotta make this look real," he said.

Rahman Aziz was in his glory, for today he and his followers would drive another stake into the heart of the Great Satan. By his conservative estimate at least 300 people would die and perhaps 1,000 others would be severely injured when 500 hundred pounds of C4 wrapped with 100 pounds of nails and ball bearings tore through the crowd. He almost valued the injured more than the dead, because they would go through life remembering, revisiting, and replaying the events of this day.

He was especially glad that many of the victims would be the Muslim turncoats who cared more about living than destroying non-believers. A special good riddance, he thought, to the cowardly hot dog vendor who cried like a girl when given the honor of becoming a martyr. Yes, today ISIS New York would strike another devastating blow for the righteous. In time Rahman Aziz and his brothers would bring New York City to its knees.

Aziz watched Khan carefully for any signs of disobedience. If this hot dog man failed him in any way, he would call upon his brothers to kill the man's wife and children. Perhaps he should have them all killed anyway, since obviously they had fallen just as far from the path as this mongrel of a hot dog seller. Yes, he would make that call when he drove away from the blast site. Aziz also kept checking his mirrors, looking for potential problems, most especially the man and woman he had seen talking with Khan while buying their hot dogs. But, no, they were long gone. After eating their disgusting meals they had probably gone to some park where they could mate like pigs in the bushes before going back to work. May they return just in time to be consumed by the holy flames at One Police Plaza!

Aziz noticed the drunk who spilled beer on himself as he staggered into buildings and even some of the people he passed. The filth that passes for human life! he thought. Look there, a woman turns and yells at the man for almost knocking into her baby carriage. Aziz uttered a brief prayer: please let this drunken infidel be among those who are sent to hell this very day.

As Nazareth approached the black Accord he noted that the passenger window was fully open. Plan A, he told himself. You get only one shot at doing this right.

He wobbled to his right as he pretended to drink his beer, banged clumsily into a brick building, and seemed to lose his footing as he staggered left toward the car. A quick look told him that Aziz still had both hands free -- left arm out the driver's window, right hand stroking his gray beard. When he was eight feet away from the vehicle Nazareth took three powerful strides and dove head first through the open window, fists and forearms locked in front of his face so that he became an airborne battering ram. Aziz barely had time to turn toward his attacker when the detective's 165 pounds slammed into his upper body, ripping the right shoulder from its socket and shattering the collar bone. The terrorist stopped screaming when Nazareth's punch fractured his jaw and rendered him instantly unconscious.

"Looks as though I don't get target practice today," Gimble said as she appeared at the driver's window, gun in hand.

"No, but it's nice to know you were there, Tara," he smiled.

"Glad to be of service, Pete. Do you see his cell?"

He fumbled around on the front seat. "Ah, wait, it's on the floor." He picked the phone up and looked it over. "Lucky us," he grinned. "The number is already punched in. All he had to do was push SEND."

Gimble suddenly looked ill. "Or all you had to do was roll on it while you were playing Superman."

"Or that," he said mildly.

"You okay down there?" Matt shouted into Nazareth's earpiece.

"Except for my deaf left ear, Matt. Yeah, we're cool. Aziz is ready for his ambulance."

"On the way," D'Elicio said. "And all's well over at Sameer Khan's house. Four guys in the car, just as Sameer's wife had said. Our Special Ops gentlemen left three of them dead and one who wishes he were. Bomb Squad is already with Sameer taking care of the cart."

"Terrific, Matt. Many thanks for walking us through this."

"Hey, for you, always. And remember, Pete, dinner's on you."

"You heard that, huh," Nazareth said.

"Yep. I'm Tara's witness. Have a good time, you two."

21.

Officers Paul Bledsoe and Jason Wyatt had the heat turned up in their patrol car as they rolled through the side streets of Lower Manhattan on another chilly November night. It was shortly after midnight, early in their shift, and both were having trouble adjusting to the oddball weather. Some recent days had felt a lot like summer, but others -- today was one of them -- were definitely borderline winter. Tonight the temperature would dip into the upper twenties, and the Channel 7 meteorologist was calling for at least a half inch of snow.

"Who the hell ever heard of snow in November?" Bledsoe complained.

"Crazy, right?" Wyatt said. "Actually the snow isn't the problem. I still have a few pink tomatoes in the garden, and the freeze will finish them off."

"Can't you cover them?"

"Nah, that only works with frost," he explained. "With a hard freeze you lose everything. I can't complain, though. It was a really good season for tomatoes."

"It wasn't a great season for golf," Bledsoe said. "I swear the more I golf, the worse I get. Last year I was under 90 every round. This year I was closer to 100. And I had brand-new clubs."

"There you go," Wyatt laughed. "Dump the new clubs and go back to the old ones."

"You might be right about that."

"I had the same problem with skiing a few years back. I had just bought new skis, and . . ."

His story was cut short by the dispatcher, who had a report of a body being stuffed into a white van about six blocks from the officers' location. A neighborhood resident had looked out her bedroom window and spotted a guy across the street lugging the body to the van's side door, then taking off in the general direction of the FDR Drive. The frantic woman woke her husband to tell him what she had seen; the groggy husband told her to mind her own damn business; and 10 minutes later she finally found the nerve to call 911.

"Oh, great," said the disgusted Bledsoe. "After 20 minutes we're supposed to find a white van that was headed toward the FDR Drive. Hey, Jay, grab that crystal ball in the back seat, will you?"

Wyatt just shook his head in dismay. "After 20 minutes at this time of night the guy could already be in Long Island City or the middle of Brooklyn somewhere. So now we should stop every white van we can find? Shouldn't be more than 100 of those on the street right about now."

A few minutes later, as they cruised East 14th Street heading toward the FDR Drive, they spotted a white van parked under a tree across from the Stuyvesant Town apartments.

"Hey," Wyatt said, "odds are only one in 10 million that this is a white van with a body stuffed in the back."

"I'll flip you to see who gets out and freezes his ass off," Bledsoe answered. "Or do you just want to take turns? I figure we won't have to search more than 30 or 35 white vans tonight."

They rolled up behind the van, and Bledsoe hit the flashers. As soon as Wyatt got out of the cruiser and took a few steps, the van roared off in a fog of burning rubber, took a hard right on Avenue B, and began flying south. The officers were half a block away when the van jumped the curb at Tompkins Square Park near East 9th. As soon as the vehicle screeched to a halt, the driver threw open the door and ran for the trees.

"Aw, shit. I really want to run through the damn park tonight," Wyatt complained. "This jerk really thinks he's going to disappear in a park the size of a pool table?"

"Who the hell knows? You jump out here, and I'll drive around to the other side. I'll also call for backup."

"Yeah, make sure you stay nice and warm."

Ten minutes later Wyatt found the middle-aged suspect up against an oak tree with a knife to his throat. The knife belonged to 22-year-old Nathan Chambers, who had been sucking down a can of malt liquor when he heard someone running toward him. It is generally a mistake to run toward a stranger after midnight in Tompkins Square

Park, and Chambers explained that unless the older guy came up with some money, he would lose his right ear, his nose, and his privates in rapid succession.

"NYPD!" Wyatt yelled. "Drop the knife, and both of you hit the ground."

Before Chambers could think about running, Officer Bledsoe ran up from the other direction, gun drawn. "You heard the man. Down. Now."

Bledsoe and Wyatt handed Chambers off to the first two cops who had responded to the call for assistance. Then they walked the older guy back to his van. He said his name was Ted Hayes and claimed he hadn't been driving the van in question. Curiously, however, they found the van's registration in his wallet.

"Will you look at that," Bledsoe said in mock amazement. "Another guy named Ted Hayes dumps his van and runs into Tompkins Square Park. Did you two bump into each other while you were hanging out with Mr. Chambers?"

Hayes was dumb, but not so dumb that he thought he could talk his way out of being the van's owner. "Okay, look, it's my van. But I didn't do anything wrong. A month ago I was beaten up by four guys who pulled me over with a phony police light in their car, and I wasn't going to fall for that again," he told them.

"Gee, they had flashers on the roof of their white sedan with blue stripes?" Wyatt asked.

"I didn't see what kind of car you guys were driving. I saw the lights and freaked. I thought it was the same punks who beat me the last time."

"So you decided to run around in the park," Wyatt said, "instead of staying in the vehicle and trying to find a police car?"

"Yeah, I did."

"Playtime is over," said Bledsoe. "Open the doors so we can see what's in the back."

"Don't you need a search warrant for that?" Hayes asked timidly.

"After you took us on a high-speed chase through Manhattan and tried to escape into the woods? Did your friend Chambers perform a lobotomy before we found you?"

The guy was offended. "Hey, nobody performed anything on me. I'm not into that stuff."

Bledsoe looked at Wyatt as though Hayes had just levitated. Wyatt simply shrugged.

"Open the van right now."

They found the body nestled in a thick layer of bubble wrap. Slender female, 5-8, 100% fiberglass. "A store dummy?" Wyatt said.

"I bought a bunch of them from a dress shop that went out of business," Hayes said nervously, "and I sell them online."

Bledsoe rocked the mannequin back and forth to see whether it was heavier than it looked. "No drugs in this thing?" he asked.

"Hell, no. It's just a damn mannequin."

Bledsoe locked the guy's eyes in a cold stare. "How about that big plastic bag under the blanket?" he said. "Any drugs in that?"

The large bag in question was filled with smaller plastic bags, each containing a white powder that Bledsoe assumed wasn't flour. Total street value of the coke was north of $40,000.

"That's not mine," Hayes yelled. "Someone must have thrown that in there while I was in the park."

"Tell you what, Mr. Hayes. We'll find out whose fingerprints are all over the bags, and we'll arrest his ass for you. Sound like a plan?" said Wyatt.

"I'm not saying anything else," Hayes countered.

"Good. Because, in fact, you do have the right to remain silent. Anything you say can and will . . ."

As Bledsoe read Hayes his rights, Wyatt noticed the vehicle that drove by. "Check it out, Paul. Another white van."

"Yeah, only 10,000 more out there," he smiled.

As he passed the crime scene Ryan Driscoll smiled and nodded amiably to the two officers.

22.

Driscoll had spent a long night upgrading the safe room in his 13th Street basement. For less than $100 he was able to outfit the space with a remote security camera featuring two-way audio. Now he could check his cell phone at any time to see and hear what was going on. But installing the system had been a major chore. First he had to cut a hole in the ceiling's soundproofing shell, then fit the camera's lens inside the mesh of the steel security cage. Once finished with the basic system set-up he had to repair the soundproofing and test-drive the new device. After downloading the communications software for the fourth time, he finally got the spy cam up and running. Now all the room needed was its next occupant.

As he drove toward the Downtown garage where he kept his van, Driscoll spotted the flashing lights alongside Tompkins Square Park. He rolled by slowly and was unpleasantly surprised to see a white van whose apparent driver was in cuffs. What in God's name, he wondered, would cause police to stop a white van almost identical to his own? What did the cops find that caused them to arrest the driver? And what if they had accidentally stopped him instead? What would the police make of his unique delivery apparatus? Was there any trace of his victims in the cargo hold? Had any witnesses yet linked a white van to the RTS killings? He was spooked, no doubt about it.

But not so spooked that he wouldn't remain faithful to his mission. After all, his basement headquarters was now fully equipped and very much open for business.

23.

Nazareth and Gimble sat in the conference room finishing their reports on the foiled terrorist attack. How can it be, they wondered, that you spend more time on paperwork than on the actual arrest? Truth is indeed stranger than fiction. But their written accounts of the takedown would be agonizingly dissected and criticized by Rahman Aziz's legal team, which had already claimed that their client was innocent of all charges. Just a devout Muslim sitting in his car praying for peace, they said. And along came the NYPD thug and injured Aziz simply because he had "the wrong look."

Gimble took the call on her cell phone shortly after 9:00 a.m. Elena Munoz, girlfriend of the late Rafael Tejera, had some information she hoped might be helpful to the detectives. She and Gimble arranged a noon meeting in Midtown, where Munoz worked for one of the City's top banks.

"What does she have?" Nazareth asked when his partner told him about the meeting.

"She was just heading into a big meeting with her boss," she said, "so she didn't have time to give me the details. Sounds as though Tejera left a note, but that's all I know."

They went back to their written reports.

"Can you imagine any defense attorney on the planet claiming that Aziz is an innocent victim?" Gimble asked.

"Hey, Tara, some of these attorneys are bigger dirtbags than their client, and this is never going to change. But don't worry about Aziz. We've got Sameer Khan's testimony as well as the cell phone that was already programmed to detonate the bomb. He goes down."

"I hope you're right, Pete. But I still wonder when the courts began caring more about the civil rights of murderers than justice for dead victims. If you hadn't gotten Aziz when you did, he would have killed people. And now his attorneys argue that you entered his vehicle illegally. Am I the only one who thinks the system is broken?"

"Not at all. Everyone thinks it's broken," he smiled, "except for the murderers. But, trust me, this one is over. The only issue for Aziz is what size cell he gets in what prison. Either way, I figure he won't last a week no matter where they send him."

"Prison justice?"

"You bet. Even in prison people won't ever forget 9/11. Guys like Aziz should hang themselves rather than face what's waiting for them inside."

"Here's hoping."

At noon sharp they sat in a pricey coffee shop on East 51st with Elena Munoz, an attractive dark-haired young woman who wore a medium-blue lightweight wool dress and a black jacket, both Armani. Gimble figured the outfit had set Munoz back at least two grand. She had heard that top executive assistants in Manhattan earned as much as $70,000, and this seemed to prove the point. Not bad money. A detective with Gimble's experience earned more, of course, but executive assistants don't normally get shot at as part of the job.

"I hope I didn't waste your time, detectives," Munoz began. "I know you haven't had many leads on Raffi's murder, so I figured something was better than nothing."

"Whatever you have for us is well worth the trip, Ms. Munoz," Nazareth assured her. "We're after someone who's motivated by hate, but right now we can't tell you much more than that. You told Detective Gimble that Mr. Tejera left a note of some sort."

"Yes, I finally found the strength to pack up Raffi's things," she said softly, "and I found this in a drawer under his sweaters. It was an odd place for a note, and it seems awfully cryptic to me." She handed Nazareth a yellow sticky note on which someone had printed *Adolphus Fleischer, deli 14th nr 2nd, 10:30.*

"Is this Mr. Tejera's handwriting?" Gimble asked.

"Yes," she said. "Very strong, highly stylized lettering. I always told him he was meant to be an artist."

"Does any of this mean something to you?" Nazareth asked.

"Absolutely not. I've never heard of Adolphus Fleischer, and Raffi certainly had no need to visit a deli at 10:30 p.m. We were always asleep by 9:30 or 10:00 because we both got very early starts in the morning."

"Yet on the night he was murdered he was indeed out after 10:00," Gimble noted.

"Yes, on that night he was. I went to bed before 10:00, and he must have -- well, I mean, he obviously went out. He didn't tell me he was going anywhere. When I woke up in the middle of the night, I found his note saying he'd be back shortly. But I already told you about that note in my missing-person report."

"Right," Nazareth said as he looked carefully at the young woman's face. "You did tell us that earlier, but now I'm a little puzzled. According to the report, you weren't surprised that he had gone out, but you've just told us it would have been highly unusual for him to be anywhere but sound asleep after 10:00. Those two statements seem contradictory, no?"

She studied her folded hands for a moment. Thin, elegant fingers and a $100 nail job for good measure. No rings.

"I didn't know he was going out that particular night," she said, "but he had told me he needed to fix a problem."

"What sort of problem?" Gimble asked.

Munoz took a deep breath and seemed to ponder how much she could say without tarnishing Tejera's reputation. In the end, she opted for full disclosure.

"He needed money, much more than he had," she told them. "He was in the country illegally and was facing deportation. But he had found someone who could arrange for him to stay."

"An immigration official?" Gimble asked.

"Yes. I never got a name and didn't want one. I was really torn. I loved Raffi. He was a wonderful, hard-working man. And I tried to convince him that bribing an official wasn't the way to handle this. Unfortunately, he was way too proud to accept my help. He said it was something he needed to take care of on his own."

"How did he plan to raise the money?" Nazareth asked.

"He told me he had some jewelry he had brought with him from the Dominican Republic." She looked down at her hands again. "I'm not sure how or when he got the jewelry, but he had it. And he was trying to get a pawn shop owner to buy it from him."

"But that wasn't working, right?" Gimble said. "The pawn shop owners all wanted proof of ownership."

"Exactly. Raffi had seen too many bad movies, I guess. He thought pawn shops would take anything."

"Some still do," Nazareth said, "but the odds of finding the right one are definitely against you. So he struck out?"

"Yes. But when I found this note, I thought maybe he had come up with the name of someone who could arrange for a buyer."

"In other words, he had identified a middleman," Gimble said.

"Yes, precisely. Raffi never mentioned the names of any pawn shops or this person Adolphus Fleischer," she told them, "but I can only assume he had found the right person."

"More than likely the wrong person found him," Gimble told her. "I'm truly sorry for that, Ms. Munoz, but my partner and I really appreciate your help. You've definitely given us something to work with, and we'll keep you in the loop."

"I would appreciate that, Detective Gimble. I hope you catch this sick person before he takes more lives."

When they were back in the car and headed for the office, Nazareth turned to Gimble and said, "Okay, it's time for you to put that psych degree of yours to work. You're the profiler-in-chief on this case, so tell me what's inside your head."

"I still think we'd be better off bringing in the FBI profiler."

"No," he shook his head, "what we got the last time was so generic it was meaningless. You're right here in the City and understand how the place works. Your conclusions mean more."

"All right, then. But I'm operating under duress," she laughed.

"Understood. If this all goes to hell, you'll get full credit."

"What a guy."

"Hey, I try," he smiled.

"We agree that this guy is motivated by hate -- specifically hatred of people he doesn't want here. Three victims, all foreign-born. All three bodies left on the street outside a consulate so that we couldn't miss the RETURN TO SENDER message. Interestingly, none of the victims was physically abused prior to death."

"What does that tell you?" he asked.

"Two things. One, he took them down without violence. It's as though they each walked right into his arms. Two, torturing or butchering them isn't necessary to his plan. It's all about the symbolism -- packaging the bodies and in a sense shipping them back where they came from. If he mutilated the victims in some way the press would no doubt focus on that rather than his sick message."

"What does he look like?"

"It's a pretty safe bet the guy is white," she answered. "And I'm guessing he's middle-aged. A kid couldn't take control of these victims in this way. Shoot them, yes, but not get them to walk into whatever trap he sets. He's also young enough to haul the bodies and dump them on the street. So I'd say fifty or thereabouts."

"Motivation? Just a guy filled with hate?"

"Lots of Americans, including politicians, don't like immigrants much, but they don't kill over it," she offered. "Since this guy obviously isn't an out-of-control impulse killer, we should assume he's got a personal axe to grind. I'd bet my last dime he or someone close to him has been harmed in some way by immigrants."

"*Harmed in some way* could mean almost anything. Harmed in business, beaten up, robbed, you name it."

"Agreed. So we're still basically nowhere, Pete. We're looking for a middle-aged white guy who feels wronged by immigrants. That could be any of a million people."

"Not really. Lots of people feel wronged by immigrants for one reason or another, even though all of our families came here as immigrants. But in New York City we have only one sicko who's killing over it. We're looking for someone whose level of hatred is way, way over the top. In addition -- and very importantly -- this guy also obviously has the means and the opportunity to set up the murders. As you've said," Nazareth continued, "he somehow gets his victims to walk into his open arms." He sat quietly as he considered what he had just said.

"The victims find him."

"Exactly," he nodded. "Consider the note that Ms. Munoz found. If this Adolphus Fleischer is in some way connected to a pawn shop -- that's a big IF right now -- and Rafael Tejera was desperate for money, then maybe Fleischer set the guy up."

"Sounds reasonable. So I guess we try to find a pawn shop owner by the name of Fleischer."

"Not until we've had lunch," he insisted. "I'm starving. That $6 cup of coffee didn't do it for me."

"Ditto. Dim sum Downtown?" she asked.

"Absolutely. And maybe dinner Saturday night?" he said.

That Saturday night they pulled up to the valet at Cafe Boulud.

"Whoa, when you say dinner, you really mean dinner, don't you?" she said. "I'm somewhere between impressed and floored."

"Enjoy it," he grinned, "because after tonight it's back to Sameer Khan's hot dog stand or take-out pizza."

"I'm okay with both."

"I know that," he said. "That's one of the things I like about you."

"Simple tastes in food and men," she kidded.

"And partners."

"You're still struggling with the partner thing, aren't you?" she asked.

"Well, we're on a date, so I'm not struggling that much. But I am worried about whether we can pull this off. So for now I'm simply putting my concerns on hold and going with your idea: let's see where this leads before we overcomplicate things."

"Great idea, Pete. This will be fine."

The menu was dazzling, as expected. Gimble chose the chanterelle risotto, and Nazareth opted for the seared duck breast. To celebrate their first official date they each had a $38 glass of champagne. After they had ordered their meals Nazareth took two small boxes from his jacket pocket and placed them on the linen tablecloth.

"I bought something," he said. "Two somethings, actually. One for you, one for me."

"I hope you didn't spend too much time wrapping them," she laughed as she looked at the plain boxes.

"Hey, it's not Christmas, Tara. I just thought these would be a good idea for us to have."

She opened her box and examined a powerful tracking device small enough to be clipped on her keychain.

"His-and-her tracking devices," she smiled. "Does this mean we're going steady, or does it mean you want to know whether I go out with someone else?"

"Wrong on both counts," he laughed as he took out his cell phone. "It means that we should be able to find each other if we're running after bad guys in separate dark alleys some night. You can turn it off when we're not on duty so you don't need to worry about Pete the Stalker."

"They're a great idea, Pete. They should actually be standard equipment."

He connected her phone to the GPS device. "I agree with you completely. If you only need it once, it's worth the money."

"A toast, then," she smiled. "To our his-and-hers spy trackers."

They touched glasses. "To that," he said, "and to us."

24.

"So tell me, Tarek Elkady, did you dance in the street and cheer when the Twin Towers fell?" Driscoll sat in the shadows of his 13th Street basement and spoke with his latest prisoner over the newly installed security system. He watched Elkady frantically explore every square inch of the small safe room, but escape was impossible. No one who entered this room would leave unless Driscoll set him free, and that was never part of the plan.

"You are a crazy man," Elkady screamed. "I love this country. This is why I moved to America."

"Oh, I doubt that, my young Egyptian thief. You came here so that you and your brothers-in-arms could help bring America to its knees. That terrorist they arrested Downtown the other day, he was one of yours, wasn't he?" Driscoll demanded.

"God help me!" Elkady yelled at the camera in the corner of the ceiling. "That man was a Muslim fanatic. I'm a Christian. Why do you have me here? I came only to do business with you."

L.E.S. Pawn & Loan was the seventh shop that Tarek Elkady had visited in his search for someone who would buy his stone cat statue. He claimed that the tiny artifact, small enough to fit in the palm of his hand, had been taken from a pharaoh's tomb and found its way into his family more than 100 years ago. Elkady was a handsome, athletically built 34-year-old whose brown skin and chiseled features made him look like someone descended from Egyptian royalty. He was, in fact, a minor-league scam artist who had succeeded in charming a succession of wealthy old women as the exiled Prince Tarek Ahmed. When not fully occupied with a woman of means, he survived by selling "ancient artifacts" skillfully fabricated by his cousin in Abnub, Egypt.

"Tell me, Mr. Elkady, how long did it take you to create that piece of junk you tried to sell me? Fifteen minutes? Less?" Driscoll asked. "And if you say it came from a pharaoh's tomb, I'll pull out your tongue with a pair of hot pliers."

"I don't make them," Elkady said tentatively. "My cousin in Egypt makes them and sends them to me."

"And who in New York City is stupid enough to buy this junk?"

"Many people. Sometimes even experts. It is very difficult to know what is real and what is fake."

"Yet I knew right away, didn't I?"

"Yes, that is true. But I tell you this," he continued, "if you work with me, we can make a great deal of money with these antiquities. I can supply the product, and you can sell at a huge profit."

Driscoll laughed derisively. "That's what you think I do for a living, you sorry excuse for human life? You think I devote myself to defrauding people who come into my shop? Let me tell you something. While your grandparents were herding camels in the desert my grandparents were here building an honest business. It was honest then," he insisted, "and it remains honest to this day. That has never changed. Only the clientele has changed, and I am fixing the problem."

"I can pay you, then. Name your price and set me free. I am a man of my word."

"And I am a man of mine. So listen to this. The only place you're going is back to Egypt. As a gift I will send you there for free. As a mummy!" he laughed. "Yes, indeed, as a mummy returning to the old country."

Elkady proved to be the most stubborn of Driscoll's victims. For two days he refused to eat or drink anything his captor dropped into the safe room. Eventually, though, thirst became a fatal enemy. He drank the bottle of juice that Driscoll provided, then passed out. Two hours later his wrapped body lay at the curb on 2nd Avenue between 58th and 59th, a few steps from the offices of the Egyptian consulate.

So many countries, Driscoll mused as Elkady's body hit the street, and so few hours in a day. How much can one man do?

25.

"I'm old, not stupid," Miriam Goodwin snapped. "And I'm also not blind. I know exactly what I saw."

"Mrs. Goodwin, I'm not the police. But I need to make sure I get the facts straight before I can file a story." Reporter Andrea Wilson of the *Times* was the newspaper's top crime reporter, so she was accustomed to interviewing some hard-bitten cops and criminals. But Goodwin was a real challenge. The old woman was furious that the NYPD had dismissed her report of a body being dumped into a white van, and she was on the warpath.

"I've given you the facts, same as I gave them to the police. I saw a body being put into a white van right across the street from our apartment. But the police said it was a mannequin. Don't you think I'd know a dead body from a mannequin?"

"It was late, Mrs. Goodwin," Wilson said gently, "and it was dark. Isn't it possible that you saw the shape of the mannequin and simply assumed it was an actual body?"

Goodwin judged that she was walking a fine line here. She wanted to blast Wilson for challenging her, but she also wanted the interview to result in a story. That was the only way her husband and friends would stop mocking her over the incident.

"Let me ask you something," she said, choking back her anger. "If you see a single strand of spaghetti on a plate, how do you know if it's cooked?"

Wilson wanted to slap the old lady, but this story could be important to her series on the RTS Killer. So she smiled when she would have preferred to scream.

"I suppose it will be wet and floppy instead of dry and stiff."

"Correct," Miss Wilson. "And that's how you can tell the difference between a body and a mannequin. One of them bends at the waist when you throw it into a truck. The other one doesn't bend because it's stiff as a damn board. I looked out the window and saw a man dragging a body to the side door of his van. He grabbed the body around the chest with both arms, lifted it to the floor of the van, and then pushed it in. While he was pushing it in the body was as floppy as a strand of cooked spaghetti."

Wilson refrained from strangling the woman and completed the interview. As she drove back to the office she was finally able to look past Goodwin's difficult personality and focus exclusively on the facts the old woman had presented. It was hard to fault her logic: a mannequin doesn't flop around like a rag doll when you lift it. Furthermore, you don't need to hoist a mannequin by wrapping both arms around it. A body, yes. A mannequin, no. The thing just isn't that heavy. Probably 50 pounds or less. In the end, Wilson decided that Goodwin was a credible witness whose account had been dismissed too quickly by the police. They had caught a drug dealer with a fiberglass "body" in the back of his white van and therefore dropped the idea of a second white van with a corpse in it. An honest mistake.

Her story found its way to page one on a relatively slow news day, and the headline caught a few people by surprise. One of them was Miriam Goodwin's husband Harry, who had laughed at her overactive imagination and told her to get some professional help. Though a skeptic since birth, Harry Goodwin accepted at face value anything he read in the *Times.* So when Andrea Wilson gave credence to his wife's story, Goodwin knew he was in the doghouse. Even the offer of lunch at the Carnegie Deli couldn't get him out this time.

Another surprised reader was Vince "The Spider" Spinelli, who had fractured Aldo Guerra's skull with a twelve-inch length of carbon steel pipe filled with cement. He had planned only to beat some sense into the guy for not paying off a gambling debt on time, but Guerra had smart-mouthed him rather than take his punishment like a man. Maybe Guerra had thought he was safe because he was walking along a sidewalk in some frou-frou part of town. But you were never safe if you ran afoul of The Spider, a 34-year-old thug who would willingly write off a bad loan before tolerating disrespect.

How the hell is life fair? Spinelli asked himself as he scanned the *Times* article. Guerra shoots his mouth off, I whack him with a pipe, and suddenly I'm on page one. The police would never find Guerra, who had been remodeled by an industrial wood chipper at a farm near

Morristown, N.J. But the white van was highly problematic. It was the vehicle he used most frequently when collecting funds from his clients, and it doubled as a rolling arsenal. Selling guns was becoming an increasingly important part of his business mix, because the demand for premium weapons was skyrocketing. If he had to dump the van and rely on something smaller, his profit margin would suffer.

As he debated whether he was being overly skittish about the news article, his phone rang. Mario Lombardi. Major pain-in-the-ass old guy, Spinelli thought. Wants a discount on this, an extra that, a free whatever. What Mario should have gotten for free was a steel pipe on his forehead before he turned 70. But he was too old to beat on now.

"Hey, Mario," he said. "How you doin'?"

"I'm doin' fine," Lombardi chuckled. "How about you and your famous white van?"

Spinelli's stomach did a few quick flips. "What the hell you talkin' about?"

"What, you don't read the newspapers anymore? Big article in the *NY Times* about some stiff being dumped in the back of a white van. And get this," he laughed, "I hear through the grapevine that Aldo Guerra's missing. Not that anyone's going to miss him. I'm just sayin'."

"Hey, Mario, how many white vans do you think there are in New York City?"

"Magic white vans that make bodies disappear?" Lombardi said. "Maybe one or two. Listen, Vinnie, if you have any enemies at all out there, you better lose the van in a hurry."

"I don't have any enemies," Spinelli said calmly. Well, no enemies that are still breathing. "But I appreciate your words of wisdom, consigliere. We need to have lunch at that fish place in Flatbush sometime."

"Yeah, sometime after you get a new set of wheels."

Spinelli recalled life being simpler for his father. In the old days you paid off the right top cop, and no one cared if some lowlife ended up in the Fresh Kills dump on Staten Island. A "Seagull Special" his old man had called it. Somebody refuses to pay or tries to push his way into your business, and you turn him into a "Seagull Special."

And nobody, but nobody, would pick up the phone and bust your chops the way Lombardi had just done. My father would've used him for chum off the back of his fishing boat, Spinelli told himself. But nowadays too many people think they don't need to show respect. They're all willing to speed-dial 911 if you look at them funny. And the cops? Yeah, the cops will show up and cart your ass off for nothing. You can't bribe anybody anymore. Everything is squeaky clean. How the hell is a man supposed to earn a living?

That night Spinelli removed his guns from the van and stored them in a highly secure cinder-block garage in Queens. Then he stripped out anything that could identify him as the owner -- well, not officially the owner, since the van had been stolen off a lot in Bridgeport, CT -- and drove it to 163rd Street and Amsterdam Avenue. There he rolled down the windows, left the key in the ignition, and hopped the C train for Downtown.

Spinelli's fix for the van problem was relatively simple compared to the challenge Ryan Driscoll faced. He, too, had been surprised by the *Times* article, and he quickly concluded that a white van was no longer the anonymous vehicle of choice in the City. Some crude gangbanger had spoiled this for everyone. One lousy body dumped in one white van, and suddenly people are suspicious of all white vans. But getting rid of the van wasn't an option for Driscoll. He had far too much time, energy, and money invested in the vehicle to let it go. Besides, this was a van designed for dumping bodies. How do you explain that to some doofus at a used-car lot?

Later the same day, with a little help from Craigslist, he paid $375 up front for the use of a private garage on the West Side off 11th Avenue. He came prepared with a long story on how he was going to be working in the area and needed a safe place to park, but the garage owner never asked. All the guy wanted was $375 cash this month and every month. No questions, no problems. And the white van didn't raise any eyebrows in this neighborhood where nothing short of mass murder would attract attention.

The next day Driscoll left his Downtown garage for the last time and pulled the van into its new but temporary space. All he needed here was enough time to repaint the vehicle before moving to a new parking garage closer to home. This wasn't going to be the most professional paint job of all time, but that didn't matter. White was white; blue was blue. He taped everything that didn't need paint, then over the next several evenings used a foam roller to apply two coats of auto primer, sanding the rough spots in between. After that he rolled on two coats of dark blue Rustoleum mixed 50:50 with mineral spirits. Total cost was under $100, and the van looked pretty good for a DIY job. Shiny and bright.

Driscoll finished the second coat of blue paint just after 1:00 a.m. and began walking toward the 8th Avenue subway and home. He hadn't gone two blocks when he noticed the three guys -- late teens or early twenties -- standing half a block ahead of him. They had gone out of their way to find a spot where there were no lights to interrupt whatever it was they had on their minds. His heart began pounding as he crossed the street. If they think I'm gutless, he said to himself, so be it. Let them laugh if they want.

But when Driscoll began crossing, so did the three. He decided that his best move was to turn back for the garage, but as soon as he moved in that direction, they followed. Escape was out of the question. He would never be able to outrun them, and it was clear they wanted to get in his face. So he took a deep breath, kept his hands in the pockets of his down jacket, and walked toward the subway.

As he got closer to the three young men he saw that at least two of them were holding weapons of some sort. Knives? Screwdrivers? He couldn't tell.

"Good evening, gentlemen," he said as they moved a few feet apart from each other and slowly walked toward him. The largest guy -- 6-3 and nearly 200 pounds, Driscoll figured -- wore a nasty smile. The other faces showed nothing but hate.

"Yeah, we're gentlemen, asshole," the big guy said. "Where the hell do you think you're going?"

"Subway," Driscoll said mildly. "Just going home."

"You won't be going anywhere unless you drop your wallet and your coat on the sidewalk, then go back wherever you just came from."

"Cut him, man," said one of the others. "He's just some street bitch lookin' for guys, you know?"

"That right, you some bitch?" the big guy asked. "You out lookin' for a man like me?" They thought this was the funniest thing they had heard in a long time. "Maybe you like all three of us, huh?"

The big guy waved his hunting knife back and forth menacingly as Driscoll pulled the Glock 20 from his pocket, aimed in the general direction of the punk's chest, and fired. The 10mm round lifted the guy off his feet and delivered him DOA to the sidewalk. Before the second punk could react, Driscoll squeezed off a round at his face, which immediately disappeared in a shower of red slime. The third would-be assailant sprinted into the dark, zigzagging as he ran, and Driscoll didn't bother wasting a shot. He was no expert marksman, and it was a safe bet the guy wouldn't be going to the police about this anyway. He pocketed the gun and walked toward the subway. Driscoll wasn't especially upset over how things had turned out. This was, after all, New York City. A man's gotta do what a man's gotta do.

26.

Ryan Driscoll lived modestly but comfortably in a two-bedroom, one-bath condo on Madison Street not far from the pawn shop. He had bought the place for a song after his parents died, and now, to his great surprise, it was worth more than half a million. For that kind of money he could buy a spacious home and 10 wooded acres in Upstate New York. But then how do you earn a living? he wondered. That was the million-dollar question. Would he be able to sell the condo and the business, then use the proceeds to buy his way into the good life in some hick village up north? Sure, but only if he was ready to exit the pawn business. Not a bad idea, actually. Business kept getting tougher and the clientele nastier. On the other hand, what else did he know? He represented the third generation at the Lower East Side shop and had never even thought about trying something else. Probably never would if he was honest with himself.

So here he was in a neighborhood that literally smelled like America's melting pot 24/7, thanks to what often seemed like more restaurants per square mile than people. You couldn't spit here without hitting a restaurant: Chinese, Thai, Vietnamese, Japanese, Mexican, Spanish, Brazilian, German. God, it never stopped. As soon as one restaurant closed, the next one opened, often in the same space. What is it with chefs? he wondered. Do they all think they've got the secret to success that has eluded every failed chef before them? The latest pending disaster had opened two weeks ago to horrific reviews: a Cuban-African fusion eatery that featured things like toasted grasshopper and wood-grilled python medallions. A local food critic had risked his life by accurately reporting that "the dining room smelled like ripe hyena carcass, and the food matched." The restaurant had already set a new Board of Health record for violations, chief among them an active rat's nest in a plastic grain bin and two dead pigeons in the meat cooler.

Unfortunately, the neighborhood had much more than restaurants. It also had bountiful crime. The local realtors' organization gave the area a moderate-crime rating, which meant there were several days each month when someone wasn't beaten, raped, or shot. His grandparents were no doubt turning in their graves, Driscoll thought, if they saw what the streets of their beloved America had become. Back in the day these same streets were tough but honest. If you didn't look for trouble, you didn't find it. A husband and wife could take a walk on a summer evening and not worry about coming home a widow or widower. People knew each other . . . said hello . . . looked out for the neighborhood.

Those days were gone forever. Nowadays you didn't know the person across the hall much less someone down the block. And if you didn't carry a gun, you had no business walking the streets after sunset. Unless you're suicidal, of course. Then it was okay.

He always carried now. During the day it was his legal concealed-carry weapon, and at night it was the one he had used to blow away the two punks. He couldn't help but smile over the incident. New York City was safer today because he had eliminated two more feral animals. Too bad he hadn't been able to nail the third. But at least he had contributed to the welfare of the West Side before moving his blue van to its new parking garage four blocks from the apartment.

Driscoll was in the middle of his customary breakfast of black coffee and buttered rye toast when the paperboy dropped the *Times* at his apartment door. Coffee mug in hand, he went and got the paper, then flipped it open as he walked back to the small dining table. He choked on a mouthful of coffee and dropped the mug to the tile floor when he saw his image on the newspaper's front page.

The police sketch artist hadn't gotten the eyes or the mouth quite right, but Driscoll recognized his own face when he saw it. Short hair parted on the left. Broad forehead. Sharp, slightly crooked nose. Full cheeks trending toward jowls. Thick neck. The sketch showed the eyes larger and farther apart than they should be, and the lips were a bit too thin and perhaps a little wide. But it was a damn good likeness under the headline, **POLICE HUNT WEST SIDE KILLER**. West Side

Killer? He had defended himself against three young punks who almost certainly would have left him dead in some alley, and now he was a wanted man!

Luis Cabrera, the 19-year-old who had run for his life that night, placed an anonymous call to the NYPD and claimed that his two dead friends were innocent victims of a robbery gone bad. The three of them were just hanging out listening to music and texting their girlfriends, he said, when this old guy came up and propositioned them. When they told him they weren't interested, he demanded their wallets. His two friends hesitated, and the guy shot them at point-blank range while Cabrera took off down the street.

The investigating detectives had no trouble identifying the two dead men. To begin with, their wallets and cash were still in their pants. In addition, and perhaps more to the point, they each had long records and were well known to local cops as grade-A prison material. It had been a matter of when, not whether, they did hard time.

Early in the investigation the police found their way to Cabrera, and the kid crumbled under questioning at his home. He admitted the old guy hadn't tried to rob them, which explained why the valuables had been left behind. But he stuck to his story about being propositioned. The police didn't care about that one way or the other. Someone had killed two people, and it was up to them to track the guy down even though he had most likely done the City a favor.

Young Cabrera was not only a felon in training but also a rather talented artist who had a sharp eye for detail. His description of Driscoll had been as accurate as possible under the circumstances -- poor light, shots fired, being high from sharing a couple of joints with his friends. What he saw in the police sketch was precisely what he remembered having seen on the night of the shootings. But portraits are mostly about the eyes and mouth. Get those wrong, and you get the face wrong. So the sketch was well wide of the mark and in fact did not look much like Ryan Driscoll. It might have been any middle-aged white guy in America. The only two people who thought otherwise were Cabrera and Driscoll.

By the time he left for the shop that morning Driscoll had done his best to look like someone else. N.Y. Mets baseball cap. Sunglasses.

And plenty of stubble on the face that he feared was going to attract the attention of every *Times* reader in the City. All he did at the shop that day was use a black marker to make a crude CLOSED FOR VACATION sign on a sheet of typing paper. Having affixed it to the shop's front door, he walked to the garage, tossed the small overnight bag in the back of the freshly painted van, and hit the road for Harrah's in Atlantic City. For under $75 a night he would take a well-earned break from reality while working on the new Ryan Driscoll.

You have to roll with the punches, he told himself. You need to stay flexible if you want to survive. But he was angry. He had simply been defending himself from street trash, and now his face was on the *Times'* front page -- the victim branded the criminal. This, he told himself, was simply one more bit of evidence of the decline and fall of the American way. He saw the signs everywhere.

American schools were forced to teach classes in every bizarre language under the sun. Why? Because the courts didn't dare offend immigrants who didn't feel like learning English.

More than three-quarters of immigrant families with kids were now on welfare. More than three-quarters of them! Why? Because bleeding-heart politicians cared more about the wretched refuse than the country's native-born sons and daughters.

We're all supposed to stop saying Merry Christmas. Why? Because we might offend some heathen who hates America in the first place. And for the first time in nearly 100 years kids at the elementary school down the block weren't allowed to have a Halloween parade. Why? Because the ones who recently jumped off the boat think Halloween is Satan's work.

Enough already! America's soul was being gnawed to pieces by immigrant vermin, and Driscoll would take no more. Shame on me, he told himself, if I sit back and do nothing while rats devour the seed corn.

27.

After only a few days on the job Acting Mayor Elliot Dortmund was sick of the RTS Killer complaints flooding his office. Even though Manhattan was under attack by religious extremists like Rahman Aziz, more than 75 immigrant advocacy groups had descended one by one on City Hall to demand "serious police action" and an arrest in the RTS case. The most vocal of the protesters was Marguerite Della Rossa of Protecting Immigrant Society, an organization that Dortmund and his key staffers had labeled the PIS-ants.

Della Rossa -- born Marguerite Barlowe in Greenwich, CT -- had come from big money, married even bigger money, and decided to burnish her image by speaking out against injustice. After considering animal rights, gay rights, and abortion rights, she and her husband decided that immigrant rights made the most sense. Immigrants had high potential as a key voting block, and Marguerite's husband, Danelo Della Rossa, was a wealthy radio station owner who had visions of running for mayor one day. So it was no surprise when wife Marguerite began pounding the airways with a message whose primary goal was to trash City Hall's temporary incumbent.

"Elliot Dortmund was a do-nothing as the City's public advocate," Della Rossa huffed one morning during her heavily promoted rush-hour talk show, "and nothing has changed. He went from being the worst #2 in City government to the worst #1. Can you guess who's paying the price for his incompetence? New York City's immigrants! They're being killed both figuratively and literally while Dortmund hides behind his desk and his p.r. flacks. How many more bodies do we need to carry from the gutters before someone cordially invites the NYPD brass to get off their asses?"

Not surprisingly, Della Rossa's scorched-earth assault during prime listening time prompted the acting mayor to call the police commissioner, who called the chief of department, who called the next guy, who called the next guy until finally Deputy Chief Crawford invited Nazareth and Gimble into his office for an energetic discussion of the facts.

"The only bigger imbecile than Della Rossa is Dortmund," Crawford began, "and I'm praying that both of them get hit by delivery trucks before the day is over. But in the meantime I have to provide this jerk with a formal report explaining why we have four dead immigrants but no suspect in custody."

"Any chance you can give him the old we-don't-have-a-crystal-ball excuse?" Nazareth asked.

"Doubtful," Crawford said. "Dortmund actually believes that all he has to do is call and tell us to arrest someone, and we do it. As public advocate he spent all day every day picking up the phone and having people kiss his butt and agree with him. So as far as he's concerned that's how the world really works."

"I have a better idea," Gimble offered. "Why don't you tell him to check on the illegals who dust and polish Danelo and Marguerite Della Rossa's $20-million brownstone? From what I hear . . ."

"Oh, God, don't go there, Tara," Crawford interrupted. "I don't care if they keep slaves . . ."

"Basically that's what they do," she shot back.

"Okay, got it," he said. "And it's probably true. But no way do I raise that subject with Dortmund. He wants to be the permanent mayor, so he's not going to war with the Della Rossas. He's gutless."

"In that case just give him what he wants, Chief," said Nazareth. "Tell him that Tara and I are working this case 24/7 and that we're getting close. We've got an unhinged middle-aged white guy who hates immigrants and is sending New York City a very carefully orchestrated message. He's clever, he's careful, but he's made some mistakes. And we're on his tail. We'll close this case before the end of the year."

"And all this is true?" Crawford asked solemnly.

"I'd say so. How about you, Tara?" he asked.

"Pretty much."

"How much is *pretty much*?" Crawford said.

"I think all of it's true, Chief," Nazareth nodded. "Listen, if this case isn't closed soon, the three of us will get transfers to hell anyway, right? So what have we got to lose by talking tough? Let Dortmund shoot his mouth off to the press and tell the world we're about to arrest this lunatic. Hey, it might even help. Maybe the guy stops killing for a while. Or he panics and does something stupid. No downside, Chief."

Crawford weighed his options and decided to go with the bold approach. "Okay, I'll lay it out for him this way and see what he says. Just make damn sure that you stick to the story if he decides to stop by for a photo op."

"After what happened to his predecessor I doubt Dortmund will be looking for photo ops," Gimble noted.

"Good point," the chief grinned. "He'll probably just call."

"Speaking of which," Gimble said, "I have a couple of calls I need to make if we're finished here."

"Let me catch up with you, Tara," said Nazareth. "I need two more minutes of the chief's time."

After Gimble left the office Nazareth turned to Crawford and took a deep breath. Over the years the chief had carefully nurtured a reputation as a growling, ill-tempered sort who was all business all the time. But Nazareth had seen a more human side of his boss a few months ago, following the shooting death of Nazareth's former partner, Detective Javier Silvano. So he figured Crawford was the right guy for this conversation.

"I need some personal advice, Chief," he began.

"Is everything okay with you and Tara?" Crawford asked.

"Oh, yeah, she's a fabulous partner."

"I didn't mean as your partner," the chief smiled at the surprised look on Nazareth's face. "What, I'm stupid as well as a pain in everybody's ass? I knew you two were a couple before you did. So what's the problem?"

"Chief, if I had false teeth I'd be picking them up off the floor right now," Nazareth said, obviously stunned by Crawford's comment. "Tara and I have been pretty discreet about this."

"You've been very discreet, which is good. But I'm not a mailman, am I? I'm a detective, so I detect things. What's your question?"

"Well, I had planned to ask whether this was going to be a problem for you."

"As your boss all I care about is the job you two do," Crawford said, "which is always excellent. As a friend I can tell you that a good team is a good team. If somewhere down the road you two should decide to get married, then we need to rethink the partnership. But in the meantime, just keep doing what you're doing."

"I really appreciate that, Chief. I was hoping you'd be okay with it, but I hadn't thought you were already clued in."

"Well now you know. And listen," Crawford growled, "if you tell anyone I've gone all touchy feely here, you'll be a crossing guard in East Jabip. Are we clear?"

"We're clear, Chief."

"Good. Want a cup of coffee?" Crawford said as he filled his cup from the old pot behind his desk. He waved some of the steam toward his nose. "Today I'm catching just a hint of wild raspberries and paint thinner."

"I've, uh, had enough for one day, but thanks."

"No guts, no glory, Pete," Crawford said. "Now go forth and catch me an RTS Killer."

The detectives spent the remainder of the day piecing together the few facts they had on each of the four RTS victims, hoping to find a common thread. Had the four men ever met? Did they have a friend, or enemy, in common? Did they shop in the same stores? Useful information on the four was scarce. Nazareth and Gimble had trolled for details among acquaintances of Saliou Ba, Kevaughn Brown, and Tarek Elkady, and what they had come away with wouldn't fill a shot glass. All three men had lived on the fringe of society. They were too new to the country to have many close friends, even inside their ethnic communities, and all three had apparently made ends meet through a variety of quasi-legal or outright illegal activities. So their acquaintances either didn't have much to say about them or simply refused to talk for fear of being linked to whatever crimes the three may have committed. The only victim they understood reasonably well was Rafael Tejera, whose girlfriend, Elena Munoz, had provided the detectives with a solid lead about someone named Adolphus Fleischer who might or might not be a pawn shop owner.

"We're sure that Tejera was trying to connect with a shady pawn shop owner," Gimble said, "and it's possible that the other three were doing the same thing. It might even be likely that all four of these guys were trying to unload hot merchandise."

"And in this great big city of ours they all happened to stumble across the same pawn shop?" Nazareth said skeptically.

"It's not all that far-fetched, Pete," she continued. "Think about it. On any given day you have hundreds of recent immigrants going into pawn shops all over the City for some reason. But we don't have hundreds of victims. We have four. So we may have a serious whacko who runs a pawn shop and cherry picks immigrants who come into his store. If he's extremely careful about who he chooses, he could definitely find four victims who are basically shadows -- people who come with almost no strings attached."

Nazareth considered the idea. "The outlier is Rafael Tejera," he said. "Full-time job, steady girlfriend, pretty stable guy. Not much in common with the others except possibly a need for quick cash."

"Right. Tejera wouldn't have fit into this at all except that he was clearly trying to unload something he shouldn't have owned. In all likelihood he stole it before he left the Dominican Republic and cleaned up his act. Didn't want to get his girlfriend involved."

"And ended up meeting with this guy Fleischer in the middle of the night."

"There you go. My research indicates that there are only three Adolphus Fleischers in Manhattan," she told him. "No links to pawn shops as far as I can tell. But as of fifteen minutes ago I have all three home addresses."

"Outstanding. We're ready to hit the road, then?"

"Absolutely. And on the way you can tell me what the chief had to say about us." Nazareth looked like that proverbial deer in the headlights. "Oh, come on, Pete. You've been obsessing over this partner thing for weeks, and I was sure you'd end up talking with him. He's fine with it, correct?"

"Yeah," he grinned, "he is. And how did you know that?"
"Your girlfriend is an NYPD detective, Detective."

28.

Driscoll was shocked by what $73 a night got him at Harrah's. The king bed with a top-shelf mattress and fancy sheets put the junk in his apartment to shame. Large TV, writing desk, couch, A+ bathroom, and even a small fridge. And the view! When he looked out the window he saw the Atlantic Ocean, not a couple of winos rummaging through trash cans under the Manhattan Bridge. A man could get used to this.

But first things first. After hanging up his clothes he followed the GPS app on his cell phone to the nearest salon that offered services for men. He invested $85 in an extra-short haircut and some coloring to get rid of the gray. When he left the place, having spent enough to buy five haircuts at Mario's barber shop back in Manhattan, he was satisfied that he already looked substantially different from the face in the police sketch. In a few days he would have a good start on a mustache and goatee to assist with the makeover.

In the meantime, he needed one more piece of equipment. He drove to a local optometrist and purchased an inexpensive pair of clear-lens eyeglasses with thick brown frames. The man he saw in the mirror looked little like the old Ryan Driscoll. He was confident that when he returned to the City at the end of the week, no one would mistake him for the man wanted for eliminating the two West Side punks.

Although he was pleased over the successful change in his appearance, he grew increasingly angry over the toll the process was taking on his finances. He wasn't a rich man by any means, yet here he was paying the price for having been victimized. Hotel room, meals, hairstyling, glasses, and all the rest. Not to mention the closed shop. His small business generated no revenue when the place was closed, and he had no way of knowing how much income would walk away from his locked door while he was in Atlantic City. You defend your life, and suddenly you're a wanted man. And on whose say-so? Luis Cabrera! A 19-year-old hoodlum who probably swam ashore with his parents after slinking out of some tropical hellhole. Welcome ashore, Driscoll mused, where immigrants can do nothing wrong and real Americans can do nothing right.

His anger had reached the ignition point by the time he returned to the hotel and walked into the casino. It was too early for dinner, and he was certain it would be a mistake to sit alone in his room while his mood blackened even further. So he decided to blow a few more dollars by playing the slots. He would play until he lost a hundred bucks or calmed down, whichever came first.

Things had changed quite a bit since his last trip to Atlantic City 15 years ago. He was surprised to learn that slot machines are equipped with buttons instead of handles, while slots that actually accept coins are virtually extinct. Two really dumb changes, he thought. The thrill of pulling a handle and waiting for actual coins to come rattling into the tray was the best part of the experience. Now all you do is sit there pushing the button like a damn robot. This might not help his mood after all.

He walked around for a while watching the crowd, then took a seat that had just been vacated by an obvious loser -- a disgruntled guy whose wife was jawing at him for having dropped half a mortgage payment into the machine.

"I go get a facial and you lose more than $700?" she screamed. "And you tell me you don't have a gambling problem?"

"Not here, not here," he complained as he headed for the exit.

"Not here, Frankie? Not here? It's your brain that's not here!"

Driscoll didn't know anything about the game other than that it cost money and had just cleaned out some schlump named Frankie. But on his seventh try he won nearly $3,000, cashed out, and left the casino floor with a big smile on his face for the first time in weeks. He had just recovered the cost of shutting down his pawn shop for a week, and he suddenly found himself able to enjoy a couple of fine meals on the house. Hey, maybe he'd even get a massage. He hadn't gotten a massage in more than 20 years.

He dined at McCormick and Schmick's inside the hotel that night. Since the casino was buying, he decided to go for broke. A dozen fresh New Jersey clams on the half shell to start, a nice Caesar salad, and then an eight-ounce filet mignon, medium rare, accompanied by a lobster tail. He washed everything down with a bottle of Prosecco. The total tab ran to over $200 with tip, or roughly four times the most expensive meal he had ever enjoyed prior to his big casino win. Tomorrow night it's a hamburger, he vowed, but before heading back to Manhattan he would spring for at least one more deluxe meal.

While he was sipping his black coffee and relaxing, a group of five men a few tables away began half singing, half shouting a song in some language that Driscoll didn't recognize at first. Throughout the dining room heads began turning, and folks who were paying big money for their meals began badgering the waiters for some relief. Finally the maitre d' visited the offending table and asked for some quiet, earning a hard elbow to the gut for his efforts. The guy who hit him yelled something to his friends in what Driscoll now took to be Russian, and they all began hooting and cheering. Diners from the neighboring tables scrambled away as four large casino security guards stepped up and appeared ready to break some heads. But the incident abruptly ended when one of the five partiers -- a burly guy in an expensive suit -- held up his hand to the four others, and they immediately fell silent. The five of them walked out of the restaurant without paying the bill while one of the security guards helped the maitre d' to his feet.

"Goddamn thugs," said a guy at the table next to Driscoll's.

"Can you believe that?" Driscoll said to him.

"Oh, yeah, we can believe it," he answered. "My wife and I have been here a week, and that's the third or fourth time those same guys have caused trouble. But no one will touch them because the top dog is such a high-roller."

"They're all Russian Mafia," the wife added confidentially. "One of the security guards told us."

"Yeah, high-rollin' Russian Mafia," the husband said. "They do whatever the hell they want, and they get away with it."

"Shouldn't be like that," Driscoll said shaking his head. "The hotel should throw them all out."

"Don't count on it," the husband said. "The hotel manager probably likes having two arms and two legs."

On the way back to his room after dinner Driscoll stepped onto the elevator and leaned against the far wall. He heard someone yell, "Hold it!" as the door began to close, but he figured he couldn't catch it in time, so he didn't bother trying. Just before the door slammed shut a meaty hand reach in and smacked the doors open. Unfortunately for Driscoll, the hand belonged to the large Russian who had elbowed the maitre d' in the stomach.

"You deaf, asshole?" the guy roared at Driscoll. "I told you hold doors."

"No, I didn't hear anything," he answered nervously.

"*I didn't hear anything,*" the Russian mocked in a simpering tone as his companions laughed. "Maybe you hear better if I put foot up your fat ass, huh?"

Driscoll wanted to kill all five of them right here, right now. But his gun was hidden in his room, and killing five Russian Mafia members on the elevator probably wasn't the best idea he'd ever had anyway. So he bit his lip and prayed for the ride to be over.

"You don't care what I say, huh, little girlie?" the guy taunted. When Driscoll refused to respond, the Russian grew angrier. "What, now you don't talk? You don't like me so much, huh?"

As the Russian leaned closer to Driscoll, the group's head man barked a one-syllable command that stopped the guy cold. He glared at Driscoll but didn't move. When the elevator slowed for his floor, Driscoll stepped around the large Russian and waited for the door to open. As it did, the guy grabbed Driscoll's collar with his left hand, pulled him backwards off balance, dug a vicious right fist into Driscoll's lower back, and then tossed him out of the elevator. Driscoll fell to his knees holding his back, then collapsed on the carpeted floor in paralyzing pain. Behind him the Russians laughed as the elevator doors closed.

For the next two days Driscoll stayed in his room while the blood gradually disappeared from his urine. His lower back looked as though it had been hit with a baseball bat, and it hurt worse than it looked. So he spent much of his time soaking in the bathtub and popping Tylenol.

Whenever he felt strong enough to eat he called room service and went with light, inexpensive meals. Because of the pain, fine dining in one of the hotel's restaurants was out of the question.

What he mostly did while in seclusion, though, was read up on the Russian mob. He was at his laptop at least six hours each day, learning as much as possible about their various enterprises, which embraced everything from arms trafficking to kidnapping to drugs to Medicare fraud. They were widely viewed as insanely brutal and willing to kill anyone for almost any reason. Doing business with them, said one former FBI agent, was like walking on eggshells with a live grenade in your hand. If you didn't fear these guys, he said, you were either stupid or already dead.

It didn't take Driscoll long to find an article on the leader of the five Russians with whom he had shared the elevator. Anatoly Volkov, age 58, was headquartered in Brighton Beach, N.Y., a place that several reporters had identified as ground zero for the Russian Mafia in America. Volkov was a legitimate businessman who owned a bakery, a restaurant, and a car dealership. But the consensus was that Volkov used these businesses to help launder the many millions that his illegal activities generated each month. Two years ago an undercover cop had penetrated Volkov's organization, but the investigation ended abruptly when the officer was found lying under the steel track of a massive bulldozer at a construction site in Queens.

Taking revenge on Volkov and his crew was not something that any sane person would attempt, Driscoll realized, but it should be relatively easy to find a worthy substitute. If Russian immigrants had become a cancer within America, then someone needed to eradicate it. He memorized the address: 9 East 91st Street, home of the Russian Consulate in New York City. His mood improved markedly. Before the year was out he would return a Russian to his sender.

29.

The Adolphus Fleischer whose East Village address was first on Gimble's list had died a month earlier at 83. When the detectives reached his apartment they found the man's son and daughter-in-law carting old magazines, dilapidated furniture, and a large collection of beer bottles downstairs to the dumpster.

"No, he was never involved with a pawn shop," the son told Nazareth, "but he should have opened one with all this crap. When he came to America after World War II he had nothing, so he refused to part with anything he ever got. Yesterday we threw out canned food he must've bought in 1950. Hope to hell he wasn't eating that crap."

"What did he do for a living?" Gimble asked.

"He was a tailor, and a damned good one at that. At 78 he was still making custom suits for CEOs of big companies," the son said. "But then the arthritis got so bad he had to stop. By the time he died his hands looked more like claws than hands. It was awful."

"No chance he might have hooked up for some reason with a pawn-shop owner?"

"Not possible, detectives. He hadn't been out of this apartment for nearly two years before he went to the hospital. He watched TV, drank, and ate whatever food I brought. No one visited except me," he said, "and he wouldn't set one foot outside the door."

As they left the building Gimble said, "Seems like the old guy was a prisoner in his own home."

"Happens a lot in the City, Tara," Nazareth said. "At a certain age this is no place to live. If you're 80 and get whacked on the head while you're walking to the grocery store, you're finished. So a lot of old people simply lock their doors and hide."

"Depressing."

"No doubt about it. So where are we headed next?"

She checked the second address. "First Avenue near 38th."

"Ah, Murray Hill," Nazareth said.

"And not just Murray Hill," Gimble replied. "The Corinthian."

"Whoa, big time. I doubt this Adolphus Fleischer runs a pawn shop." The Corinthian was a stunning fifty-seven story apartment tower whose finest units sold for $4 million or more. If you wanted to rent instead of buy, a four-bedroom retreat would set you back as much as $20,000 a month. "No idea what he does?"

"None. But I can tell you he has two vehicles registered. A Ferrari 458 Italia worth over $300,000, and . . ."

"Wait, let me guess. A 1969 VW bus."

"Very close, Pete. Actually it's a Rolls-Royce Phantom that cost nearly $500,000."

"You've got to be kidding me," he said. "Why is he living in an apartment instead of on his own private island somewhere?"

"I guess we'll find out, won't we?"

They did. Adolphus Fleischer's luxurious place at the Corinthian was simply his weekday home, he told them after inviting them in and offering them whatever they felt like drinking. Nazareth was sorely tempted by the Glenfiddich 50-year-old single malt scotch, because he had never sipped from a $25,000 bottle of anything. In the end, though, he and Gimble settled for water while Fleischer explained that his real home was a $75-million gem situated on nearly 100 lush acres in Westchester County. The 46-year-old stayed in the City for most of each week and traded his own portfolio from an array of ultra-high-end computers in a small office next to his bedroom.

"I can actually do the trading anywhere," he told them, "but I often like having breakfast or lunch with former colleagues as well as officers of companies in which I'm investing. So Manhattan still works for me, but I refuse to commute here from Westchester."

Fleischer howled with delight when the detectives explained why they had visited him. "A pawn shop! That's absolutely wonderful. No," he smiled, "I have never needed to visit a pawn shop. Three years ago I retired from the hedge-fund business with about $7.3 billion in the bank. Well, not a bank, actually. I wouldn't put a dime in a bank."

"And you're still a full-time trader?" said Gimble, clearly amazed that a billionaire still worked every day.

"This is what I do, Detective Gimble," he said warmly. "It hasn't been about money for a very long time. Some people play golf; I trade.

It's what I love to do. Every now and then my wife decides we should take a trip, and we go. But otherwise this is where I like to be. If I stopped doing it, I'd be an old man in a hurry."

Nazareth and Gimble thanked him for his time, and as Fleischer opened the apartment door for them a gorgeous young woman who might have stepped from a magazine cover prepared to enter. She had her key out and was obviously startled when the door swung open.

"Oh, God," she laughed, "you scared me, Dolph."

"I'm so sorry, Morgan. Please say hello to Detectives Pete Nazareth and Tara Gimble. They came to see if I'm in the pawn-shop business."

"A porn shop?" she said.

"It's a long story. I'll tell you all about it."

She smiled sweetly at the detectives and gave Fleischer a peck on the cheek. "Nice meeting y'all," she said as she glided toward the kitchen.

Fleischer winked at the detectives. "What happens in New York City stays in New York City, right?" he said as he shook their hands.

The next Adolphus Fleischer lived on West 109th Street a few blocks away from Central Park. "Third time's a charm, Pete," Gimble said. "Let's hope the next guy means something to the case."

"He can't possibly mean less than the first two, can he?"

"Not likely. But anything is possible in Manhattan."

"Can't disagree with that," he nodded.

The man who answered the doorbell looked like a cross between a clown and a visitor from another galaxy. Pudgy, 5-8, hair down to his shoulders, and covered from head to toe with brightly colored dust and glitter. Nazareth and Gimble wondered what they had stumbled onto this time.

"Please tell me you're not the models!" the guy squealed in a tinny voice.

"No, sir, I'm Detective Pete Nazareth and this is my partner, Detective Tara Gimble. Are you Adolphus Fleischer?"

"That's the name on my driver's license," the guy said, "but in the art community I'm known as Ronay. Why are you looking for me? If it's about the parking tickets, I'll just pay the damn things."

"Not parking tickets," Nazareth told him. "Can we come in and talk to you for a few minutes?"

"Lucky for you I just finished shooting the first scene. So, yes, I have some time," Fleischer said. "But I'm expecting two models, and as soon as they get here I'm finished talking with you. Models get paid by the hour as soon as they set foot on location."

He offered the detectives seats on a large couch from which he removed a rumpled sheet and bedspread. "I sleep here because I use the bedroom as my art lab," he explained. "I usually do two ensembles a month, and I can't sleep in the bedroom while those are in progress."

As Fleischer sat down on a heavy wooden chair he sent a cloud of multi-colored dust billowing from his clothes. Gimble's curiosity took charge.

"Forgive me," she smiled, "but I'm trying to figure out exactly what sort of art you do. I'm completely baffled."

"You came here to ask me about my painting?"

"No, sir, but you've certainly aroused my curiosity. If you'd rather not discuss it, though, that's okay."

"Please, that's quite all right," he said eagerly. "Come look at the work space."

He led them to the lone bedroom of his unkempt apartment and opened the door. They saw nothing but blackness. When he flicked the switch on a small spotlight mounted in the corner of the floor, they found that the entire room -- walls, floor, and ceiling -- had been painted high-gloss black. Good luck getting the paint off the hardwood floor, Nazareth said to himself. We'll be back here for the murder investigation once the landlord sees this.

"What I do is called dimensional expressionism," he explained. "I use a network of fans and strobe lights to manipulate colored particles in a closed space. The result is what I call an ensemble. What happens is I adjust the room's airflow and lighting according to the theme of the current artwork, turn on the video camera, then throw handfuls of colored dust and glitter into the room's atmosphere.

When you got here I had just finished the first element of *Mayan Dream*. The two models who should arrive shortly will help create the second element. They'll strike a variety of poses while the atmosphere operates around them."

"Ah," said Gimble. "Sounds very interesting. I'm not familiar with dimensional expressionism."

"I'm the first to work in this medium," Fleischer said proudly. "Some artists work in three dimensions -- sculptors, for instance -- but I work in four by adding time to the mix. Each work of art lasts only a few seconds. I keep a video record of each ensemble, but that's not the art. The art is solely what happens in this room."

"How exactly do you make money with that?" Nazareth asked.

The guy was horrified. "Money has nothing to do with it, Detective. This is about expressing one's soul."

"But you still need to eat, right?"

"Yes, quite true, detective. I do need to eat, and I eat quite well," he said as he turned off the room lights. "Full professors earn quite a lot these days, especially at the University."

Nazareth dropped the subject, appalled that a university would pay someone a lot of money to blow colored dust around in a black room. So he told Fleischer why they had visited, and the professor shook his head.

"Insanity is one of the primary themes that I explore in dimensional expressionism," he said seriously, "and what you're describing is totally insane. It's insane that someone is murdering immigrants, and it's insane that you're here questioning me about this. I have no time to hang out with pawn-shop owners and murderers."

It might be better than what you're currently doing, Nazareth wanted to say.

"Mr. Fleischer . . ."

"Ronay," the guy corrected.

"Right. As far as we can tell there are only three people in Manhattan named Adolphus Fleischer," Nazareth said coolly, "and that name is the only possible link we have to a growing list of dead bodies."

"Well, I wish you well, but I can't help," he said. "I assume you've already translated the name."

"What do you mean *translated*," said Gimble.

"Adolphus Fleischer. It's one of the reasons I use the name Ronay. I've hated my real name since I was about 11 years old," he told her. "The German name *Adolphus* means *noble wolf.* The *Fleischer* part means *butcher.* This is news to you?"

"Yes, absolutely," she replied.

"Then perhaps I've helped you after all, detectives." The doorbell rang. "And now it's time for me to concentrate on art, if you don't mind." He opened the door to a couple in their late teens. The guy had strong Latino features that seemed perfect for Fleischer's Mayan art project. The girl, on the other hand, looked about as Mayan as Alice in Wonderland. Fleischer seemed displeased as the detectives thanked him for his time and walked out.

"Dimensional expressionism?" Nazareth said to Gimble.

"Sort of like the emperor's new clothes," she laughed.

"And someone actually pays him to teach that sort of thing?"

"I hate to break the news, Pete," she said, "but if he's a full professor, he's probably making $200,000 a year."

"For teaching students how to throw colored powder in front of a fan?"

"No, for helping them explore the meaning of their existence in space and time," she grinned.

"I need pizza," he said.

"So do I. Right after I get all this colored dust off me. But first, tell me what you make of the German translation."

"Right about now I wish I had taken German instead of Spanish."

"You're better off with Spanish in New York, Pete."

"Yeah, I guess. But if I had known about the meaning of the name before, we would have taken a shortcut."

"How so?" she asked.

"Instead of assuming we were looking for an actual person," he said, "we would have realized it's a pseudonym for the murderer's other self. We've known from the beginning that this guy is in the message-sending business, what with the RETURN TO SENDER stamp and the wrapped bodies. But now we also know he's convinced of the rightness of what he's doing. He's the *noble wolf* whose job is to *butcher* the undesirables."

"Another major-league sick puppy."

"You and I seem to be magnets for them," he said, shaking his head. "If I had to guess right now, I'd say this guy passes as a perfectly respectable pawn-shop employee or owner who's constantly trolling for victims."

"Who end up in the back room being wrapped in plastic."

"Maybe, maybe not," he said. "We know that Rafael Tejera disappeared late one night after his girlfriend went to bed. If in fact he met someone who was using the name Adolphus Fleischer, they didn't meet at the pawn shop. There's no pawn shop anywhere near the address on the note we looked at."

"So this guy lures the victims to another place?" she asked. "If that's how he's operating, he's playing a dangerous game. What if the vic shows up with a friend? Or a gun?"

"We've already concluded the guy is smart and has plenty of potential victims, so I'm guessing he simply waits for loners. So far that's been the case except for Tejera. But remember," he added, "even Tejera was a loner when he went out that night. If the killer watches from a distance, he'd easily make sure things look right before moving forward."

"Easily?" she said.

"Too strong a word. Nothing about this would be easy. But he could certainly control things quite a bit and bail out if he didn't like what he saw at the meeting place."

She considered that for a moment. "I wonder whether he's used the same meeting place each time."

"If he has a safe place -- an apartment or a favorite alley, for instance -- then probably. But otherwise I assume he would change things up just in case the police got hold of the address."

"In that case the only place we're going to find him is in a pawn shop," she said.

"Of which there are roughly 600 in New York City."

"Are there really that many?"

"Yep."

"Let's go get that pizza," she laughed. "I can see we're going to be burning lots of calories."

30.

Driscoll returned to Manhattan a new man. He looked different, and that alone made the trip to Atlantic City worthwhile. But he was also surprisingly well rested. The Russian's punch hadn't done any serious damage, so the net effect was that Driscoll had relaxed for the first time in years, eaten well, slept more than usual, and saved some cash from his brief slot-machine encounter. Above all, he had come home with a mission. He was going to bag a Russian bear, no doubt about it.

Finding the right one would take some time, of course, because not many Russians came into his shop. Most of them lived in Brighton Beach and stuck close to home, where pawn shops were relatively plentiful. So he coached himself to be patient. Good things take time, and he wasn't going to rush the process and risk making a major mistake. He also had plenty to keep him busy in the meantime.

At the top of his list was deflecting some of the attention that the RTS Killer had been garnering in Manhattan lately. He was somewhat alarmed to read that the NYPD considered an arrest imminent. Were the detectives handling the investigation actually making progress? Or was this just bluster, a case of someone trying to cover his butt in the press? Driscoll didn't believe he had left any damaging clues behind for the police, but he decided that his next victim would come from New Jersey. It was time for Adolphus Fleischer to become a Garden State immigrant, at least temporarily, and he was going to begin by dedicating himself to some unfinished business.

His niece, Meryl Connolly, had been gang-raped in Brooklyn by what he still referred to as "a pack of South Asian mutts." He didn't care where the rapists had come from. India, Pakistan, Bangladesh, Nepal, or some other hellhole were all the same to him. Someone must pay for destroying young Meryl's life.

His first step was to search online for New Jersey's immigrant groups, and it took only a few minutes to learn that those from India led the way with nearly 11 percent of the state's total population. Next he researched New Jersey homes for sale. A minimum price of $600,000 seemed about right, but above all the place needed to offer a full measure of privacy. Driscoll didn't need any nosy neighbors interfering with his plans. Proximity to Manhattan would be a plus, but he would be flexible for the right property. After less than 10 minutes he found a lovely colonial on a large, relatively secluded lot in Ridgefield Park, only 14 miles from Downtown via the Lincoln Tunnel.

Now he needed the right real estate agent. This search took a bit longer, but after looking through the agent lists at three large firms he finally found Vishesh Joshi, who advertised himself as a million-dollar producer and had a bunch of fancy professional designations after his name. Vishesh Joshi! How many Americans are out of work today because Vishesh Joshi and the rest of the Indian horde have moved in? he wondered. He desperately wanted a Russian, but for now an Indian would do nicely.

Driscoll called the agency and asked for Joshi.

"He's just finishing a phone call," the woman said. "Would you like to wait?"

"Yes, thank you."

"Can I tell him who's calling?"

"Yes, my name is Adolphus Fleischer. I'm calling about a home in Ridgefield Park," Driscoll said.

"Okay, thank you. Please hold."

After 30 seconds Joshi picked up the line. "Good afternoon, this is Vee. How can I help you Mr. Fleischer?"

Driscoll forced himself not to laugh. The guy probably flew here on a damn magic carpet, he thought, and now he calls himself Vee. Just one of the good ol' boys down at the bowling alley. Tony and Hank and Joe and Vee.

"Yes, good afternoon, Vee. And please call me Dolph," he said. "I found your name on a list of New Jersey's top real-estate agents and wonder if you might be able to help me with a home in Ridgefield Park." Driscoll gave him the MLS number, and Joshi was eager to show a $600,000 home to a buyer who had simply fallen into his lap. If only the business were always this easy!

"I haven't seen the home yet," Joshi said, "but that's certainly a lovely neighborhood. Are you just moving to the area?"

"No," Driscoll chuckled, "I've lived in Manhattan for many years. I'm looking to buy a home for my daughter. She's getting married in two months, and this will be my wedding present to her and her husband." He pictured the agent drooling all over his phone.

"Will you be financing the home for her?" Joshi asked discreetly.

"No, I'll be paying cash. I'm hoping that an all-cash transaction will help me get the best price possible," Driscoll explained.

"Oh, most definitely," Joshi told him. "Cash is best. When would you be able to close?"

"Once I find the right property," he said, "all I need is an inspection. I want very much to close well ahead of the wedding."

"Well, Dolph, I see that this home has been on the market for 132 days, so the seller should be ready to negotiate. I can help you move very quickly if this is the right property."

Driscoll had set the hook and would now reel the guy in. He asked to see the home at 7:00 the following evening. "I can't get away during the day, so I hope an evening appointment isn't a problem for either you or the sellers."

"That's not a problem," Joshi said. "My time is your time, Dolph."

"Well, I certainly appreciate that, Vee. Sounds as though you're just the person I've been looking for."

At 6:50 the next night Driscoll pulled up in front of the home in Ridgefield Park. Joshi was waiting in his car, keeping himself warm on a blustery, 21-degree early December evening, and he got out as soon as Driscoll walked toward the front door.

"Dolph?" Joshi called.

"Yes, good evening, Vee. I almost called to cancel," Driscoll said. He had concluded that his hand-painted van might be a liability to someone pretending to have $600,000 in cash lying around, so he had concocted a story for it. "My car had a flat, but luckily I was able to borrow my future son-in-law's van. It's a piece of junk, but it got me here in one piece."

"Oh, I'm so glad, because I am sure you will like this home."

Driscoll quickly eyed the neighborhood and was distressed to see seven cars parked in the driveway and alongside the curb at the home across the street. A football party perhaps? The home's blinds were open, and through the bay window he saw at least eight or nine people wandering around the living room.

"The home looks nice from the street, Vee," he said, "but I'm not so sure I like the location. I really want something more secluded than this. I'm a little put off by all the cars across the street."

"I know exactly what you mean," Joshi nodded as he pulled the collar of his winter coat tighter against his throat. "This seems to be a very busy street. But, you know, I have another home that could be exactly what you're after."

"Okay, then I guess we can meet again later this week," he said, disappointed that he wouldn't be able to send Joshi on his way to hell tonight.

"Actually we can see it right now," Joshi said. "It's my own listing, and the owners are in Florida for the winter. I can show the home whenever I like. Five bedrooms, four baths, and nearly two acres. The only problem is that the home is listed for nearly $800,000."

"The price really isn't an issue, Vee," Driscoll said calmly. "I want the right home in the right neighborhood for my daughter."

"It's a wonderful thing you're doing, Dolph," Joshi said brightly, "and you will absolutely love this home. No more than 10 minutes from here." He tried to conceal his excitement as he got into his car, but he was definitely flying high. He had done some online snooping after his phone conversation with Driscoll the day before and had found a news item on an Adolphus "Dolph" Fleischer who had been one of the country's top hedge-fund managers before retiring a few years earlier. He hadn't bothered to look for another story, and it hadn't occurred to him to search for a photo. Who else has $600,000 just sitting there waiting for something to buy? he asked himself. This had to be the same Dolph Fleischer.

When he had parked in front of the second home he grabbed the listing sheet and got out to meet Driscoll, who had already left his van and was happily surveying the neighborhood. He liked what he saw. The huge home was the last one on a dead-end street and sat on an exceptionally private, heavily treed lot. The nearest neighbor was 50 yards away on the same side of the street. Across the street: woods. Lovely, dark, and deep. Joshi had done himself proud.

"Do you like the location, Dolph?" Joshi asked as he walked up to him.

"This is precisely what I had in mind, Vee. Precisely."

"Excellent, excellent. Then let's go take a look inside. That's the best part," he smiled.

"Let me get my briefcase, Vee. Is it okay if I take some photos for my daughter?" Driscoll asked.

"You're really not supposed to," Joshi said confidentially, "but if you don't tell, I won't tell."

"I promise not to tell anyone," Driscoll grinned as he opened the van's side door. He pretended to fumble with something in the cargo area and said, "Vee, can you help me with this for a second? My briefcase is stuck under a mountain bike."

"Oh, yes, let me help you, Dolph."

As soon as Joshi leaned into the van, Driscoll put a gun to the man's ribcage. Joshi looked down, and his eyes widened.

"If you do anything other than what I say," Driscoll hissed, "I will blow you all over the street. Do you understand?"

"Yes, but why are you doing this?" he stuttered.

"It's very simple, Vee. I'm kidnapping a million-dollar producer," Driscoll told him, "and your family will pay $100,000 for your safe return. Once I get the money, you will go home to your family."

"I'm not a rich man, Dolph," Joshi pleaded. "That's not what million-dollar-producer means."

"I don't care what it means, Vee. Your family will pay for your safe return. But if you cause me any trouble," he said, "you'll go home in a body bag. Understood?"

"Yes, I understand," he whimpered.

"Very good. Then put those handcuffs on." Driscoll had attached the cuffs to a length of chain bolted to the van's floor. "Put your right wrist in and lock it, Vee. Good. Now the left." Driscoll checked both wrists to make sure the cuffs were securely fastened, then ordered Joshi to climb into the van and lie down. Finally he pulled a length of cloth across his prisoner's mouth and tied it tightly behind his head.

"Now we're going for a short ride, Vee. And if you cause me any trouble at all I'll pull into the woods, douse you with gasoline, and set you and the van on fire. Does that sound like a plan?"

Joshi nodded, and Driscoll slammed the van door shut. The ride to Driscoll's prisoner quarters on 13th Street took slightly more than an hour, during which Joshi did nothing to arouse his captor's anger. He focused instead on the $100,000 ransom and wondered whether it was customary for a hostage to negotiate a lower amount. If he believes I don't have more than $50,000, he thought, I will save a great deal of money. But what if he somehow already knows how much I have? Or what if he threatens my family? Or what if he tortures me into telling the truth? Before Joshi could decide on the best strategy, the van reached its destination.

When Driscoll opened the side door he immediately placed the gun to Joshi's forehead and removed the gag. "Remember to do exactly as I say," he ordered, "and we'll be finished with this in a few hours."

"I will do exactly as you say."

"Then listen carefully. When I remove the cuffs, you will sit up, get out of the van, and walk alongside me. If you make any sound or try to call attention to yourself, I will shoot you in the head. This is a promise, Vee, not a threat."

Joshi did as ordered and entered the basement one step ahead of Driscoll. A minute later he sat alone, locked in the safe room while Driscoll checked to make sure the remote camera and sound system were operating properly.

"Now give me your home phone number and your wife's name," Driscoll said over the speaker, "and I'll take care of the rest."

"She will not know how to get the money," Joshi complained. "For that I will need to speak with her."

"Oh, please, Vee," Driscoll laughed, "I'm not going to let you talk to her in your Hindu jibber-jabber and tell her where we are. Am I that stupid?"

"No, Dolph, you are not stupid. I will speak English to her. You can listen. But if I don't tell her how to get the money," he said nervously, "she will not know how to do it."

"Tell you what, Vee. We'll pick this conversation up again tomorrow night. Perhaps by then you will realize that I make all the decisions. I set the rules. I tell you what to do. I decide when you leave this room."

"Fine, Dolph, I will give you my phone number so that you can speak with my wife," Joshi pleaded, "but please don't leave me in this room until tomorrow night."

"Too late for that, Vee. You should have learned better manners before you jumped off whatever boat brought you here. I don't like ill-mannered immigrants. In fact," he said angrily, "I don't like any immigrants."

He turned off the speaker and was gone.

31.

Nazareth fell asleep around 10:30 p.m. on his living room couch and didn't wake up until nearly 1:00 a.m. He turned off the 70-inch flat-screen TV, killed the lamp on the end table, and walked over to the window that looked out on the East River. From the 12th floor of his East 24th Street apartment the City looked almost gentle in the dark. Without the noise, the jostling, and the smells, he thought, the place is actually quite beautiful. He savored the mesmerizing display of glittering lights, reflections, and third-quarter moon. All seemed peaceful.

He knew better. He understood better than most that down there on the streets life was anything but peaceful. That message got reinforced every day when he stepped out of the apartment building and hit the pavement after another night in his safe cocoon.

His two-bedroom apartment was well above the means of the average NYPD detective, but some money his parents had left him and a bit of wise investing had made the purchase possible. Maple hardwood floors gleamed from the entry all the way to the far end of the living room, where the huge TV graced the wall. The galley kitchen featured stainless-steel appliances and eye-popping marble countertops with silver and gray veins swirling through a black background. The bedroom nearest to the kitchen had been converted to a high-end gym fit for a former Marine. All in all the apartment was a haven from the dangerous realities of Manhattan.

But time was running out on this portion of his life. You can live here only so long, he reminded himself, without becoming a captive. The older you get, the more hazardous the place becomes. And the more you try to insulate yourself from those hazards, the more hardened and cynical you grow. Before long you forget what it's like to let your guard down and just live. You begin looking over your shoulder constantly, wondering who's going to try to threaten you or rob you or stab you.

I get more than enough of that on the job, he thought. If marriage is in the cards, maybe even a family, it can't be here. There needs to be another place where all this goes away -- a place where you can sit on the patio and drink a beer while listening to the birds sing, where you can look up and see a billion stars in the night sky. It was out there somewhere, and he felt it getting closer.

How in God's name did a city like this one become a haven for every form of lowlife on the planet, he wondered. Scammers, muggers, rapists, murderers. Predators of every size, shape, color, religion, and nationality preying upon people who just want to earn a living and raise their families. Do they come here because of the sheer numbers of potential victims? It's like hunting in the zoo, he thought. Everywhere you turn you can find the elderly, the sick, the frightened, and the disabled. If you want to do bad things, this is certainly the right place.

But is it more than that? Is there something about the City that makes criminals feel at home? Are the side streets, alleys, slums, subway tunnels, bridge underpasses, and parks so inviting that New York City is the place where every dirtbag on the planet wants to settle? And does the madness ever end, he asked himself, or do we keep throwing more cops and more money at the problem until the planet ceases to exist in another million years?

Nazareth was able to get his head around a poor kid making terrible choices. He didn't excuse it, but he understood it. Hunger can make you do bad things. What he could not fathom, however, was someone like the RTS Killer. Here's a guy who probably passes for normal, works a regular job, and has a few drinks with his buddies at a local bar. Then when the spirit moves him he kills people because they left another country and came looking for their share of the American dream.

When the hell did Americans ever do otherwise? This is how we all got here! he wanted to scream. We're all immigrants! We're the ones who made the City great. And now this sick SOB is killing people because he doesn't like . . . what? Skin color? Language? Dress? Religion? All of the above?

What's driving him? Hate, yes. But hate triggered by what? Is it possible to know? Hell, is it even worth knowing? How could a person be prompted to kill over something as absurd as "differentness." There had to be more to it. In the end, though, motive no longer mattered in this case. All that mattered was taking a madman off the streets. The RTS Killer was making the City -- and by extension the Department -- look bad. Nazareth took that personally.

As he studied the night he thought about Tara Gimble. A great partner, yes, but also perhaps the woman he had been waiting for. They made a great all-around team, and he could easily imagine settling down with her in a quiet spot somewhere in the heart of America. She had been born and raised in Brooklyn, the daughter of an NYPD sergeant. Would she ever move? Was being a detective what her life was all about? Did she ever think about being a wife and mother? He didn't know, and it was too soon to ask. But that conversation was coming. At some point soon they would decide where they were headed.

He checked his cell phone. The tiny tracking device he had given Gimble showed that she was in her apartment, safe for another night. But that would change once again when she reported for duty in this life-or-death business they had both chosen. Nazareth would never forget that his previous partner had been gunned down during what had seemed to be a low-risk arrest. Bad things do, in fact, happen to good people.

He prayed that nothing bad would happen to Tara Gimble . . . and wished that she were with him right now.

32.

When Driscoll visited Joshi the next night around 10:00 he found him crying at the table in his cell. The guy was sobbing so loudly that he almost didn't hear Driscoll's voice over the speaker.

"Crying like a little girl, Mr. Gandhi?" he taunted.

"My name is not Gandhi," Joshi screamed, "and I am thirsty and hungry. Why are you doing this to me?"

"You have a short memory, my friend," Driscoll said. "It's all about money. And you're in luck. I spoke with your wife, and she's going to pay $200,000 for your release."

"What? We do not have that much money. It's impossible," he wailed. "You said you wanted $100,000."

"She's going to sell your house. Isn't that wonderful? You'll get to go home, and I'll get $200,000. America really is a land of dreams, isn't it?" Driscoll had not spoken with Joshi's wife, but he took cruel advantage of this opportunity to exact one further bit of revenge on his captive. "Well, actually you won't get to go home, because the house will be gone. But at least you and your wife will be together, eh?"

"Please, Dolph, I have done nothing to harm you. I do not deserve this."

"Oh, really? Tell me, then, when was the last time you were in Brooklyn?"

"Brooklyn? I have been there, but I can't remember when."

"Do you have friends in Brooklyn, Vee?"

"Friends, yes, and family. I know many people in Brooklyn."

"Then tell me, Vee, what went through your mind after your friends and relatives gang-raped my niece?"

"What? Are you mad? My friends and relatives are good people!" he yelled.

"Don't make me laugh, Vee. You and I both know that raping women is just a bit of harmless fun where you come from, isn't it?"

"You are insane. The only woman I have ever touched is my wife."

140

"I read the papers, Vee. India is the rape capital of the universe. Rape is your national pastime. Don't insult my intelligence by denying it."

"I am sorry for your niece, Dolph. But my friends and I have never hurt anyone, and we would never think about raping a young woman."

"I didn't tell you she was young," Driscoll snapped. "How did you know that if you weren't one of the rapists?"

"I, I just assumed she was young," he stammered. "I have no idea how old she is."

"You sound like a guilty man to me, Vee. Perhaps I should have you sign a confession, eh? That would make me very happy."

"I would never sign a confession to something I didn't do," he said angrily. "You could kill me, and I still wouldn't sign."

"If I killed you, you wouldn't be able to sign, would you?" he laughed. "The hunger has gotten to you." Driscoll opened the small access door and dropped in the customary bottle of iced tea and a granola bar. "Let's take this up again after you've eaten."

Joshi finished the iced tea and the snack bar in less than two minutes. Five minutes later he was unconscious on the floor. Shortly after 2:00 a.m. Driscoll slowed the van as he passed the Indian Consulate on East 64th Street, opened the van's cargo doors, and watched in the driver's-side mirror as the body hit the pavement. He saw no one, and no one saw him. He turned right on Park Avenue and calmly drove home.

Another successful mission under his belt, Driscoll was pleased to have avenged the brutalization of his niece. But the fire in his gut burned for a Russian. The thugs in Atlantic City had probably come close to killing him, he thought. A knife instead of a punch, and it would have been all over. At the same time the humiliation of being laughed at and taunted as he lay injured on the floor was even more infuriating. What kinds of cold bastards are these people?

His face grew red as he looked back on the encounter. Sooner or later the right one would come along. When he did, Driscoll would be ready.

Somewhere in New York City a dead Russian walked the streets.

33.

The long letter from Sabni Yaseed almost never reached the right hands. It was mailed from the ancient city of Al Qasr on the northern edge of Egypt's Dakhla Oasis. Nearly two weeks later it landed on the desk of an overburdened functionary at the Egyptian Embassy in D.C. After being kicked up the chain for three days, the letter was finally overnighted to the Egyptian Consulate in New York City, where it fell under a secretary's desk and went unnoticed for two days until a meticulous janitor picked it up and placed it on the young woman's chair. Twenty-four hours later the letter finally reached the Consul General, who called Nazareth.

"Detective Nazareth, this is Dr. Ashur from the Egyptian Consulate," he began. "You asked me to call if I learned anything at all about the late Tarek Elkady."

"Yes, sir," Nazareth said. "It's kind of you to remember me." Nazareth and Gimble had met with Ashur following the discovery of Tarek Elkady's body, but at the time no one at the Consulate had any information about the victim. Everyone was outraged by the hate crime, naturally, and the Consul General had vowed to call the detectives if he learned anything that might be useful to their investigation.

"I have just received a letter from Mr. Elkady's cousin in Egypt," he explained, "and it contains information that may be helpful to you. I do not know how this man, Sabni Yaseed, learned of the murder. I must assume that a friend or family member here in New York City notified him, but I have not been able to find anyone who claims to have known Mr. Elkady."

"If we could find that person here in the City," Nazareth said, "he or she might prove to be an extremely important witness. Can you reach Mr. Elkady's cousin by phone?"

"I have already tried that, Detective, with no luck. Sabni Yaseed may not have a telephone, or his name may not be Sabni Yaseed at all.

When you read this letter," he continued, "you will understand why the cousin might not wish to be found."

"Can I have someone pick the letter up?"

"I doubt the actual letter would be of use to you unless you read the language," Ashur told him. "I have had it translated as accurately as possible, and I will gladly fax it to you."

"That would be great. But please keep the original in a safe place because it's always possible that we can pick up clues from it."

"I will certainly do that, Detective Nazareth. You will have the letter momentarily."

Nazareth snatched the translated letter as soon as it came through the fax machine, and he stopped by Gimble's desk on his way to the conference room.

"What've you got?" she asked.

"Could be big, could be nothing," he said. "A letter sent to the Egyptian Consulate by Tarek Elkady's cousin. Just came in, and I thought we should look at it together. You read Egyptian, don't you?"

"Oh, absolutely. Not as well as Chinese or Vietnamese, but I do okay for a Brooklyn kid," she grinned. "But as a matter of fact, Pete, in order to read the letter I'd need to be proficient in Modern Standard Arabic, because that's the official written language."

"You're serious?"

"I am."

"How did you know that?" he asked.

"It's a bit of completely useless information that infiltrated a few of my brain cells at Stanford, and now I can't get rid of it."

"In that case I can forget it," he said. "If I ever need to know, I'll just ask you."

"That's why I'm here," she laughed.

They both stopped laughing when they read Sabni Yaseed's two-page letter, which the guy had marked "extremely confidential" before sending it to the Egyptian Embassy. Why he thought the information contained in the letter would remain confidential was anyone's guess, but the detectives knew immediately that they had just been handed a key to understanding Tarek Elkady's brief American life and death.

In his letter Yaseed pleaded with the Egyptian ambassador to help him locate "a great sum of money" -- estimated to be at least $100,000 U.S. -- which Elkady had been preparing to send back to Egypt at the time of his murder. Yaseed provided an account number for his late cousin's bank in Manhattan along with evidence of having received wire transfers from that account to his own account in Cairo. All of this was straightforward and well documented. What was not at all clear, however, was the precise nature of the business in which Yaseed and Elkady had been involved.

Yaseed claimed to be an antiquities dealer of some renown and said that his cousin had sold a number of important artifacts to U.S. museums and private collectors. He briefly described the items as statues, figurines, jewelry, and pottery dating back to the pharaonic period, which meant they were as much as 3,000 years old. What Yaseed failed to mention was how he had come into possession of such antiquities or precisely how his cousin had found his "many esteemed clients" in the City.

He did, however, provide some highly useful information about his cousin. Elkady, he said, had been living in a small Brooklyn apartment with two Egyptian families, though Yaseed didn't have the address. He also said that Elkady had worked exclusively with Manhattan clients because there was no market for antiquities in Brooklyn's Egyptian community.

"What he meant to say," Gimble said, "is that Egyptian immigrants probably aren't interested in fake artifacts."

"I'm absolutely with you on that," Nazareth replied. "If Elkady was a legitimate antiquities dealer, he managed to keep it a secret. If no one at the consulate knew of him, it's far more likely that he was a scam artist. My guess is that he was peddling fakes to anyone who would bite."

"It's a huge online business," she nodded, "and it seems to be getting bigger all the time. Even some high-end buyers are willing to pay thousands for junk that's *guaranteed* to be authentic. A few years back I worked a case involving a Mexican drug dealer who had laundered some of his money through an online business that sold

Mayan antiquities -- most of them fake, of course. I'm assuming the market for Egyptian relics is even greater."

"Tell you what. Two floors away is a guy in Major Case who I bet can shed some light on this."

"Eddie Lightner?"

"The very same."

Lightner was something of a star within the NYPD ranks because of the number of important art-related cases he had closed as a member of the Major Case Squad. The guy was widely known to be brilliant as well as tenacious as a pitbull, and he also happened to hold both undergraduate and graduate archeology degrees from Boston University. He still spent two or three of his vacation weeks each year on an archeological dig in some exotic and usually godforsaken spot, so Nazareth thought it was a pretty safe bet that Lightner could shed a little light on the Yaseed-Elkady enterprise. He wasn't disappointed.

"I've been on several digs in Egypt," he began, "and I can promise you that most of the antiquities being sold today didn't come out of the ground -- at least not in their present form. My guess is that at least 90% of the statuary currently available has been carved from chunks of limestone that some guy living in a mud hut dug up within the past six months."

"And it actually passes for authentic?" Gimble asked.

"Without question. Once the piece has been carved in the old style," he explained, "it's given an aged look through any of several methods -- being buried in camel dung among them -- then marketed to wealthy collectors who are looking for a bargain."

"And wealthy collectors can't tell a fake from an original?" Nazareth said.

"Hell, no. These are sleazy collectors who think they're operating in the black market for genuine antiquities, and they're delighted to pay $10,000 for a piece they assume should be worth $30,000. Of course, what they're getting is actually worth maybe $25. When these buyers die, they often leave their collections to museums, and even museum curators often have trouble knowing what's real and what's fake. Testing an object to see if it's genuine can cost a ton of money, so many museums don't even bother."

"So what did this guy Elkady and his cousin back in Egypt have going?" Gimble asked.

"Let's back up a step," Lightner said. "First off, the guy in Egypt probably isn't your vic's cousin, and his name sure as hell isn't Yaseed. He provided an account number for a bank in Cairo, but he didn't show either the owner's name or the current balance. My guess is Elkady actually did wire money to that account, but as soon as it hit the bank in Cairo it was sent through a network of banks to its final home somewhere far away from Egypt. There's no way this guy would show you the money."

"Okay, and second?" Gimble asked.

"And second, the guy who wrote the letter probably isn't the person who's fabricating the fake artifacts. He's more likely the line boss," Lightner said. "Under him he most likely has a dozen people who create extremely careful replicas of ancient artifacts. When they're finished he distributes them through his sellers all over the world. The cheaper items get sold online, but the pricier fakes need to be marketed face to face. I'm guessing your dead guy Elkady was one of the most important sellers, because Manhattan is serious big time."

"So his market was the wealthy," Nazareth said.

"That would have been his primary market," Lightner nodded. "He would never have tried to sell directly to museums, but he would definitely have been selling to private collectors here in the City. It takes time, but eventually he would have learned who's in the market for stolen antiquities."

"So it's unlikely Elkady would have been peddling to pawn shops?" Gimble asked.

"On the contrary. I think that would have been a regular part of his operation. It might take weeks to close the deal on a $15,000 or $25,000 major piece, but the guy needs to eat every day, right? So he would have been peddling a large number of smaller pieces to anyone he thought could be conned. People on the street, people who answer online ads, and, yeah, pawn shop owners. A lot of those owners have back-door businesses that would benefit from artifacts that can't easily be proven to be fake."

"In other words, if a buyer ultimately learns the item is a fake, the pawn shop owner can argue that even an expert would have been fooled." said Nazareth.

"Sure. If museum curators don't know fake from real, why would some pawn shop guy? You can move a lot of junk to the right people, and chances are you'll never get caught. And besides," Lightner added, "who's actually harmed? No authentic antiquities have been stolen, and the people who got fleeced are buyers who were willing to rip off Egypt's cultural heritage. Is it still fraud? Sure. Do I care? Hell, no."

"Have you had any big cases involving pawn shops, Eddie?" Gimble asked.

"Big cases, yes," he said, "pawn shops, no. They wouldn't hit my radar screen. But for whatever it's worth I'm guessing your guy wouldn't have worked pawn shops anywhere near the high-rent neighborhoods where he was peddling expensive junk to Mr. and Mrs. Richie Rich. The last thing he needed was for a wealthy client to see him mucking around in a pawn shop. I'd say he would have trolled for business either way Uptown or way Downtown."

"Makes sense. We have no solid basis for assuming that a pawn shop is involved in these murders," Nazareth said, "but we also can't rule that out. Each of the victims was operating on the fringes of polite society, so it's possible they all walked into the wrong storefront."

"You just touched on the problem, Pete. The word *storefront* covers a hell of a lot of territory," Lightner told him. "All of your victims could be connected by the same convenience store, the same liquor store, the same deli, or the same bar. No telling. My gut tells me a pawn shop is the likeliest common denominator, but don't forget about the other places."

"Got it. Thanks for your help on this," Nazareth said as he shook Lightner's hand.

"No problem, guys. And if I run across any connection that might be helpful," he said, "I'll absolutely tell you."

By the time they got back to their own corner of One Police Plaza, Nazareth thought the next steps were reasonably clear.

"Our best approach for the moment is to get a list of pawn shops and start showing the vics' photos around in those neighborhoods."

"Makes sense to me," Gimble said. "But I'm not liking our odds."

"I hear you, Tara. But it's the only plan we've got right now. So," he smiled, "do we begin Uptown or Downtown?"

"How about we begin north of 90th, then head Downtown if we strike out?"

"Done. Wear your walking shoes tomorrow."

"Fine by me. In the meantime, can I buy you a pizza tonight?" she smiled.

"I never say no to pizza. My place or yours?"

"Since I hate my place and love yours, let's dine at Nazareth's Bistro tonight."

"I'll make the reservations."

34.

New Yorkers had certainly sat up and noticed the RTS Killer's ambitious efforts, and Driscoll was elated by the recent press coverage. He didn't like being referred to as a *madman, sicko,* or *psycho,* but he considered this a small cost for so much benefit. As he saw it, he was helping the City in two ways: first by ridding the streets of immigrants, and second by igniting a nasty debate between pro-immigrant groups and Americans who, like him, saw that the country was being overrun by freeloaders. The anti-immigrant sentiment was especially vile on the Internet, where some of Driscoll's brethren on the lunatic fringe had begun referring to him as "the Great White Hope." Although he hadn't begun his killing with any long-term goal in mind, he now hoped his efforts might succeed in triggering the race war he believed was long overdue.

But that was a matter for the future. This was the here and now, and he viewed the present state of affairs as completely unacceptable. He stared at the headline on the front page of the day's *Times:* **BRIGHTON BEACH VENDETTA LEAVES FOUR DEAD.** Even by New York City standards this one was over the top. Five armed men had beaten, tortured, and then executed four family members -- a father, mother, and two sons in their twenties -- in what the police stated was mob-related retaliation for the ultimate sin: testifying against one of the gang's members in court.

Although the brutal murders had taken place on a busy street in broad daylight, the detectives working the case could find no witnesses. None. Zero. An anonymous phone call alerting them to the crime was all they had, and they didn't expect to get more. The message had been delivered to everyone in Brighton Beach: rat out the Russian mob, and you'll die badly.

The Russians are a different and dangerous animal, Driscoll told himself, and he would need to take extra precautions when dealing with them. Unfortunately, dealing with them wasn't an issue at the moment, because not a single one had come into his shop since he had gotten back from Atlantic City. He could occupy his time with immigrants from elsewhere if he wanted to, of course, but his insides were being eaten away by hatred of the Russian crew that had assaulted and humiliated him. And what had he done? He hadn't held the elevator door for a group of thugs.

What would have happened if he hadn't been inside the hotel? Or what if they had put a gun to his head and made him go outside? Would they have killed him and left him in a ditch? Would they have beaten him so badly that he'd never walk or talk again? They're worthless scum, he thought, typical of the breed.

Driscoll viewed the *Times* article as a call to action. Waiting for the right Russian to enter his shop might take weeks or months, and he wasn't prepared to wait that long. So he decided to push the pace while maintaining complete anonymity. In less than 20 minutes at a neighborhood Internet cafe he created a free online classified ad targeted to zip code 11235 -- Brighton Beach. The ad was brief and to the point: *Glock 19. Priced to sell.* To this simple message he added the number of the first of his ten disposable cell phones, which he had bought for less than $10 each. So little money for so much security! He was pleased at how technology could be put to work so easily. Now all he had to do was wait for calls.

By the end of the ad's first day he had taken three calls, all from men speaking without a Russian accent. In each case he asked for a phone number and said he would call back, but he never bothered to write the numbers down. Instead, he turned the cell phone off and tossed it in a dumpster near his apartment. The next morning he ran a new ad with the number of his second disposable phone. On the fourth call his stomach did a backflip when he heard the gruff Russian voice.

"You sell Glock 19?" the caller said.

"Yes, I do," Driscoll replied, "as long as you're the right buyer."

"What is right buyer?"

"Not the police."

"Police? Speak like me? Maybe in Moscow," he laughed, "not Brooklyn."

"Then you and I can talk," Driscoll said.

"This gun is good shape?" the guy asked.

"Perfect shape. I have several of them," he said, "all new. But I don't need them all."

"Ah, you stole them maybe?"

"Are you the police?"

"I'm not police."

"Then you shouldn't care where I got them," Driscoll said. "Do you want one or not?"

"How much?"

"Cash, $300. No cash, no gun."

"Is very cheap $300," the Russian said.

"I need the cash in a hurry," Driscoll told him, "so I'm selling cheap."

"Okay, you come here?"

"Where's here?" Driscoll asked.

"Brooklyn," the Russian told him.

There was no chance at all that Driscoll would venture to Brighton Beach. Besides, he had no reason to change a system that had been working perfectly, so he told the guy they would meet at the usual 14th Street address. The Russian said he couldn't be there until two nights later but was fine with 10:00 p.m. "When I'm certain you've come alone and aren't being watched by the police," he told the guy, "I'll call and tell you where to meet me."

"Why come alone?" the Russian asked warily.

"Because last year two guys robbed me," Driscoll told him. "While I was doing business with one of them, the other guy hit me over the head with a pipe and nearly killed me. So now I work face to face, one on one. If that's no good, you need to buy your gun someplace else."

"No, this is fine. I just wonder, is all. Now I understand."

"Good. My name is Adolphus Fleischer. What about yours?"

"Timur Gorokhov," he said gruffly. "But you do not share with anyone."

"Understood. Then I'll see you Thursday night at 10:00, Mr. Gorokhov."

The rage that had howled inside Driscoll ever since the Atlantic City encounter would soon be unleashed. Too bad it couldn't be one of the men who had injured and insulted him, he thought, but this would still be highly satisfying. Two nights hence he would embark upon the most intensely personal of his missions, one that would take revenge to a frightening new level.

The Russian bear was going to suffer horribly for its crimes.

35.

Nazareth and Gimble got an early start the next morning after having identified more than 20 pawn shops between Central Park and 190th Street. If they really hustled, they might make a dent in the Uptown group before working their way south. Coordinating their travel would be easier than usual since Gimble had spent the night at Nazareth's place after they had dined on pizza, salad, and a bottle of chianti. Her overnight stays had become frequent enough that she now kept a few outfits at his place, and they both were growing more comfortable with the arrangement. They were a couple who also happened to be professional partners, and so far they had successfully managed to keep the two roles separate. Precisely how this would play out was still anybody's guess, but for now they were both deliriously happy.

"So we split up and hit the places separately?" she asked as they approached the first large cluster of pawn shops near the George Washington Bridge.

"Why don't we hit the first few together and see what we turn up, then take it from there?"

She looked at him curiously. "You're not worried about me, are you, Pete? Because you know I can take care of myself."

"Actually," he smiled, "I was thinking more about myself. I like having you cover my back. This neighborhood is better than it used to be, but it's definitely not the Upper East Side."

"Understood. But don't ever feel as though I need special treatment on the job. Off the job," she grinned, "you can treat me as specially as you'd like."

"Deal."

They spent the first 45 minutes stopping by local businesses -- groceries and check-cashing stores among them -- and interviewing random people on the street, but no one recognized any of the victims. Finally they hit the first pawn shop at 9:35 just as the owner, Trevor

Franklin, was opening for the day. Gimble showed him 8x10 photos of each victim while Nazareth explained why they were asking.

Franklin studied the photos carefully and said, "Three of them I have never seen, for sure. But this one," he said as he tapped Rafael Tejera's photo, "maybe he was in here. It was weeks ago, possibly more, but he looks familiar."

"Do you remember anything about him?" Nazareth asked.

"If it's the same guy, I remember I was a little surprised," Franklin said. "He seemed legit, not like some of the scammers that walk in here, and I liked what he was trying to sell. But he had no ownership papers, so that was that."

"No way around the rule?" Nazareth continued.

"No, sir. This sign here," he pointed to the wall behind him, "is the same as the one in the front window. Most people see it in the window and walk away. But if they miss it out there, I show it to them in here."

WE DO NOT LEND OR BUY
UNLESS YOU HAVE BOTH
-- PHOTO I.D.
-- PROOF OF OWNERSHIP

"Did he seem upset that you wouldn't buy from him?" Gimble asked.

"Nope. He may have asked me for the name of a shop that didn't care so much about the rules," he said, "but I never try to help people find dirtbags. A few sleazy pawn shops give all of us a bad name, so I won't lift a finger to help them get business."

"I need to ask you a very important and confidential question, Mr. Franklin," Nazareth said seriously. "Let's assume this guy left here and went to other pawn shops in the neighborhood. Could he find one that wouldn't care about the rules?"

The guy seemed spooked by the question. "Detective, I don't need to get in the middle of somebody else's business, and I sure as hell don't need to end up dead in a dumpster."

"You think there are pawn shop owners who would harm you if you said the wrong thing?" Nazareth asked.

"That's a fact," he said. "Up here it's strictly live and let live."

"Just point me in the right direction," Nazareth said, "and I promise you that your name will never come up in any way. We just don't want to waste all day hitting every clean pawn shop in the City. If we can take a shortcut, that would be terrific."

Franklin thought hard, then said, "If you visit Paco Avala's shop two blocks down, you won't see any sign like mine in the window. That's all I can say, Detective. But I tell you this confidentially. If you mention my name, you may be coming to my funeral."

"You have my word, Mr. Franklin. We'll visit two other shops before we hit Avala's," Nazareth assured him, "just in case someone saw us come in here."

The next two pawn shops earned the detectives nothing but blank stares. If any of the victims had set foot in these stores, no one remembered. But both shops seemed like well-run businesses, not the sort that would handle dirty, off-the-books transactions. Paco Avala's shop, on the other hand, looked like the sort of place where you could buy or sell anything, no questions asked. Avala was behind the counter when Nazareth and Gimble walked in, and he didn't look at all pleased to see them. His stringy black hair looked as though he might have combed it several days earlier with an egg beater, and the black T-shirt with the silver skull clung to his large gut, making him look about 10 months pregnant.

"Good morning," Nazareth said. "Are you Mr. Avala?"

"Depends on who's asking," he shrugged.

"Detective Pete Nazareth, NYPD," he said as he flashed his gold shield, "and this is Detective Tara Gimble."

"You haven't busted my chops enough already about that guy?" Avala said.

"What guy are we talking about?" Gimble asked.

"If you don't know, then it's none of your business, is it?" he said.

Nazareth cut off the non-conversation by laying the victims' photos on the counter. "Any of these men ever come in here?" he asked.

Avala didn't bother to look. "Never seen any of them."

"And you can tell this without even looking?"

"Yeah, I'm psychic. I never seen any of them."

"But if you had seen one of them, you'd tell us, right?" Gimble prodded.

"If I saw one of these guys hack an old lady to death on the sidewalk right outside my door, I wouldn't tell you jack about it. Okay?"

"No problem, Mr. Avala," Nazareth smiled. "Sorry to waste your time."

"Yeah, go waste somebody else's time."

"Will do. Oh, and please say hi for me when the Consumer Affairs people get here later. They'll have an officer with them," Nazareth said, "just to make sure you're extra polite while they tear your place apart."

"Hey, hey, okay, I'll look at your damn pictures."

"Have a lovely day," Nazareth called over his shoulder as they walked out the door.

When they hit the sidewalk Gimble asked, "Are you really calling for someone to check the place out?"

"No reason not to," he answered. "Obviously the guy's dirty as hell, so they'll find something. I didn't see any guns on display, so I'm guessing he does that business in the back. If so, he has a really bad day ahead of him."

On the way to the fifth pawn shop they approached a large grocery store that despite the chilly weather had several heavily laden fruit stands on the sidewalk. As they neared the main door they heard shouting from inside, and at that moment three men wearing black ski masks bolted from the store, one of them with his arm tightly wrapped around the neck of a young woman who was screaming for help. The first guy out the door stood about 6-4 and carried a lot of muscle on his frame, but he made a major mistake when he waved a long switchblade at Gimble's face as he ran for the van waiting at the curb. In one fluid move she deftly blocked the knife aside, wrenched the guy's arm behind his back with her right hand, and locked her left arm around his throat in a vise-like choke hold. When he dropped the knife

Gimble drove him face down into the pavement and threw all her weight on his bent arm, which fractured at the elbow and shoulder.

While Gimble was handling the first attacker, the second guy out the door raised his gun toward her but hesitated, afraid of shooting his partner. That moment of hesitation cost him his life when Nazareth put a single round through his heart. The guy fell backward into a fruit stand and sent oranges, pears, and apples spilling across the sidewalk.

The guy who held the young woman around her neck was only halfway out the door. He began raising his gun to her head when suddenly he arched backward, released the weapon and his hostage, and stood motionless with his hands at his sides. He fell forward to the pavement with a cleaver buried deep in his upper back across the spine. The burly Hispanic man standing behind him wore a bloody butcher's apron and a large smile. He laughed as his eyes met Nazareth's. "You want some nice steaks, officer?"

Nearly an hour later the two detectives turned the scene over to the large NYPD force that had responded to multiple 911 calls. What everyone had assumed was a robbery gone bad was actually a kidnapping, plain and simple. The three punks plus their driver had been paid handsomely to bring pretty Daniela Estrada back to a Manhattan drug kingpin who had taken a fancy to her. Estrada and the two surviving hired hands would most likely spend the rest of their lives in prison, while Wilfredo Medina -- the jovial 52-year-old butcher at Aguadilla's Grocery -- would spend the rest of his life finishing each version of the story with the same line: "It was just like splittin' a chicken, man, but not quite as tender."

Nazareth and Gimble were finished canvassing pawn shops for the day. As soon as Nazareth was cleared for duty again -- he would have to sit out for a few days because of the shooting -- they would start in again. But this time, they agreed, they would move Downtown, where things promised to be quieter.

36.

The killing of New Jersey real estate agent Vishesh Joshi reignited the firestorm of anger within the City's ethnic communities. Although Joshi wasn't a New Yorker, he was one of their own -- an honest, hard-working husband and father who had broken his butt to earn his piece of the American dream. That he was slain simply because of his accent, skin color, or status as an immigrant was more than New York City's immigrant-support organizations could take. Desperate to keep his election campaign on track, the acting mayor vowed to accelerate the investigation into the RTS Killer's crime spree while at the same time volunteering Nazareth, as the NYPD's lead detective on the case, to meet with a coalition of the City's civil-rights groups.

"Sorry to hand this one to you, Pete," said Chief Crawford in his office, "but this came directly from the mayor."

"And what does he expect me to tell everyone? Does he think we're sitting on our asses waiting for the killer to turn himself in?"

"You already know he doesn't give a rat's ass what you tell them. You solve crimes; he plays politics. As long as he doesn't have to answer their questions himself," the chief said, "he's fine with whatever happens. If they demand your head on a platter, he'll give it to them. That's a given."

"This is no way to run an investigation, Chief."

"It's no way to run a city, Pete. But we play the hand we're dealt. I'll be there, and I'll do whatever I can to help you get through it. I'll let you decide whether you want Tara in on this. The mayor didn't specify both of you, so do whatever you think is best."

When Nazareth told Gimble about the upcoming trial by fire she was incensed -- first by what she termed a "kangaroo court," and second by the suggestion that maybe she wouldn't want to be part of it.

"I don't need to be protected from anyone, Pete. We're doing everything we can to catch this guy," she said, "and I'll stand by our work. If the mayor wants us off the case, let him take us off the case.

But we leave or stay together. That's the deal. So don't even think about not having me at the meeting."

"Somehow I knew that's what you'd say."

"Damn right. Win or lose together."

"We'll win, Tara. No doubt about it."

The next morning at 9:00 the two detectives walked into the large City Hall conference room and faced off with 24 leaders of the City's most prominent civil-rights and immigrant-support organizations. The acting mayor kicked things off by apologizing for the lack of progress on the case and declared he would do everything in his power to energize the investigation. He then turned the meeting over to Deputy Chief Crawford and split as fast as his feet could carry him.

"Within the NYPD the buck stops with me on this case," the chief began. "I'm the senior man in charge of the investigation, and every day the case goes unsolved is another mark against me. So let me tell you how I'm attacking this. From Day One I put the NYPD's top detective team on the case. Out of all the crimes they could be solving, this is the only one they're working on -- seven days a week. These are the same two detectives who recently stopped a terrorist attack Downtown, they're the same two detectives who recently stopped a kidnapping Uptown, and they're the same two detectives who just a few months ago brought down a serial killer who had been preying on widows.

"No one else is better equipped to nail this RTS Killer, and they will do it," he vowed. "In the meantime, I have given them full authority to call upon any resources they might need to help them get the job done. I have complete confidence in their abilities, ladies and gentlemen. And I must tell you that if these detectives should get pulled off the case for any reason, everyone in New York City will be less safe tonight."

The chief's strong opening statement seemed to ratchet down the group's fury, but it was Nazareth who closed the door on debate.

"Earlier this year my friend and partner Detective Javier Silvano, a loving father and husband, died in the line of duty while working on the Rosebud Killer case that all of you remember. You hadn't heard of Detective Silvano until he died," Nazareth said softly, "but each and every day before that he was on the job, putting his life on the line to protect what's best about New York City. A couple of days ago we nearly lost my new friend and partner, Detective Tara Gimble, while she was taking down a kidnapper. And less than a month ago I almost died on the street while working the RTS Killer case.

"Javier Silvano paid the ultimate price for you, and for me, and for everyone else who wants New York City to be a place where we can all live without fear and where everyone, regardless of color, religion, language, or nationality can pursue the American dream. Detective Silvano would do it again for us if he could and if that's the way it had to be. He accepted the fact that good people sometimes will die so that the rest of us can live.

"Detective Gimble and I have much to live for, but it's a fact that a lot of people who choose this calling of ours will die while trying to make sure everyone in this room -- each and every one of you -- can walk the streets without fear. You or your ancestors came to America for the same reason my great grandparents did: to build a better life. Today Detective Gimble and I are hunting down a madman who hates not only you but everything this country stands for. I can't promise you that she and I will both be alive when this guy is finally brought to justice. What I *can* promise you," he told them boldly, "is that we *will* bring him to justice, and I'm willing to bet my life on it. More than that I cannot do."

The room was absolutely quiet when Nazareth finished speaking. He opened the floor to questions and got only one: "What can we do to help, Detective?"

"There are two things that will help us close this case," he began. "First, have your organizations get the word out that we need leads. If they hear someone preaching hate, they have to call us. The person they're calling about could very well be the killer. Second, help us learn everything we can about the victims. Too many people have stonewalled us, for whatever reason. We need your help in learning as much as possible about these men so that we can connect the dots. There's a common thread," he assured them, "but we can't find it without help."

Before leaving the room all 24 community leaders asked for copies of the victims' photographs and promised to feed as much information to Nazareth and Gimble as they could.

"I came here thinking we might get the boot," Chief Crawford told his two detectives as they walked to their car. "Instead we now have 24 major community organizations trying to help us. That's a pretty amazing turnaround, Pete. But, please, no more talk about dying."

"We're in the dying business, Chief," he said with a sad smile. "That's just how it is."

Early the next afternoon the two detectives began visiting Downtown pawn shops, hoping for better results than their Uptown excursion had provided. The first four shops they hit produced no useful information, but together Nazareth and Gimble fielded nine phone calls as a result of the previous day's meeting with community leaders. True to their word, the leaders who had witnessed Nazareth's presentation had been hammering their respective constituencies for information about the RTS victims or hate crimes in general.

"It's an embarrassment of riches, Pete," Gimble said. "There's nothing hot in what we've gotten so far, but it's really encouraging that people are willing to help us."

"This is how it's supposed to be," he nodded. "When the people of this city work together instead of against each other, they can accomplish anything. I mean absolutely anything."

Just as they were about to enter L.E.S. Pawn & Loan, Nazareth's phone rang yet again. Ryan Driscoll stood at his counter and studied the two detectives on the sidewalk as they engaged in an impromptu conference call with the pastor of a neighborhood church. The Rev. Malcolm Green had several days earlier provided counseling to two members of his congregation who had been the target of some particularly vicious trash-talking.

"The young man and his wife were having sandwiches at a neighborhood pub," Green told them, "when two men sitting at the bar began insulting them. The men didn't address them directly, but they were apparently quite loud, and it was obvious to everyone in the place that they were talking about the young couple."

"Had the couple ever seen these men before?" Nazareth asked.

"One of them, yes," the pastor said. "The young woman works in the neighborhood and had seen this man before. She remembered him because he always stared at her when she walked by. But he had never said anything until this incident. I should tell you," he added, "that I don't approve of drinking alcohol, and I told the couple they should not have been in a pub even if only to eat. But still . . ."

"But still," Gimble finished his thought, "they have a right to be wherever they want to be without getting abused."

"Exactly, detective. And they were most definitely abused. So when a colleague of mine called earlier today and told me about your investigation, I decided I should report this."

"And we thank you for that, Pastor Green," Nazareth said. "Can you give me an idea of what the men at the bar said?"

"Apparently a great deal was said," Green told them, "but I can't give you all the details. What alarmed me the most was that one man said *kill them all and let God sort them out.*"

"Did they describe the two men?" Nazareth asked.

"Both white and middle-aged," Green said, "but they were focused on the loudest one -- the one the young woman had seen in the neighborhood. They said he was an overweight, drunken Irishman."

"An Irishman?" Gimble said.

"I can't say whether the man is actually Irish. They were in an Irish pub, and for some reason the man struck them as being Irish."

"Okay, Pastor Green, it would be good for us to visit the young woman," Gimble told him. "If she works in the area and has seen this man before, we'd like to spend some time with her right now."

"I'll need to call her first because I'm sure she's still pretty shaken by this. She and her husband are lovely young people who should not have to feel threatened in their own neighborhood."

"All the more reason for her to meet with us. No one needs to know she spoke with us," Gimble assured him, "but this is obviously a man we need to find. This is precisely the kind of lead that could help us nail the RTS Killer."

A few minutes later Green called back to say that the young woman had reluctantly agreed to meet with them at her office. As Nazareth and Gimble headed off toward the John Street address, Ryan Driscoll noticed that his hands were trembling. He had no way of knowing who these two were, but his instincts told him they were most likely NYPD. His lunch rose dangerously close to the back of his throat. How in God's name had they found their way to his door? And why had they left without speaking with him?

Was it time to run?

But if he were truly a suspect, he reasoned, they wouldn't have walked away without confronting him. That would make no sense. What did make sense, he decided, was to hang the CLOSED FOR THE DAY sign in the door and stop by his favorite pub on the way home. A couple of pints would help settle his nerves.

Tamia Wilson was a 27-year-old assistant vice president at a private investment firm, and her roomy, well-appointed office suggested that she was a young woman on her way up. She closed the door and joined the detectives at a small conference table near the window overlooking John Street. After listening to her account of the hate-filled remarks that had been directed at her and her husband, Nazareth asked for the most accurate description she could provide. The man she remembered could have been any of a hundred thousand guys in Manhattan, but that was the best she could do. Returning to the pub and identifying him was out of the question. She would not return there.

"Okay, graying hair, maybe 55 years old, about 200 pounds, round face, and reddish complexion," Gimble said as she consulted her notes. "Rev. Green told us you think the guy is Irish. Why is that?"

"When my husband and I first sat down the two men were singing some sort of Irish song," she said. "I don't know the name, but it's one of the songs that's always popular around St. Patrick's Day. He didn't speak with an accent, but for some reason I assumed he was Irish."

"And the incident took place around 6:00 p.m.?" Nazareth asked.

"Yes. We sat down about 5:50, and a few minutes later they started in on us."

Nazareth looked at his watch, thought a bit, then turned to Gimble.

"I wonder if Shirley could join us for a drink in about an hour. Want to see if she's available?" he said.

"I guarantee you she'd love a piece of this," Gimble smiled. She speed-dialed her close friend, Detective Shirley Anderson, and quickly laid out the story.

"Hell, yes," Anderson told her. "You just made my whole week, Tara."

Gimble gave her partner a thumbs-up. "Game on. You and I get there at 5:45," she told him, "and Shirley will join us at 6:00."

Wilson seemed somewhat confused by what was happening, so Nazareth filled her in. "Shirley Anderson is one of the top detectives on the force," he explained. "She also happens to be black as well as a member of our Hate Crimes Task Force. So if this guy is at the pub tonight, one of us could very well end up taking him down."

"And you're sure he won't know I'm the one who identified him?" she asked nervously.

Nazareth shook his head and smiled. "It'll just be him and us. If he shoots his mouth off, one of us may be compelled to shut it for him."

At 5:45 Nazareth and Gimble sat down at a small table in Megan's Pub, a dimly lit place featuring a huge, well-polished bar and a dozen tables where you could dine seven days a week on corned beef and cabbage, shepherd's pie, or whatever else chef/owner Megan Brody decided should be on the menu. It seemed like a cozy, neighborly place, and the detectives ordered a couple of coffees and a plate of appetizers.

At 6:00 sharp Detective Shirley Anderson walked in, waved to Nazareth and Gimble, and joined them at their table. A pleasant young waitress took Anderson's drink order -- Coke with a twist of lime -- and left the three detectives to chat. By 6:15 most of the tables were occupied by chatty young white-collar types who had spent the day shuffling papers for the area's banks, brokerage firms, and insurance companies. The nearly full bar, on the other hand, was the domain of serious drinkers who were more interested in the next pint than the next conversation. For the most part these were blue-collar guys who had spent the day lifting, hauling, or pounding, and they were here to forget their jobs, get a buzz on, and go home to wait for the next day to begin.

There was no interaction between the two distinctly different crowds until a loud-mouthed guy with graying hair and a boozer's red face grabbed a stool and pulled his large belly up to the bar. He yelled to a couple of his friends, then ordered a Harp lager and a shot of Jameson Irish whiskey. As soon as he finished the first boilermaker he ordered another, immediately downed the whiskey, and drained half the beer. He then slowly turned toward the detectives' table and glared at Shirley Anderson, the only non-white patron in the entire pub.

"And sure enough it looks like someone left the cage door open again, Patrick," the guy bellowed. "Now we've got an ape among us."

A few of the guys at the bar snickered into their mugs, but the fat drunk next to him nearly choked on his Guinness from laughing so hard. "If Megan isn't careful," Patrick replied, "the Board of Health will shut the place down because of the wildlife."

"Right you are, Patrick," his compatriot said loud enough for everyone, but most especially the detectives, to hear. "We don't need any wildlife roaming among the humans, do we now?"

The detectives pretended to ignore the guy, and that seemed to set him off even more.

"A deaf ape we have, Patrick. A deaf ape and her two white handlers. They don't seem to know they've been invited to leave," he growled before ordering his third shot and beer. When he turned back to look at Anderson, she smiled at him. He shoved the stool away and went for her. "What in the hell are you smiling at?"

Nazareth kept his seat and calmly said, "Get lost." The guy grabbed Nazareth's left arm, which felt remarkably like cast iron, and instantly knew he had made a big mistake. The detective ripped a vicious right into his assailant's lower belly, and the guy went down fast and hard. Two burly men from the bar began moving toward

Nazareth but stopped where they were when all three detectives held up their shields. Detective Anderson smiled broadly as she slapped the cuffs on the man who lay in a pool of his own beer, whiskey, and urine.

Six blocks away, at The Kilcolgan Pub, Ryan Driscoll nursed his second Guinness and munched on chicken wings. He was thinking clearly again and had convinced himself that he had left no clues for the police to follow. Let them visit the shop whenever they want. And may they kiss my Irish ass when they do.

He grinned into his beer. Here's to the Russian.

37.

The next morning Nazareth and Gimble battled the snow flurries and strong gusts that ripped along the streets of Lower Manhattan driving the wind chill near zero. They were heading back to L.E.S. Pawn & Loan to pick up where they had left off the day before. Danny Rowan, the loud-mouthed racist they had arrested for menacing Detective Anderson, had been in Texas throughout October and November as a heavy equipment operator for his employer, a large national construction company. So they quickly ruled him out as the RTS Killer. He was, however, a useless mutt, and New York City would be a kinder place while Rowan was off the streets.

"It's only a few blocks, says the ever-observant NYPD Detective Pete Nazareth," Gimble muttered into her scarf as snowflakes battered her eyes. "Let's just walk, he says."

"Okay, my bad, Tara. But it wasn't this windy before, was it?"

"You mean when we were driving to work this morning? No, it wasn't windy in the car," she laughed. "But people were practically being blown over on the sidewalks. Did you not notice that?"

"Not really," he said. "I was actually thinking that we're a few weeks from Christmas and hoping we don't have another RTS killing in the works. I don't suppose this guy cares about the calendar, but another murder right around Christmas would really make people crazy. It's tough to believe in peace on Earth when someone is killing out of pure hatred."

"Pete, right now I'm hoping you and I live until we get to the pawn shop. I'm really cold."

"Is that the warmest coat you've got?"

"No, but my down ski jacket doesn't really go with this pant suit."

"Well, how about after work today we get you an early Christmas present?" he said. "I don't need my partner freezing on the job."

"Your partner could use a month in Florida."

"The sooner we catch this guy, the sooner we can talk about getting away. And if we don't get him soon," he added, "we may be looking for jobs in Florida."

The snow and the wind picked up just as they reached the pawn shop door, and they welcomed the blast of warm air that greeted them when they walked in. Once they had both removed their hats and Gimble had pulled the scarf from her icy face, Driscoll recognized them as the couple that had stood outside his shop the day before. Steady, he told himself. They know nothing.

"Good morning," he said confidently. "Tough day to be walking the streets of Manhattan."

"You've got that right," Nazareth said as he rubbed his frigid hands together. "Feels more like late January."

"In Alaska," Gimble added.

"Well, you're my first customers of the day," Driscoll told them, "and I've got a full pot of coffee."

"Thanks very much for the offer," Nazareth smiled, "but we're really not customers." He and Gimble showed Driscoll their shields. "Detective Pete Nazareth and Detective Tara Gimble."

Driscoll's stomach lurched, and he could feel his face turning red. He thought about the gun behind the counter and hoped he wouldn't need to use it. But if they were on to him, he would have no choice. He wasn't going to spend the rest of his life in prison being brutalized by the same lowlifes he was trying to eliminate.

"Ryan Driscoll's the name," he said, offering his hand. "All my records are up to date, and I'll gladly share any information you need. L.E.S. has been in business for over 100 years, and we've always played by the rules."

"I'm sure that's the case," Nazareth said, "but that's not why we're here." He took the victims' photos from a large brown envelope and placed them on the counter for inspection. "We're looking for anyone who has seen one or all of these four men."

Driscoll studied the photos, hoping that his terror wasn't obvious to the detectives. The last time he had seen these faces they were covered by plastic and rolling toward the curb, so the pictures were a major jolt to his system. He suddenly felt trapped. What if the detectives had already traced one of the victims to his shop? If he said he didn't recognize the guy, would they be all over him? But if they had any credible evidence, wouldn't they skip the charade and just bring him in for questioning? He took a deep breath and boldly rolled the dice.

"This one might be familiar," he said, tapping the photo of Saliou Ba. He squinted and held the photo closer to his face, making a great show of trying to remember. "I'm not sure, but either he or someone who looks a lot like him was hanging around outside my shop a month or so ago. I always notice when someone does that, because we've been robbed before. But this guy never actually came in."

"You were afraid he was going to rob you?" Gimble asked.

"When someone just hangs around outside and doesn't come in, yeah, I worry. I have no idea whether he's waiting to make sure I'm alone or is just out there waiting for someone. Pays to keep your eyes open around here."

"Did you see him just the one time?" Nazareth asked.

"If it was him, yeah, just that once."

"And you're sure he didn't come in?" Gimble said.

"If he had come in," Driscoll answered, "I probably wouldn't have remembered him at all. A lot of people come in every day, and I can't remember them all. But someone who spooks me for some reason, him I remember. So can you tell me what this is all about?"

While Nazareth explained the reason for their visit and prodded Driscoll to take a closer look at the other photos, Gimble wandered around the shop and checked out the hundreds of items for sale. One piece in particular caught her attention. It was a small, badly worn statue of a small animal. Driscoll noticed her looking at it and said, "Can I show you something, Detective?"

"This piece here looks pretty old," she said as she pointed out the statue.

"No telling how old it is," he told her. "It's been in that case for 50 or 60 years, and it's supposed to be thousands of years old. My father bought it and claimed it was a limestone cat from an Egyptian tomb. But I don't know one way or the other."

"When you buy something like this," Gimble asked, "do you keep a record of the seller, the date, the price, and so forth?"

"Absolutely," Driscoll assured her. "All of my inventory since about 1996 is on a computer. Something like this piece, though, would still be written up on a file card in the back somewhere. My grandfather and father only filed items by date, because the business was simpler back then. To find details on this statue I'd have to go through tons of old cards."

"Okay, I was just wondering," she smiled. "It does look like an original, doesn't it?"

"Something that's been here in the shop for so long probably is legit," he explained. "But things like this that hit the market nowadays are usually junk. Fake artifacts are big business, and I don't give them a second look when someone brings them in."

"Has anyone tried to sell one here recently?" Nazareth asked.

Once again Driscoll felt trapped. What if the detectives already knew he had seen something like this recently? They'd cuff him as soon as he denied it.

"Sure, I see fake stuff every month or so. But I never spend any time with it. As soon as someone puts it on the counter," Driscoll told them, "I say I'm not interested. I have no idea whether it's real or fake, so I pass."

The front door opened, and a young Oriental man walked in carrying a guitar case that was dusted with light snow. Driscoll's smile quickly turned to a frown when he saw who it was.

"Same guitar, right?" Driscoll snapped. "Same answer: not interested. It's a piece of crap."

The young guy glared at him, eyed the two detectives, and went back into the cold.

"These people can't even remember who they show their garbage to," he said, plainly disgusted. "Instead of keeping track of what shops they visit, they keep hitting the same places again and again. That guy was in here last week with the same guitar and the same attitude. Gimme a goddamn break."

"Well, we appreciate your time, Mr. Driscoll," Nazareth said as he and Gimble began bundling up for their trek to the next shop. "If you think of anything that might help us, please give either one of us a call."

"I'll absolutely do that, detectives. Stay warm out there, okay?"

"We'll do what we can," Gimble said from under her scarf.

As soon as the door closed behind them, Gimble said, "Mr. Driscoll has a bit of a short fuse, doesn't he?"

"Especially with *these people*," Nazareth replied.

"You caught that too?"

"Most definitely. He's not a big fan of Oriental customers, apparently."

"And I'd love to learn more about that Egyptian statue."

"It's enough that it's there," he said emphatically. "Maybe it's been there for 50 years, and maybe it's been there for a week. We may never know. But we do know that Tarek Elkady was peddling bogus antiquities before he was murdered, so Ryan Driscoll just hit the radar screen."

"Your radar screen works in the snow? It's coming down harder, in case you hadn't noticed."

"Yep, the radar works in the snow. I'm not so sure about the car, though. We may be sleeping at the office tonight if this doesn't let up."

"Uh, no, you'll be sleeping at the office," she said seriously. "I'll be taking the subway home."

"Where's your sense of adventure, Tara?"

"I'm saving it for the RTS Killer," she said. "My gut tells me we're closing in."

"From your lips to God's ear, Tara."

38.

Driscoll brooded once again over his pathetic gutlessness. Two detectives -- one of them barely old enough to shave, the other just pretty window-dressing -- had walked into his shop, and he had damn near lost his breakfast! So much for being the most feared man in all of New York City. His insides had turned to jelly at precisely the moment they should have turned to steel. He would not, could not, allow that to happen again.

He also wanted to kick himself for not removing that old piece of crap statue his father had bought nearly half a century ago. The damn thing had nothing whatsoever to do with Tarek Elkady, but obviously the detectives had made a mental note of it. How ironic it would be if he were linked to the dead Egyptian by a scrap of sandstone that had been gathering dust in a display case all these years. Enough second-guessing! What's done is done.

If the detectives returned, he told himself, it would be because they considered him a suspect, and he would act appropriately. He would not allow them to nibble away at him bit by bit while they built their case. No, if they came back to the shop, they would never walk out.

But precisely what would he do? Naturally they would give up their weapons as soon as they looked down the barrel of his shotgun. Then he would lock the front door and order them into the back room. Next? He could force both of them into the antique gun vault his grandfather had bought nearly 100 years ago. Yes, he needed to clear that thing out. Once empty it would easily accommodate two people. And since the vault probably weighed 600 pounds, there was absolutely no way the detectives would be able to tip it over once they were locked inside. A few turns of the old handle on the steel door, and the vault would become their tomb.

This was a manageable plan, he decided, as long as the two detectives came to his shop alone. He would lock them away, then disappear from New York City forever. But how could he simply walk away from his entire life? No way in hell. A better option would be to kill the detectives and get rid of the bodies before any other police showed up. Precisely how he would do that required some additional thought.

All he was sure of at the moment was the outcome. If the two detectives returned to L.E.S. Pawn & Loan, they would die there.

39.

After Nazareth and Gimble had thawed out, assisted by some black coffee and hot chocolate, they decided to put Ryan Driscoll under the microscope. They had absolutely no solid clues tying him to the RTS crimes, and on the surface he appeared to be a highly unlikely suspect. He was pleasant, polite, and very well established in the community. Hell, L.E.S. Pawn & Loan was one of the oldest businesses in Lower Manhattan, and the guy seemed to be running a clean operation.

On the other hand, the detectives still believed that a pawn shop might be the thread linking the four victims. So in the broadest possible sense Driscoll fit the bill. In addition, they had noticed an abrupt change in his attitude when the young Chinese man had entered the store. Was that really just fallout from the man's previous visit, or were "these people" a sore spot for Driscoll? Finally, they were intrigued by the presence of the Egyptian statue. Would the murderer have been dumb enough to put that item on display? Probably not, but this wouldn't be the first dumb mistake that had unmasked a killer.

"One of the things bothering me about this," Gimble said, "is that I don't see a connection to the New Jersey victim, Vishesh Joshi. As far as we can tell he had absolutely no need to visit a pawn shop, least of all one in Manhattan, and his wife swore that all he ever did was work or hang out with his family. This is not someone who had a secret life, Pete."

"Joshi is an outlier, no doubt about it," he nodded. "But if you look at the crime itself, everything fits exactly. I'd say there's no question one person killed all five men. Why the murderer worked outside Manhattan is anyone's guess, but it's possible he felt we were getting too close."

"Even though we weren't?"

"Right," he nodded, "even though we weren't. Remember, the press had us solving this case weeks ago, so it's possible he believed what he read. On the other hand, we may never know why he went after Joshi."

"Okay, so where would you like to go from here?" she asked.

"I'd like to dig into the pawn shop itself and see if anything stands out in the City's records. Unpaid taxes, municipal disputes, consumer complaints, bankruptcy filings, and anything else that might point to a motive."

"Okay, and while you do that," she offered, "I'll get as much personal background on him as I can. In fact, I'd like to take a hard look at the whole family. There's always a chance something relating to his parents or grandparents set him off."

"Sounds good. Between City records, the Internet, and the FBI database, we should be able to get a good feel for what Driscoll's life has been like. If anything seems to match up with the RTS Killer's profile, we pay him another visit."

"But not during a blizzard," she smiled.

"But not during a blizzard."

40.

The snow that had raked Lower Manhattan that morning blew out to the Atlantic after less than an hour, leaving little more than a half inch of white stuff on the ground. But Driscoll decided to check with Timur Gorokhov to make sure they would still meet that night. The Russian was greatly offended by the call.

"You think this is snow?" he growled. "I'm afraid of winter, maybe? Let me tell you, in Russia this like spring. Day like this I swim maybe."

You'll be swimming in a gutter soon, you Commie bastard, Driscoll wanted to tell him. Instead, he swallowed his anger and said, "Okay, I'll see you tonight," then clicked off. Next he turned his attention to the old gun vault. It would take at least an hour, maybe more, to clean the thing out and to decide what items could safely be stored in the basement temporarily. Life would definitely be simpler if the two detectives didn't return to his shop, but he planned to be ready for whatever came his way.

At 9:45 that night Driscoll stood in the shadows on East 14th Street, not quite a block away from the address he had given Timur Gorokhov. The wind had died down since the morning, but his fingers and toes were numb nevertheless. It might be necessary to revise the meeting arrangements after tonight because waiting out here in the cold was not something he could get used to. When he was a kid his mother practically had to drag him inside when he and his friends were playing out in the snow. And now he was always cold in winter.

Maybe he should just pack it in, move to Florida, and sip margaritas on the beach while the blood-sucking immigrants took complete charge of his beloved Manhattan. Could one man really stem the ugly tide? Probably not. On the other hand, if he remained faithful to his mission, wouldn't other warriors join him? Wouldn't his actions become a call to arms for all the real Americans who were tired of picking up the tab for the riffraff flooding the country's shores? And when that happened, would he really be satisfied growing fat and old in Florida while patriots won back the homeland? No, he wouldn't. The mere thought of caving in made him angry. Game on.

At 10:05 a black sedan pulled up in front of the assigned spot, but from where he stood Driscoll was unable to see whether Gorokhov had come alone as directed. This wasn't good. He had no idea how many people might be sitting in the car -- or perhaps crouching in the back -- and he wasn't about to walk over and find out. Suddenly he felt something other than his hatred of all Russians creep into his system. This was now about Gorokhov. Driscoll found him arrogant and threatening. Putting him down like a stray dog would be intensely satisfying.

He called the guy's cell number.

"Gorokhov," is all the Russian said. But the way the word came out of his mouth seemed like a challenge to Driscoll.

"Fleischer here. You can leave your car and lock it," he said. "You'll only be walking a couple of blocks."

"No, is cold. I drive."

"You told me you like the cold," Driscoll said calmly. "So walking a couple of blocks should be fine."

"Car is better. Nice and warm," Gorokhov told him.

"How many men do you have in your car with you?"

The Russian paused and looked around the neighborhood, hoping he would spot Adolphus Fleischer. He saw nothing but shadows and the lights of passing cars.

"I am alone," he said.

"Then get out and lock your car. I'll tell you where to walk. You do it my way," Driscoll said, "or you wasted a trip to Manhattan."

"Fine," he grumbled, "I do it your way. But this is stupid. I am alone, as you told me." Driscoll drew a sharp breath when he saw the giant that emerged from the black sedan. Gorokhov stood nearly 6-6 and weighed close to 250 pounds. He buttoned his long dress coat and turned up the collar against the chill. "Okay, what next?"

Driscoll had him go to the corner before giving him further directions, just in case the guy had accomplices in the vehicle. Only then would he tell him where they would meet on East 13th Street.

Gorokhov complained about having to shut off his cell phone, but Driscoll told him it was the only way to make sure he wasn't tracked by the police. The Russian finally complied and began walking toward the rendezvous point. Driscoll waited to see whether anyone left the guy's car, but there was no activity. He then trotted in the opposite direction, taking the long way to East 13th so that he and Gorokhov would end up walking toward each other.

When they were about 20 feet apart Driscoll said, "I'm sorry for all these precautions, my friend, but being careful is how I stay in business." He eyed the guy carefully, looking for signs of a weapon -- not that he really needed one. The guy was frighteningly large, and his mirthless face might have been chiseled from granite.

"Is cold, is late," Gorokhov answered. "We do business, I go home."

"Absolutely. My place is right over here." He led him to the basement door, stepped aside so that the Russian could enter, and locked the door behind them. The space was dark except for the hanging bulb in the safe room where Gorokhov would spend some time in hell before being wrapped for shipment. "Here, let me get the light for us."

Driscoll kept his right hand in the pocket of his down ski jacket, squeezing the grip of his Glock 20. He breathed a bit easier when Gorokhov passed through the metal detector without setting it off, therefore was taken completely by surprise when the Russian spun around and slashed at him with a ceramic tactical knife.

Driscoll jumped back but not before the blade's tip had sliced through the point of his chin, hitting bone as it carved a two-inch gash. As Gorokhov began to swing the blade a second time, Driscoll fired three shots through the pocket of his ski jacket into the center of his attacker's silhouette. The huge Russian groaned, grabbed his eviscerated gut, and slumped to the floor.

Warm blood from Driscoll's chin ran down his neck and soaked into his jacket and flannel shirt. When he gingerly put his hand to the wound he nearly passed out from the blinding pain. He threw off his jacket and slowly lowered himself to the floor, leaned back against the cold concrete wall, and gradually pressed his forearm against his chin, fighting the pain in order to stop the bleeding. He would need stitches, and soon. But at least he was alive. If the Russian had been half a step closer he would have sliced Driscoll's neck in two.

Before his heart had stopped pounding he heard panic in the street outside the basement door. Two men, possibly more, were screaming Gorokhov's name along with other Russian words that might have meant anything. But to Driscoll they meant only one thing: his life was over. What chance did he have of overpowering two or three thugs who were probably well armed? And if they took him alive, would he beg for death long before it arrived? As the terror washed over him he resolved to fire at the men until he had one final bullet. That one he would take to the side of his head.

He waited for someone to kick the door open. How the hell had they followed Gorokhov here? The Russian's cell phone had been turned off, and Driscoll had watched to see whether anyone else had gotten out of the black sedan. Had they arrived in a separate vehicle? Had they taken positions on the street before Gorokhov's arrival? And why would they have gone to all this trouble over one damn gun anyway? Surely there was more to it than that. Did they think he was a gun dealer and hoped to steal everything he owned? Or did they view him as a threat -- someone who was trying to do business on their Brighton Beach turf?

He would never know. As he sat in the dark basement, bloody and frightened, the voices grew fainter. The men were still shouting Gorokhov's name, but they had split up and were moving away. They obviously had known that their comrade had walked south from 14th Street, but clearly they had no idea whether from there he had gone east, west, or farther south. For nearly 15 minutes he sat motionless and listened to the distant voices.

And then they drew closer. The men were returning to Driscoll's 13th Street corner. "Gorokhov! Timur! Gorokhov!" How long before someone called the police on these guys? Driscoll wondered. And what happens if the police come, find out that someone is missing, and begin knocking on doors? But would these thugs ever mention why they had come to this neighborhood? Of course not. They might say that a friend had wandered off, but the police would have no reason to suspect a kidnapping or murder. No, they would assume that Gorokhov had found a woman and was shacking up for the night.

Driscoll sat against the wall for nearly an hour after the voices had finally disappeared. The basement had no windows, so he didn't fear being seen. But he was terrified that any sound would bring a gang of storm troopers racing into the room. So he waited. And bled. And planned.

This was certainly not business as usual.

41.

By the end of the day Nazareth and Gimble had read every scrap of information available on Ryan Driscoll, his family, and his business. Except for cups of soup at their desks and a couple of bathroom breaks, neither had done anything but scrutinize the details surrounding the life of a man who by all accounts should not be considered a suspect.

On the surface at least both L.E.S. Pawn & Loan and Ryan Driscoll appeared to be squeaky clean. The business had never been cited for any type of infraction, and that was surely some sort of record in a city where most businesses, even the respectable ones, had at least a few black marks against them. And Driscoll seemed like the kind of person most observers would consider a first-rate citizen if not a pillar of the community. He had been a varsity player on a championship Xaverian High School basketball team, earned an associate degree in business management from Bronx Community College, had an unblemished record as owner of the pawn shop, and as a member of the local Chamber of Commerce had successfully mentored several small-business owners.

Since appearances are often deceiving the detectives planned to do some additional digging into Driscoll's background, but that would have to wait until tomorrow. Nazareth said he was getting hungry and wanted to head out before the sidewalks and streets began to freeze over. After driving to his place they walked three blocks to Ristorante Livorno, enjoying the sights and sounds of approaching Christmas along the way. Many of the shops they passed had brightly colored lights in their windows, and some of the larger stores had Christmas carols playing softly from sidewalk speakers.

"A little snow in the landscape really makes it feel like Christmas," Gimble said.

"Absolutely," he smiled. "But where I'd really like to be right now is up in Vermont or maybe New Hampshire. Lots of snow-covered woods, white mountains in the distance, and a warm cabin with an old fireplace."

"Sounds great to me," she sighed.

"Tell you what. As soon as we wrap up this RTS case, why don't we find that place and just escape for a week?"

"I'm ready when you are."

"Deal. Now I have an extra incentive to catch this guy," he grinned.

"As though you needed more motivation. You're all about motivation, Pete." She thought a moment, then added, "In fact, you're the most driven person I've ever known. You take guys like the RTS Killer personally. It's never just a job."

"And that's exactly what I like about you, Tara. Getting by isn't enough. It's always all or nothing, and that's why you've had such a great career."

"So we're the NYPD's official mutual admiration society, I guess."

"No doubt about it."

They entered Ristorante Livorno to the sound of owner Vincenza Murano's delightful welcome.

"Peter, Tara," she called to them, "it's so good to see you on such a cold, snowy night. Welcome!" Even if the food here were terrible -- and it was anything but -- Nazareth and Gimble would keep coming back simply for the experience of being greeted by this grandmotherly woman who had spent nearly 40 years nurturing what almost everyone agreed was one of the finest casual Italian restaurants in Manhattan. And that was saying something in a city where Italian restaurants are among the world's finest.

After hugging them both, Murano led them to a quiet table in the farthest corner. The restaurant would grow crowded later, as it did every night, but for the moment they were among a handful of diners. Across the room they noticed a large table for ten with a RESERVED sign on it.

"Expecting a big group later, Vincenza?" Gimble asked.

"Grazie a Dio," she answered, "thank God, yes. The same boys come here for 26 years now. But they're not boys anymore -- all grown men. They played basketball together in high school, and no matter where they live, they come here every year for this dinner."

"What a great story," Nazareth said. "That's the sort of thing the newspapers should pick up on."

"Especially around Christmas," Gimble added. "What better peace-on-earth story could you ask for than a bunch of guys who remain friends after all this time?"

Murano laughed as she poured a glass of chianti for each of them. "Believe me, they don't have time for reporters. They get here," she said, "and they never stop joking with each other. Then they eat and talk until midnight. I stay open very late for them."

The detectives shared a large Caesar salad before moving on to the main event: chicken parm for Gimble, lasagna for Nazareth, and a basket of freshly made focaccia. Everything at Ristorante Livorno, from the bread to the pasta to the cannoli, was made each day right there in the kitchen by Vincenza Murano and the head chef, daughter Chiara. The food wasn't fancy, but it was exceptional.

By the time Nazareth and Gimble got to their coffee and espresso, along with a couple of complimentary cookies that Vincenza Murano insisted they couldn't pass up, the former members of the Bishop Loughlin High School basketball team had taken their places at the large reserved table. Although the guys were now in their mid-forties, most of them looked as though they could still handle themselves on the court. This was especially true of the one they all called "Big Guy," who stood 6-9 and weighed well over 250 pounds. "Big Guy" looked to be in great shape, and he was obviously still the group's ringleader after all these years.

He eagerly traded wisecracks with his friends, giving even better than he got.

"I see guys like this," Nazareth said, "and really wish that I were more in touch with some of my old high school teammates. I think your high school friends are the best ones you'll ever have, and your teammates are the best of all."

"I agree completely," Gimble said. "Surviving adolescence together makes your high school friends unique. Nothing in college came even close to that for me, and it's a shame we lose touch with so many people. We start jobs, get married, move away, or whatever, and suddenly we're lost to each other. You don't mean for it to happen, but it does."

"The good news is that you really never lose each other completely, though. I remember two years ago I bumped into one of my best friends from high school," Nazareth grinned. "We were both ordering take-out at some place Downtown, and we ended up eating together on a bench in Battery Park. Three hours later we had to stop because we couldn't laugh anymore. It was as though we had never been apart. Unreal."

"Have you seen him since then?" she asked.

"Nope. I'm still getting around to it," he shook his head sadly. "That's what happens, you know. Life intervenes. But I'll tell you something. If you ever want to know everything about me, just look up Bobby Simonson. He knows it all."

Gimble suddenly seemed lost in thought. She was looking at Nazareth, yet she was a million miles away.

"Something I said, Tara?"

"Actually, yes. Seeing these guys at their little reunion and listening to you talk about Bobby Simonson has given me an idea," she told him. "If we're going to find out everything we can about Ryan Driscoll, we should get the names of his high school teammates. It doesn't mean we should talk to anyone yet, but if we do get to that point we'll have a short list of guys who knew him way back when."

"Great idea. Tell you what, if you track down as much as you can about Driscoll tomorrow, I'll go back to work on his family. We have all the names now, so it shouldn't be too difficult to get some facts about them. See where it goes, right?"

"Okay, we see where it goes."

"Speaking of which," he said.

"Yes?"

"Some time ago you and I agreed that we'd see where we went."

"Yes we did, didn't we," she answered.

"So . . . I think it's pretty obvious that wherever we're going, Tara, we're going together. True or false?"

"It's certainly true for me, Pete," she said as she took his hand. "We're great detective partners, but I think we're a great couple as well."

He looked deep into her eyes and liked, no loved, what he saw there. He glanced toward Vincenza Murano at the front of the restaurant, offered her a quick nod, and said, "This isn't where we came on our first date, but it's where we come whenever we want to feel at home, right?"

"So serious, Pete Nazareth. Yes," she said, "this is where we both feel at home. I think this is where we got to know each other -- relaxed, comfortable, away from the job. This is definitely our place."

She smiled at him just as Vincenza Murano arrived at the table, set down two champagne flutes, and began uncorking a bottle of Moet & Chandon.

"Is it already New Year's Eve, Vincenza?" Gimble joked.

"Drink to whatever you wish, my dear," she whispered. "Buona fortuna!"

When a rather puzzled Gimble turned back to Nazareth, she noticed the black velvet ring box that now occupied the center of the white linen tablecloth. She felt her stomach do a triple back flip when he said, "You're the one I've been waiting for, Tara Gimble. Any chance you'll marry me?"

Gimble wasn't much of a crier, but she didn't seem to mind the tears that welled up in her eyes. "Oh, there's a really good chance of that, Peter Nazareth. I would love to marry you."

He gently opened the box and placed the three-carat emerald cut diamond ring on her finger. As if on cue, Vincenza Murano led the entire restaurant, both staff and patrons, in a standing ovation for the two detectives. "Champagne for everyone!" she announced. "May God bless these two wonderful people."

When the cheering and hugging finally ended, Gimble said softly, "Pete, did you have to sell your apartment to buy this ring? I hope my arm doesn't get tired from lifting it."

"Actually I robbed a lovely store on Fifth Avenue last night," he told her, "but we don't need to broadcast that, do we?"

"Hey, whatever. I love this ring."

"The style's okay?"

"Okay? God, this is the most beautiful ring I've ever seen in my entire life. This is the ring of a lifetime."

"That's good, because where I come from you only get married once."

"I'll drink to that," she said as she picked up her champagne glass.

"To us."

"To us."

42.

The floor was thick with blood. This is generally what happens when you remove someone's insides with a high-powered handgun. Driscoll wasn't sure what made him queasier, the heap of Russian gore at his feet or his own oozing chin. In every way possible the night had turned against him, and it wasn't nearly over. Although he was desperate to remove every trace of Gorokhov's presence from the basement, he also desperately needed stitches. Since he had no idea how long a wound like his could remain untreated, he opted to take care of himself first. The body would have to wait until tomorrow night, when Driscoll would return, prepare Gorokhov for shipment, and dump the large package outside the Russian consulate on East 91st Street.

Driscoll pulled on a hooded sweatshirt, covered his chin as best he could, and unlocked the door. He cautiously walked up the stairs to the sidewalk, peering in all directions to make sure that Gorokhov's friends had finally left the neighborhood. Satisfied that he was alone, he eased into his van and drove to the Lenox Hill Hospital ER in the Village.

"Good Lord, man, what did you run into?" asked the ER nurse, Peggy Broome. "That's the worst chin I've ever seen with a live person attached to it."

"If I told you, you wouldn't believe me," Driscoll grumbled, hoping to avoid all conversation about the wound.

"Try me," she said undeterred. "If I don't list a cause, you don't see the doctor."

"Okay, I was trying to juggle knives. No seriously," he said when the nurse gave him a harsh cut-the-crap look. "A friend of mine is having a talent competition at his New Year's Eve party, and I thought I'd really wow everyone with knife juggling."

"Had you ever tried it before?" she asked.

"Not with knives, but with golf balls, lemons, bowling pins," he told her. "I'd seen guys do it with knives on YouTube, so I figured I could handle it."

"How about now? Have you changed your mind?"

"Uh, yeah, I think I may stick with lemons."

Nurse Broome wasn't buying Driscoll's story, but she wasn't a detective and had no choice but to fill out the ER form accordingly.

"Come with me, Mr. Driscoll," she said pleasantly, "and we'll have the doctor check you out."

She laughed when Dr. Seth Jurgens did a double-take between Driscoll's chin and the ER form. "You were juggling knives?" he said incredulously. "How does a knife generate this much force if you're juggling it?"

"It all happened pretty fast," Driscoll assured him. "I may have caught one of the knives too high and poked my chin into it while I was chasing another one."

"If you say so," Jurgens said, shaking his head. "I hope the other guy looks better, because you're a mess. Do you want me to call in a plastic surgeon for this? You're going to need a bunch of stitches."

"I'm already pretty enough, Doc. Whatever you do for me will be fine."

"All right. Let's do it."

By the time Driscoll returned to his apartment he was in no mood to think about disposing of Gorokhov's body. In fact, he wished he could kill the Russian twice more -- once for trying to rob him, a second time for causing him so much pain. The numbing shots to the chin had hurt like hell, and the doctor had told him to expect even more pain once those shots wore off. No pain medication, though. Just Tylenol, the doctor had said.

Screw Russians, screw doctors, and screw the world. What this situation required was four fingers of Irish whiskey neat.

43.

The new day was business as usual for Nazareth and Gimble until Chief Crawford walked into the conference room where they were sifting through information on Driscoll, his family, and his friends.

"I'm sending you two the bill for my next eye exam," the chief groused. "I was nearly blinded by the light from that thing." The thing in question was the engagement ring on Gimble's left hand.

"It's my new secret weapon, Chief," she grinned. "Once I blind the perps, cuffing them is a lot easier."

"Well that thing should certainly do the job. Let me see that up close," he said. "Holy Christmas. I assume you didn't get this from Pete, because no detective can afford something like this."

"He stole it for me."

"Hey, Tara," Nazareth yelped, "we agreed we wouldn't talk about that."

The ring had rescued Crawford from a particularly rough morning. "The ring is amazing," he smiled, "and it's terrific that you two didn't monkey around with this forever. Congratulations."

"Thanks, Chief," they said in unison. Then Nazareth added, "No problem with us as partners?"

"We'll revisit that when you're married. In the meantime, carry on. But please catch this bastard soon so that we can all get some time off around Christmas."

"We're with you, Chief," Gimble said. "We're peddling as hard as we can on this."

For the rest of the morning they collected data from every available source, including news articles about the championship basketball team that Driscoll had played on at Xaverian High. The *New York Times* archives and the N.Y. Public Library online database successfully filled in any blanks that their Internet searches had left.

"Time to compare notes?" Nazareth asked shortly after noon.

"Uh, no," Gimble replied, "it's time for lunch. Then, and only then, do we compare notes. Besides, it's sunny outside, and I want to see how the ring shines in daylight."

"In that case, I'm with you. Sameer's hot dogs today?"

"Yep, I'm a cheap date with a gigantic diamond ring."

"Okay, Sparkles, let's go."

Sameer Khan was doing a brisk business despite the brisk weather.

"How can you stand being out here all day, Sameer?" Nazareth asked him.

"At my cart," he told them, "it is never cold, trust me. I sit in front of the exhaust fan, see, right here. Feel that, Detective."

Nazareth put his hand in front of the miniature blast furnace that vented the grill on Khan's hot dog cart. "Whoa, baby, that's hot!" he yelled.

"I invented this myself," Khan said. "No more cold weather for me when I'm working."

"Just don't set yourself on fire, Sameer," Gimble said playfully. "Pete and I would starve without you."

"I will never let you starve, Detective. You two are always special to me. And," he grinned, "it looks like maybe you are special to each other, yes?" His eyes grew brighter as he admired Gimble's ring.

"You should be a detective, Sameer. You're very observant."

"No, I should be a fortune teller," he replied. "I knew four months ago that you two would one day be husband and wife."

"You did?" she said.

"Oh, yes. The first time I saw you together I could tell. And I am very happy for you. If you want hot dogs at your wedding, I will be there."

"Now that sounds like a plan," Nazareth said immediately.

"Not so fast, Pete," Gimble teased. "We love you, Sameer, but I'm not sure we'll have hot dogs on the menu that day."

"Well, it was worth a try, Sameer," Nazareth told him. "I still think it's a great idea."

"If you change your minds," Khan laughed, "you know where to find me."

Back at the office Gimble said she needed a little more time to follow a lead that seemed promising, so they continued working separately for another hour. By the time they broke to compare notes, they each seemed pleased with the results.

"You ready?" he asked.

"Oh, yeah," she nodded. "I've definitely got something hot. But how about we cover what you've got on the family first."

"Okay, two details, one of which really stands out. First," he said, "Driscoll's father shot and killed a guy -- Hispanic male, long record -- who was trying to rob the pawn shop back in 1984. No charges, but the old man was apparently never the same after that. Second, and most significantly, a few months ago Driscoll's 16-year-old niece was raped by a group of South Asian gang members while attending an outdoor concert in Brooklyn. Not sure whether they were Indian, Pakistani, or something else," he explained, "but odds are the girl will never be 100% again."

Gimble shook her head slowly. "The father's experience alone might have been enough to set this guy off," she said, "but the niece too? Yeah, that could easily push someone over the edge. How did you track the niece back to him?"

"It's not something I was looking for," he told her. "I ran a search for his sister, who lives in Manhattan, and stumbled across the information about her daughter. The girl's name wasn't in the paper, so we never would have connected Driscoll to the crime unless it had turned up in the Department database. Naturally this is all highly circumstantial, but it fits the profile, doesn't it?"

"Hell, yes, it does," she said. "And what I've got is also circumstantial, but it's pretty powerful stuff when you put it alongside what you've come up with. The star player on Driscoll's high school basketball team was a guy named Jed Butler. He was on his way to a pro career when he got injured, and he ended up carrying mail for the Postal Service. A few weeks ago he was killed while trying to protect a store owner who was being robbed. Screwdriver to the back of the neck, then through the heart."

Nazareth was on full alert now. "Any chance Driscoll and Butler were still in touch with each other?" he asked.

"Butler delivered mail to the pawn shop," she said, "so they saw each other almost every day. And guess who killed Butler."

"I'm listening."

"Jamaican gang."

"One of our vics . . ."

"Right, Kevaughn Brown," she said. "Jamaican. Murdered by the RTS Killer not long after Butler's death."

"And Vishesh Joshi, Indian," he noted.

"Right, not all that long after Driscoll's niece was raped by South Asians."

"No way in hell this is coincidental, Tara," he said. "We both know that."

"Agreed. But we have nothing that puts him near any of the victims. In fact," she added, "I'm not sure we have enough to bring him in for questioning."

He thought about that. "On paper we've got absolutely nothing," he reasoned, "so if we bring him in all we'll do is put him on notice that we're looking hard."

"In which case he stops killing people," she added, "and we never nail him."

"Right. And I don't read him as someone who'll break down under questioning. He seemed under control when we visited him, because he's probably certain we have nothing solid to go on."

"So we just keep an eye on him?" she asked.

"That's one possibility, but if he spots a tail, we might lose him for good. As you've said, he can shut down the program and let us follow him forever if we want to. No, I don't like that. I think he's good for the murders, and I want the son of a bitch."

"What about having someone go into the shop posing as an immigrant looking to do some off-the-books business?"

"That would work," he said, "but I worry about how long it might take. We don't know how long his process runs from start to finish.

Days? Weeks? No telling. Besides, I seriously doubt he targets every immigrant who walks into the shop. He's obviously highly selective, but we don't know what it is he's looking for. The victims are quite different in a number of ways."

They sat quietly for a time, each searching for some way of linking Driscoll to the string of murders. Finally Nazareth got up, sorted through his notes, and handed Gimble an address.

"We can't be sure," he began, "but we think that this address on East 14th Street was where Rafael Tejera met whoever it was killed him. That's point one. Point two is that we assume the RTS Killer needs a safe place where he can kill his victims, wrap them in plastic, and then eventually load them in whatever it is he's driving -- car, truck, most likely a van. Do we agree so far?"

"We do. And isn't it likely that the safe place we're talking about is somewhere near the 14th Street address?" she said.

"Precisely," he nodded. "All the vics have been dumped somewhere between 1:00 and maybe 4:00 a.m., which means the guy is operating at night, when he could work almost anywhere in the City without being noticed."

"Especially if all he's doing is loading a van. Why wouldn't a business owner -- someone who runs a pawn shop, let's say -- be loading a van at some crazy hour? Who would think anything's wrong with that?"

"If Driscoll's our guy," Nazareth said, "and has a warehouse or another shop that we don't know about, he's using that place as his base of operations for killing people. I agree with you that no one would give him and his van a second look. He'd normally be loading and unloading goods all the time."

"And you didn't turn up any other properties in his name when you looked at the business?" she asked.

"Just his apartment. And there's nothing off about that place at all."

Nazareth closed his eyes, folded his arms, and leaned back in his chair. Gimble knew he wasn't resting. He was visiting that special place where his brain had a long history of knitting together details that didn't seem connected. After a minute or so he opened his eyes and laid it out.

"Let's go with the idea that he has a second place," he said. "And let's assume he invites all of his victims to meet him at or near the 14th Street address. The 14th Street address is most likely within walking distance of that second place. They meet at this first address, then walk to the secret location to conduct their business. Next thing you know someone is dead."

"If that's all true, and it sounds plausible to me," she told him, "then going door to door in that neighborhood should scare up someone who recognizes Driscoll."

"Bingo!" he smiled. "There's no law that says he can't have a secret location, but my guess is that if there is such a place -- big *if*, of course -- it will contain a boatload of evidence linking him to the murders."

"Time to call in some extra bodies?" she said.

"Not yet. This is all highly speculative, so I'd hate to have 10 people working the street if there's nothing there. Why don't you and I hit some stores and apartments on our own. If we find anyone who recognizes Driscoll, we put on a full-court press. But if we get nothing, we'll need to decide whether this is worth pursuing. I don't want to be so desperate to find the killer that we latch onto a series of crazy assumptions, beginning with Driscoll as a suspect."

"You don't really believe that, Pete."

"No, I don't. There's a very good chance Driscoll is our guy," he said. "But we have no idea whether this 14th Street address is connected to him at all. At the moment it's just a hunch."

"A hunch worth acting on. Let's show his picture around."

Nazareth checked his watch. "It's kind of late now, and if we're going to do this, I'd like to give it a fair shot. How about we plan to get there by 10:00 tomorrow morning, walk the area for a while, and see what we've got?"

"I like it," she said. "And I'm betting we find someone who recognizes him. I definitely have a very good feeling about this."

44.

He didn't feel bad. He felt nearly dead. As he squinted at himself in the bathroom mirror early the next morning, Driscoll struggled to turn off the pounding inside his skull. Between the gash on his chin and the half bottle of Jameson's he had sucked down the night before, he was hitting on no more than two cylinders. Yet he had no time to lie around licking his wounds. He knew that the Russian could be stinking up the 13th Street basement by now and that the body needed to be prepped for shipment. And all that blood! What the hell do you even use to get rid of blood? He had no idea. Better find an answer fast, he told himself, because every drop of Gorokhov's blood represented the potential for life in prison.

He didn't like closing the shop because that might raise a red flag if those detectives came back. But he liked even less the thought of someone stumbling across the Russian's body. What if there were a fire in the apartment building? Sure as hell someone would enter the basement, and then it would be only a matter of time before the trail led back to him. Or what if the landlord decided to check on the place unexpectedly? Driscoll had changed the lock, but that didn't mean a motivated landlord wouldn't be able to get in anyway. Hell, 10-year-old kids were breaking into homes these days with the help of battery operated lock-picking devices that worked every time. No door was safe. And a door with a dead body behind it was the unsafest of all.

In the end Driscoll went with a compromise. After a cup of black coffee and a slice of burnt toast he walked toward the pawn shop, where he would work until noon. Then he'd drive to 13th Street and take care of the more serious business.

His heart immediately began racing when he saw the NYPD cruiser parked in front of L.E.S. Pawn & Loan, lights flashing. He nonchalantly looked all around him to see if any cops were running in his direction and hoped that his face didn't reveal what his insides felt. The adrenaline rush made his hangover even worse, hard as that seemed. Was this the beginning of the end? Were the police already inside the shop, ripping the place apart as they searched for evidence? Should he bolt while he had the chance?

His brain cells were batting zero.

Before Driscoll could decide what to do, a uniformed officer climbed out of the cruiser, walked to the SUV parked in front of it, and slipped a parking ticket under the SUV's windshield wiper. The fire hydrant, Driscoll thought. Of course. How many times a month did he see a car ticketed or towed because of that hydrant? Too many to count. It must be one of the most profitable fire hydrants in Manhattan.

His hands were shaking, his legs felt like jelly, and he was angry. Angry at himself once again for cowardice in the face of . . . well, absolutely nothing. The man who had blown away the Russian bear had nearly wet his pants over the sight of a police car with flashing lights. Were his nerves shot to hell, or was this simply the result of the injury, the stitches, and the hangover? He couldn't tell. All he knew was that he needed to get a grip on himself.

He entered the shop, turned on the lights, and made sure the shotgun behind the counter was locked and loaded.

45.

Holiday traffic in Manhattan was pure hell, so Nazareth and Gimble wasted a lot of time driving from One Police Plaza to East 14th Street the next morning. It was nearly 10:45 by the time they had found a parking space not far from the address they hoped might be linked to the RTS Killer. Nazareth tossed the NYPD placard on the dashboard, then he and Gimble walked into the first deli they found for two coffees and a few questions for the smiling Korean owner behind the counter.

Nam Lee Cho was in his mid-sixties but could easily have passed for a man in his forties. He was short but powerfully built, and his eyes seemed not to miss anything that moved inside his store. Nazareth read the guy as someone who didn't have much trouble with shoplifters -- at least those who wanted to leave the store with all body parts intact.

After ordering their coffees, Nazareth showed Cho his shield and ID, then handed him a black-and-white photo of Ryan Driscoll that had accompanied one of his Chamber of Commerce talks.

"Just wondering if you've seen this man in the store or around the neighborhood," he said while he was pushing a plastic lid on his coffee cup.

"Peter Nazareth," Cho nodded. "I watched you knock out a very good Korean fighter last year."

"Do you follow Taekwondo tournaments?" Nazareth grinned.

"Only for my students. And the young man you knocked out, he is one of my best. He's very humble now," he smiled.

"You run a Taekwondo school and this store?"

"Not the school anymore. Now my son runs it, but I still train a few students. Some of the time," he tapped the counter, "this is where I work. You still fighting, Detective?"

"A few times a year, yes, but I don't always know when I'll be available. This job has crazy hours."

"It's a good job to have," Cho said pleasantly, "and I am grateful to NYPD for all the help they give me. Too many crazy people come in here. This man," he pointed to Driscoll's photo, "is not one of them. I have not seen him. But if you leave his picture, I will call you if he comes in. I will always help NYPD."

"That would be terrific," Nazareth said as he handed Cho a business card. "Detective Gimble and I really need to speak with him."

"If you need to speak with him," he replied, "I will try to help. You can trust me."

As the detectives hit the street Nazareth said, "And, for the record, I do trust him. I didn't recognize him behind the counter, but as soon as he mentioned the tournament I knew exactly who he is. Grandmaster Nam Lee Cho, 9th-degree black belt, whose son is four-time U.S. champion and most recently Olympic gold medalist. That's why he stepped aside to let his son take over the school."

"So he opened a deli?" Gimble asked.

"Oh, I'm guessing this is simply one of several businesses he's had going for years. Guys like him don't come from Korea to sit on their butts," he said. "They work non-stop until they succeed, and some, like Grandmaster Cho, succeed big. He probably puts some time in at the various businesses to make sure his employees are on top of things."

"I assume he's the sort of person our RTS Killer would like to get rid of."

"Yeah, probably. But I'm not worried about Grandmaster Cho, believe me. He'd change RTS to DOA in a heartbeat if he had to."

"That sounds good to me," she said. "In the meantime, how would you like to proceed?"

"Why don't we visit a few more places together and see how it goes?"

"Nice try, Pete. But we can cover twice as many places if we split up, right?"

He looked at her and shrugged.

"Listen, Pete, when we're on the job, I'm Detective Gimble. When we're off duty, I'm Tara the fiancee. Cool?"

"Cool," he said sheepishly. "Okay, we split up. I want to hit a few more stores and then ring a few apartment doorbells."

"And I'll do the same," she said. "How about we meet back at the deli around 1:00 and grab a sandwich?"

"Sounds good. Call if you need me."

"I definitely will," she grinned. "And you do the same."

He gave her a thumbs-up and headed down 14th Street. Gimble tapped her jacket, felt the gun on her right hip, and casually strolled toward 13th Street. She figured that if Driscoll had a secret place somewhere in the neighborhood, it made sense to canvass between 11th and 17th. Three blocks north, three blocks south. She was determined to find out whether the 14th Street address was a link to the RTS Killer or simply another tantalizing but frustrating dead end.

For no particular reason she hung a left on 13th Street, walked past the first dozen addresses, and climbed the stairs of a pricey apartment building where she assumed units sold for well over a million. The doorman who let her in got first look at Driscoll's photo, but the face didn't ring a bell. So he helped her identify a few tenants who were in the building at the moment and arranged for her to go up. Not everyone was delighted to be interviewed, and no one recognized Driscoll. Strike one.

As Gimble crossed the street and chose another apartment building, Ryan Driscoll watched from his van half a block away. He had just arrived to clean up the basement and prepare Gorokhov for late-night shipment when he spotted the detective leaving the first apartment building. To his amazement he felt no panic. Maybe he had already expended a day's worth of adrenaline on the false alarm with the police car that morning, or maybe he was finally toughening up. Whatever. He recognized Gimble immediately and waited for Nazareth to appear.

Ten minutes later he watched Gimble leave the second apartment building, cross the street again, and walk past several more addresses before climbing the stairs to a place only a few doors from his basement hideaway. It was now 12:20, and still no Nazareth. Driscoll correctly assumed that Gimble was working the street alone and hitting random apartments. If she stuck to her current pattern, she would soon cross the street, visit another building, and cross back over near his place.

What to do about that? On the one hand, it was clear that Gimble didn't know which building was his. On the other hand, it was obvious she had somehow linked the RTS Killer's work to this neighborhood. The key question was whether the police had already pegged him as the key suspect. If so, why would they be going door to door instead of arresting him? No, he told himself, they still don't know who they're after. But they're getting close. Time to run, or time to stand tall?

When Gimble once again crossed over to the opposite side of the street, he had his answer. In her hand she carried a large photograph. Although he couldn't see whose face was on it, he already knew. "You bitch!" he muttered. "You no good, interfering bitch."

He watched Gimble ring one of the apartments and get buzzed in immediately. Remember this, he coached himself. Whenever you need to enter a building, simply hit the doorbell and identify yourself as a cop. Piece of cake.

As soon as the detective disappeared inside the lobby, Driscoll left the van, kept his face half covered by the high collar of his wool winter coat, and unlocked the basement door. Daylight spilled across the floor where the Russian lay in a swamp of congealed blood. Two rats scurried away from the body as Driscoll slammed the door behind him and flicked on the lights. Before long, he thought, you will have female companionship, Comrade Gorokhov.

He slipped the Glock from his pocket, took a deep breath, and opened the door just a crack so that he could watch the street. Then he waited. Five minutes. Ten minutes. Fifteen . . . and she crossed the street, stepped onto the sidewalk directly in front of him, then climbed the stairs at the next building. He opened the door wider.

"I'm down here, ma'am," he yelled to her. He turned so that all she could see was the back of his head silhouetted against the basement lights.

"Are you the doorman?" Gimble called.

"Yes, ma'am," he said. "Just sliced my hand on a file cabinet down here. I'll be right up."

Gimble headed toward the basement door. "Do you need help?" she asked.

"It's bleeding pretty bad," he answered.

When she reached the bottom step Driscoll opened the door wide and pointed the gun at her face. "Unless you want your entire head blown off," he growled, "get in here without making a sound." He stepped back and kept the gun trained on her.

She recognized him instantly but was helpless to do anything but comply. He wasn't close enough for her to attack, and even she wasn't fast enough to cover the distance between them in the time it would take for him to squeeze the trigger. Worse, the dead body and the pool of blood told her all she needed to know about Driscoll's willingness to waste her. This was someone who wouldn't think twice.

He closed the door and ordered her over to the safe room.

"I told you there was a lot of blood, didn't I?" he mocked. "Careful not to ruin your pretty shoes."

"I'm not alone, Mr. Driscoll," she said calmly. "You know I wouldn't have come here by myself."

"Oh, of course you would have," he sneered. "All you NYPD girls have something to prove, don't you? Want to make sure you outdo the guys. Well, this time you've outdone yourself. Get into the room and sit down. If you want to die here, just do something I haven't told you to do."

She sat at the plastic table and waited for an opportunity to reach the gun on her hip. But that wasn't going to happen.

"With two fingers of your left hand," he told her, "reach across and remove the gun that's poking through your jacket. Do it slowly and gently. Good. Toss the gun against the wall near me." She did as she was told. "Very smart. Now attach these to your right wrist and left ankle." He tossed her a pair of black double-lock handcuffs that had been hanging on the safe room's outer wall.

"Brand new, Detective," he said, clearly amused as she snapped the cuffs on. "I don't know why I bought them, actually, but here they are, coming in quite handy."

"Mr. Driscoll," she began, but he cut her off.

"If you prefer, Detective, you can call me Adolphus Fleischer," he grinned. "You recognize the name, don't you? You seem to know a great deal about me."

"I recognize the name," she told him, "but I didn't know it was you. My partner and I were still guessing."

"Well, your guessing days are officially over now. You and that foul Russian on the floor over there will take a ride together tonight. I'm afraid I won't be able to drop you off at a consulate, though. I plan to push your interfering ass into a river instead. Would you prefer Hudson or Harlem?" he laughed.

"I'm sure you realize that killing me will be the beginning of the end for you, Mr. Driscoll. The other officers who are working this neighborhood as we speak all know that I came to 13th Street," she said, "and they'll be looking for me. If they find me dead, they'll never let you live."

"I'm not terribly concerned about that, Detective. You and I will just sit here comfortably until dark," he explained, "and we won't leave until your friends are gone. They can suspect me forever if they want, but they'll never have any proof. And I seriously doubt they'll get warrants to search every single apartment on East 13th Street. You and I are quite safe here."

"Until someone on the street recognizes your photo."

He picked up one of the photos that Gimble had been showing around the neighborhood. The image was a couple of years old, but it reflected his recent makeover because a police artist had retouched the photo to show a mustache, goatee, and eyeglasses.

"Very clever of you to have included my recent changes, but the people on this block have never seen me. Today is the first time I've come here in daylight, and it's probably the last, thanks to your meddling. You do realize," he said, "that I'm performing an important service to this city, don't you?"

"By killing innocent people and then mocking them by the way you dump their bodies?" she said, disgusted by everything he represented.

"Innocent? Don't make me laugh. I chose wisely, Detective. Those men and that Russian in there were the worst of the worst -- vermin, scum, leeches sucking America dry. They came here to murder, rape, and pillage," he said bitterly, "and instead of hunting me you should be draping a medal around my neck."

Gimble didn't respond. Driscoll was getting worked up by his own hate talk, and she feared he could snap at any moment. The less she said, the better her chances of surviving. Driscoll moved toward her, quite safe now that she was cuffed like a pretzel, and patted down her pockets. From her right pocket he pulled a pair of handcuffs.

"You came prepared, I see. I could have kept my cuffs nice and new, Detective," he mocked. "Why didn't you tell me sooner?"

"Why didn't you ask?" she replied sarcastically.

Driscoll backhanded her across the face with his gun, splitting open the left side of her mouth and chipping one of her lower teeth. Her head snapped back, but she didn't make a sound.

"Very impressive, little girl. Very impressive. Not a sound," he said. "Is that something they taught you at the police academy? How to remain silent when being hit by a bad old man like me?"

Gimble licked some blood from her lip but didn't answer. She was not going to push her luck again.

Driscoll continued rummaging through her jacket, allowing his hands to linger on her chest as he felt for the inside pockets. She imagined locking his neck in a choke hold and slowly intensifying the pressure until his upper vertebrae shattered. But with only her left arm free she had no chance of overpowering him. All she might succeed in doing was getting her head blown off.

"What do we have here, my lovely friend," he said as he lifted a set of keys from her pocket. His eyes widened and his stomach lurched when he saw the small tracking device on her keyring. The swagger instantly disappeared.

"What is this?" he screamed. "What the hell is this?"

She fought back a smile, certain that it might earn her a bullet. "My partner and I each have one," she explained calmly. "It's a wireless tracking device."

"How is it tracked?" he yelled. "Tell me how this goddamned thing is tracked!"

"On our cell phones," she told him. "We're supposed to meet at 1:00 for lunch, and that's how we planned to find each other."

Driscoll felt dizzy when he looked at his watch. 12:56. He ran from the basement knowing only one thing: he needed to disappear, and fast. But where? It wouldn't be dark for another three hours at least. Would he be able to hide anywhere in Manhattan now that every cop probably had his photo and his name? He started the van, then paused before he put it in gear. How the hell could he know she was telling the truth about the 1:00 o'clock meeting? Maybe she was just screwing with his head. And he had fallen for it!

Then the other shoe dropped . . . loud and hard. Gimble was the only person able to identify him as the RTS Killer. Everyone else might suspect him, but the one person who could actually finger him was handcuffed in his safe room. One well-placed round would fix this. He knew what he needed to do.

As he opened the van door Driscoll looked up the street and saw Detective Pete Nazareth walking in his direction. Gimble hadn't been lying after all, and it was too late to shut her up for good. All he could do now was put as much distance as possible between himself and the police. He pulled the collar of his jacket as high as it would go and slowly pulled away from the curb.

Nazareth glanced at the passing van whose driver seemed to be studying something on the seat -- a cell phone or delivery receipt perhaps -- but gave it no thought. He had struck out ringing doorbells, so it was time to meet Gimble for lunch. His cell phone told him she was a few hundred feet away.

46.

Driscoll saw Nazareth look at the van as it passed and knew he would soon connect it to the RTS killings. Now the only question was how long it would take the police to throw a net over the entire city. Would he have enough time to escape via the George Washington Bridge and drive west, or would the police already be setting up roadblocks? The Queens Midtown Tunnel was just a few blocks away. Surely he could slip through before the police began searching for his blue van, but where would he go from there? Laguardia? Flying wasn't an option, he realized, because his picture would soon be on display at every airport terminal in the area. Long Island? He'd be trapped like a rat out there. North toward Upstate New York or Connecticut? No. He needed to head west as fast as possible and get far away from New York City.

He cursed himself again for not killing Gimble when he'd had the chance. Allowing her to live was the kind of horrific mistake that comes from not having enough time to plan, and he knew that from this moment forward his plans needed to be flawless if he didn't want to spend the rest of his life in a Riker's Island cell.

What he needed right now was a quiet place to think. But where, he wondered, can you sit in broad daylight when every cop in the City is about to begin hunting you down? The sign for the Queens Midtown Tunnel triggered an idea. He turned onto East 34th Street, pulled into a parking garage, and left his van in the darkest corner available. The police would eventually find it, of course, but by then he would be safely out of sight somewhere in Montana or New Mexico or Colorado, enjoying his new life.

He walked to the street and snagged a cab, telling the driver to take him to the long-term parking lot at Laguardia. Driscoll eyed the driver's ID hanging in the back and wasn't at all surprised to find a name he couldn't pronounce. When only 5% of cabbies are born in America, he reasoned, the odds of finding an immigrant behind the wheel are pretty damned good.

The driver jabbered on his cell phone the entire way, in between bites of something that to Driscoll smelled like raw sewage. The guy plainly wasn't interested in speaking with his passenger, at least until it was time for the tip. No need to worry about a tip, Driscoll thought. You won't be able to spend it where you're going.

When they reached the long-term lot at Laguardia, Driscoll had the cabbie drive up and down lanes as he searched for an area completely free of travelers.

"You not know where car is?" the driver yelled through the bullet-proof partition, irritated by his passenger's apparent confusion.

"Is the meter still running?" Driscoll answered sarcastically.

"Yes, still running."

"Then what's your hurry?"

The driver didn't like Driscoll's attitude. "I miss next fare, that's what," he snapped.

"A fare in the hand is worth two in the bush," Driscoll told him.

The driver glared at him in the mirror but said nothing. He didn't recognize the bastardized cliche and didn't care. All he wanted was for Driscoll to leave the car.

"Stop, right here!" Driscoll said. "This is it. Pull in next to the green Volvo."

"No park, eh. You get out here."

"Whatever you say." Driscoll slipped out of the back seat and began walking away. The driver lowered his window and yelled, "$57 plus tip and tolls!"

Driscoll stepped back toward the car and said, "I'll give you $10. Take it or leave it, asshole."

The enraged driver threw open the door and found himself face to face with a Glock 20. "Move your ass over to the passenger side," Driscoll told him, "or I'll blow you over there in little pieces."

"Hey, no problem. Keep your fare," he whimpered. "I just go."

"Where you go is to that seat over there. Do it now."

The driver slid over to the passenger seat while Driscoll looked around the cab to make sure they were alone Without saying a word he reached in and shot the guy once in the side of his head.

After checking that there was no blood on either his clothes or the driver's seat, he climbed in and pulled the cab into the empty parking space. Satisfied that the dead cabbie couldn't be seen by anyone driving past, Driscoll got out, settled comfortably into the back seat, and prepared to wait for the cover of darkness.

He now had plenty of quiet time to plan his route to freedom.

47.

Nazareth knocked on the door when he reached the locked basement on 13th Street but heard nothing. He knew she was in there, so he speed-dialed her cell phone. No response. Without hesitating he took half a step back, leaped forward, and with a powerful double side kick drove both feet into the door, ripping the jamb from the frame as he flew in. He froze when he saw what he at first thought was Gimble's lifeless body on the floor, but then heard her voice from the safe room. His relief at seeing her alive was quickly overwhelmed by rage. Whoever had left his partner bloody and battered in this filthy dungeon would taste Nazareth's wrath.

"Thank God you're alive, Tara. I thought I had lost you."

"It was Driscoll," she told him as he worked the handcuffs loose. "He was going to kill me tonight, but he got spooked when he found that GPS tracker you gave me. He left just a couple of minutes ago."

"Walking or driving? Any idea?"

"I heard an engine start right after he went outside, so I'm guessing he drove."

Nazareth thought about that. "I noticed a blue van going down the street just before I got here."

And I saw a blue van parked in front of the building. That was probably him, Pete."

Nazareth studied her cut lip. "He hit me with his gun," she said. "I think he may have broken a tooth." She opened her mouth for him.

"Yeah, the tip of the lower tooth is broken off," he said. "And the top of his neck is going to be broken when I find him."

Nazareth called for backup at the basement, then sent out the alert for Driscoll and his blue van.

Gimble got to her feet, wiped some blood off her mouth, and announced, "We're going to his apartment, Pete. If we're lucky, maybe he'll run there before leaving town. He has to know his life in New York City is over."

"I want you to stay here and have your mouth looked at."

"It's my mouth," she insisted, "and it's fine. I want this son of a bitch more than you do. Let's go."

They waited for the first cruiser to pull up, gave the responding officers the short story, then were on their way.

"How the hell did you find him?" Nazareth asked as they trotted for their car on 14th Street.

"I'm embarrassed to say I didn't. I thought he was a doorman, and I walked right into a trap."

"Whose body was that on the floor?"

"Some Russian he wasted. Don't know who or why. But that room I was in," she said, "must be where he kept the victims before killing them. Once that door is locked, no one gets out. Serious prison."

"The guy is smart and meticulous," Nazareth said as they climbed into their unmarked Impala. "So it doesn't surprise me he'd have a place like that way off the grid."

"Now let's hope he thinks he has enough time to hit his apartment before splitting. He's bound to need money or checks or something. Anything. I'm going to call and arrange a welcoming committee for him."

"That's fine, but tell them to send a couple of plainclothes guys. If he sees blue uniforms and flashing lights, he'll bolt."

"Understood." She noted the concern on Nazareth's face. "Don't worry, Pete, we're going to get him."

"I'm not worried about that, Tara," he answered. "But I want to be the one who takes him down. This is now personal."

"I'm fine, Pete. Really."

"Well, he's not going to be." He looked straight ahead and stomped on the gas.

They both knew that Ryan Driscoll was a desperate man who would have no qualms about leaving a trail of bodies between New York City and whatever rat hole he chose to live in for the rest of his life.

Nazareth and Gimble didn't plan to let that happen.

48.

A bit of quiet time in the back of the cab allowed Driscoll to design a plan that struck him as workable in every way, and before too many days passed he would be living the good life elsewhere in America. Colorado struck his fancy. Mountains, valleys, wilderness, and, yes, genuine Americans. He was disgusted that a patriot like him could be hunted for having done nothing more than rid the streets of filth. But that's New York City for you. The place has gotten so bad, he told himself, that the natives have forgotten it was ever good.

Well, he'd done his part. The rest would be up to someone else now.

As darkness fell he fired up his cell phone, searched the Internet for a travel website, and bought himself a one-way ticket from Laguardia to Phoenix on a flight that left that evening at 5:45. The itinerary called for roughly seven hours with a long layover in Chicago. For less than $400 he had gotten himself a great deal of insurance. He figured that since the police would no doubt be checking airlines for his name, he might as well give them something they could latch onto. The thought of half the cops in New York City racing to Laguardia on a fool's errand brought a smile to his lips.

All he needed now was a new vehicle since driving out west in a stolen yellow cab wasn't an option. Fifteen minutes later a 40-something woman in a long black winter coat stepped off the airport courtesy bus and fumbled in her pocket for the keys to her Lexus SUV. Driscoll was eager to get behind the wheel. He casually walked up to her, pulled the gun, and pointed it at the center of her chest.

"Give me the keys," he said, "and get your ass over to that yellow cab." A bullet to her head, and he'd be on his way.

"Oh, God," she whimpered, her voice cracking.

"No, I'm not God, but you'll get to see him if you don't hand me the damn keys."

She trembled slightly as she took her hand from her coat pocket. The keys dangled from a stylish pink rhinestone keychain whose petite canister was capable of delivering a stream of pepper spray and UV marking dye up to 10 feet. In this case the spray needed to travel less than two feet. She pressed the button when Driscoll reached for the keys, and he immediately dropped the gun and clawed at his eyes. While he screamed and staggered backwards, the woman put every ounce of strength in her trim body behind the right foot that slammed into his groin. Driscoll hit the pavement moaning as she jumped in her SUV and sped off.

He could barely see as he hobbled toward the cab. His eyes were on fire, and the pain in his groin was sickening, but he knew that the woman would already be dialing 911. He threw the cab in gear, hoping that the lights from oncoming cars would help keep him on the right side of the road while his vision slowly recovered. Not until he had crossed the airport boundary and passed over the Grand Central Parkway did he remember he had a large logistical problem: a dead cab driver slumped on the front seat.

His eyes began to clear as he turned down a succession of side streets looking for a place free of traffic and pedestrians. Not far from the airport he found a quiet street abutting Overlook Park and decided this would have to do. He hit the brakes, scrambled around to the passenger side, and dragged the dead driver out of the cab, leaving him in a crumpled heap half on and half off the curb. As Driscoll pulled away to tackle the next important step of his escape plan, the cab's right rear tire thumped over the dead man's lower legs, snapping them like twigs.

Ten minutes later, eyes still tearing, he made a quick stop at a CVS pharmacy on Queens Boulevard, where he spent $20 on an electric razor and another $10 on black hair dye. Since he was already there he also used the ATM machine to grab as much as he could in cash advances. He left the store with one small shopping bag and $2,000 cash in his wallet.

Shortly before 6:00 he walked into the grimy office of the most rundown motel he'd been able to find and gave the old drunk at the desk cash for one night. He was pleased that the guy wasn't watching TV, because it was highly possible -- likely even -- that his face was now being plastered on screens throughout the Metro area. Let them look all they want, he told himself, because an hour from now they'll be looking for the wrong guy. He parked the yellow cab as far as possible from his room and locked its doors.

The motel room looked suspiciously like an hourly rental. Poorly made bed, well-worn linoleum flooring, and a tiny bathroom whose shower wore a coat of furry mold. But the faucet in the sink delivered warm water, and that's all he cared about.

Twenty-five minutes later Driscoll was a new man. His hair was considerably darker than before. The mustache and goatee were gone. And the fake eyeglasses were at the bottom of the bathroom trash can. His face looked quite unlike the one in the photo that Detective Gimble had been showing around back on 13th Street, and he was well satisfied with the transformation.

Only one task remained before he began rolling toward his new life.

49.

The two detectives weren't overly surprised that Driscoll hadn't gone back to either his Lower East Side apartment or the pawn shop before running. It had been a long shot. But they were disappointed -- especially Nazareth, who longed to punish Driscoll for what he had done to Gimble.

"I think we should still have someone watch both places," Gimble said. "He can't just bail on everything he owns, including the apartment and the business."

"Maybe, maybe not. If the choice is leave it all behind or rot in prison," Nazareth said, "I assume he leaves it. It's also possible he has some money stashed away. Either way, he's certainly smart enough to realize he can't afford to be arrested. There's no defense attorney on the planet who can get him out of this."

"I really hoped he'd try to come back Downtown," she said.

"Me too, Tara," he said, slowly shaking his head. "This isn't going to be easy."

Ryan Driscoll was now simply one of the eight and a half million people who called New York City home. Nazareth and Gimble found the odds unappealing.

On the other hand, they were pleased that Chief Crawford had mobilized the entire Department on their behalf. In no time at all the full force of the NYPD had been brought to bear on the RTS Killer. Police were stopping every blue van they could find, whether on the City's streets or at bridges, tunnels and ferries. Driscoll's photo had been sent to local TV stations as well as airports, bus stations, hotels, and any other travel-related businesses he might try to use. And naturally every cop in every car and on every street corner was looking for a man matching Driscoll's description. The suspect was armed, dangerous, and most likely desperate, and he had to be taken down.

The Department's full-court press also touched the Manhattan DA's office, where two days earlier forensic accountant Thad Carter had begun investigating Driscoll's business activities for his friend and former track teammate, Pete Nazareth. He had said the report might take a week or so, but the sudden City-wide alert pushed the project to the top of his list. After working frantically on the project all afternoon, he caught up with Nazareth as he and Gimble were parking in front of Driscoll's 13th Street basement. They had gone back there hoping the Crime Scene guys had discovered some bit of evidence that might point them in the right direction.

"I'm sorry to tell you," Carter began, "that this guy is no idiot, Pete. Either he knows a fair amount about international business, or he hired the right middleman."

"International business?" Nazareth said, puzzled by his friend's comment. "He's been running a pawn shop his whole life."

"Unfortunately," Carter continued, "he technically has been running someone else's pawn shop. L.E.S. Pawn & Loan is owned by an offshore company in Belize. The official name is Donegal Enterprises, but I guess we can assume it's your guy Driscoll."

"What exactly does that mean to us, Thad?"

"It means we can't touch the property. Driscoll has been paying rent to the company, and the company can sell the property whenever it wishes."

"That's complete bullshit, and you know it!" Nazareth fumed.

"Hey, don't shoot the messenger. And, for the record, the news gets worse. Driscoll doesn't own his apartment."

"Don't tell me," Nazareth said.

"All right. I won't tell you that Driscoll has been paying rent to the owner of the apartment, Donegal Enterprises of Belize."

"Thad, this is Tara Gimble. Do you have any idea where Driscoll's cash is? We're assuming the guy can't run far without money," she said hopefully.

"What I can tell you, Tara, is that the last time he had money with a U.S. financial firm the account was slightly under a half million. I can't be sure about this, but it looks as though the money went to a bank in Belize, and from there it got dumped in Europe. Switzerland would be my guess."

"In other words, he has plenty of cash," Nazareth said, "and he'll be able to sell off the two properties. Which means no matter where he goes, he won't starve."

"Rough guess, he's worth maybe two million, guys," Carter said. "He knew enough to get everything offshore, and he most likely spent a few thousand dollars to have a specialist do all the work for him. Looks as though it might have been a Bahamian agent that sets up these invisible companies and accounts for anyone willing to pay the fee."

Nazareth sat quietly and shook his head after Carter had hung up.

"People like us are lucky to finish the day alive," he said sadly, "while some guy in the Bahamas gets rich helping dirtbags like Driscoll set themselves up for life. I mean, it's not enough that we put our lives on the line against the murderers and rapists and terrorists and drug dealers and all the rest. We have to do it while people like Driscoll are allowed to park their money overseas and live happily ever after. What's wrong with this picture, Tara?"

"You're always the first to say we need to play the hand we're dealt," she said gently, "and that's what we need to do right now. Remember, Driscoll hasn't begun living the good life yet. I've got to believe he's still in New York City. He's probably sitting in front of a TV set waiting to see if his face pops up on the screen, which it will."

"I hope to hell you're right, Tara. We need a little luck here, and so far we've haven't gotten any."

They walked into the basement and found the Crime Scene officers tagging and bagging every scrap of evidence they could find. Gorokhov's bloody remains had been carted away, but a trove of valuable information remained. Among other things, because Driscoll hadn't been able to scrub the place down before bolting, his fingerprints were all over the materials he had used in the RTS murders. In addition, the team had found numerous sets of prints in the safe room, and in a matter of hours they would link those to the RTS victims. If they ever found Driscoll, he would go away for life.

Gimble was about to photograph the safe room where she had been held when Chief Crawford called on her cell phone.

"This is Gimble, Chief."

"Is Pete with you?"

"Yep, we're at Driscoll's hideout on 13th."

"Well, your buddy Driscoll is booked on a 5:45 flight, Laguardia to Phoenix, with a stop in Chicago. My guess is he'd like to get off in Chicago and disappear," he told her, "but the flight's not leaving with him on it. That I can goddamn guarantee you."

"You've made arrangements, Chief?"

"You bet. The airline will board the flight, close the doors, then sit at the gate until our guys can get on and take him. He won't have a weapon," the chief said, "so this should be quick and easy."

"Do you want Pete and me to get out there?" she asked.

"Hell, no. Unless you've got your own private helicopter you'll never get there before this all goes down. Just sit tight where you are, and I'll call as soon as I know what's happened."

She told Nazareth what was going on and waited for him to explode over not being able to arrest Driscoll himself. Instead, he calmly shook his head.

"Not going to happen, Tara. Driscoll may be booked on a flight," he said, "but there's no way he plans to board that plane. All he's doing is forcing us to commit resources to Laguardia. He's nowhere near the airport."

Before Gimble could respond, her cell phone rang again. She listened briefly then said, "Wait, hold on. Let me get my partner on the call." She and Nazareth went into the safe room, where she put the phone on speaker.

"Okay, Andy, I've got Pete Nazareth with me. Pete," she said, "this is Officer Andy Polinski, who's out in Queens not far from Laguardia."

"Okay, so we've got two things going on," Polinski said. "First a woman called 911 about a guy who tried to carjack her fancy SUV at the airport's long-term lot. Guy had a gun, and he matches the description of the nutjob you're looking for. She dosed him with pepper spray, kicked him in the, uh, groin, and took off."

"Was she hurt?" Gimble asked.

"Bruised the top of her foot on his crotch maybe," he laughed. "Otherwise, no. The second thing is we're here on a street next to

Overlook Park with a very dead cab driver. Black dude, mid-thirties. Took a bullet to the head and was dumped at the curb. No sign of the cab."

"No witnesses?" Nazareth asked.

"In New York City?" he snorted. "Somebody who saw something? No, nobody saw a thing. There are 10 houses across the street, but nobody saw anything. Right. We got the call from a mailman about 20 minutes ago."

"This is great, Andy. Thanks for getting to us so quickly," Gimble said.

"No problem, detectives. Hope you find this son of a bitch fast."

Gimble hung up as Nazareth took a seat on top of the plastic table in the safe room. He rested his forehead in his right hand, closed his eyes, and tried to bring some order to all the details that were zipping around inside his brain. Gimble left him alone for a few minutes while she checked in with the Crime Scene specialists. By the time she came back, her partner was ready to roll.

"So what are you thinking, Pete?" she asked.

"We need to assume that Polinski's two incidents involve Driscoll. For some reason he ended up at Laguardia and tried to snag a car. He missed getting the SUV," Nazareth told her, "but he got the cab and dumped the cabbie on the side of the road."

"So he's running in a cab?"

"Yeah, but not for long," he said. "He knows damn well that every cop within 100 miles of the City will be looking for that cab. So he's in Queens. Definitely in Queens," he nodded. "And he's hunting for another vehicle."

"Another carjacking coming up."

"You bet. And I guarantee you he doesn't plan to leave a witness," he said grimly. "He's already spooked by the woman who got away at Laguardia, so this time he'll be a lot more careful."

"I'll call Crawford and ask him to get the word out," she said as she speed-dialed the chief's private number.

"Tell him to assume that Driscoll's on foot now," Nazareth told her. "He'd want to get far away from Overlook Park, then dump the cab in a relatively busy neighborhood. He can't waste all night trying to find the next vehicle, so he's going to be where there are plenty of cars available."

Gimble briefed Crawford, who immediately updated the earlier alert. In addition, he made sure local radio stations got word that a killer was on the loose in Queens, most likely trying to steal an escape vehicle. Crawford had no way of knowing that the stations would not interrupt prime-time programming for something short of the end of the world. This meant the first radio announcement wouldn't come for another three hours.

"The question now," Nazareth said, "is where you and I should hang until we catch a break. Queens makes no sense. At this time of day we'd spend an hour just getting through the tunnel."

"But if he gets another car," she said, "he could be in Ohio or Virginia before we know what he's driving."

"I'm with you, Tara, but we won't accomplish anything sitting in the Queens Midtown Tunnel. All you and I can do right now is hope someone spots him before he catches his next ride. We're overdue for a little break."

50.

Driscoll scoured the streets of Queens in search of the right person with the right vehicle. The darkness alone was enough to make him feel comfortable, but his altered looks made him feel absolutely invincible. No one was going to recognize him. Of that he was certain. So he took his time, passing up two or three possible victims because they were driving wrecks that probably wouldn't have gotten him as far as the Verrazano Bridge.

After nearly a half hour, when he was a few blocks from the entrance of the Queens Midtown Tunnel, he spotted someone leaving an Italian restaurant and walking toward a car parked on a quiet, poorly lit side street. A short, heavyset man with a slight limp was completely focused on finding his keys in one of the pockets of his huge horse blanket of an overcoat. When the guy finally hit the remote Driscoll was delighted to see the lights flash on a 2015 silver Toyota Camry. Excellent vehicle, he thought, one that was common enough not to attract attention as he cruised across America in style. Rip off a few license plates along the way, and he'd be good to go.

As the man grabbed the door handle, Driscoll walked up beside him and jammed the gun into his plump midsection.

"Do precisely what I tell you to do," Driscoll said calmly, "and I won't have to spread you and your Italian food all over the sidewalk."

"Hey, hey, hey, no problem," the guy yelped. "Take the wallet, the car, the coat, whatever you want. No argument from me. Just please don't shoot me."

Driscoll had no desire to shoot the guy here and attract attention. Plenty of time to waste him later.

"Get behind the wheel," he ordered, "and let's take a ride."

"Please, just take the car," the guy said.

"Get your fat ass behind the wheel, or I spread your guts all over this nice car."

When the guy slid behind the wheel, Driscoll jumped into the passenger seat and pointed the gun toward the man's head.

"What's your name?" Driscoll asked.

"Angelo Dinapoli."

"Okay, listen carefully, Angelo Dinapoli," Driscoll told him. "You're going to get on 278, and you're going to follow that all the way over the Verrazano Bridge to Staten Island. Once we get there, you will get out of the car, and I will drive off. Do you understand?"

"Yes, I understand," Angelo said nervously.

"Then move."

Dinapoli threw the car in gear, drove to the end of the side street, and hung a hard left on the main avenue. They hadn't gone half a block when Driscoll saw the flashing lights ahead.

"Turn here, turn here!" he yelled. Dinapoli immediately swerved right and onto the approach road for Queens Midtown Tunnel. "Shit, no, stop!"

"I've got cars behind me," Dinapoli screamed.

"Go, then, go, goddammit!"

And there was no turning back. Unless Driscoll wanted to jump out of the car amid the tunnel traffic, he was on his way back to Manhattan.

"I ought to blow your brains out!" Driscoll yelled.

"You told me to turn," Dinapoli whimpered. "What was I supposed to do?"

"Son of a bitch!" Driscoll said as he pounded the dashboard. "No good son of a bitch!"

"Listen, I'm . . ."

"Do you have EZ Pass?"

"Yeah, but . . . ."

"EZ Pass lane! Get in the fast lane."

But as soon as the car squeezed into the EZ Pass lane, Driscoll knew he had blundered. If the police came looking for this vehicle, the EZ Pass transponder would become a beacon in the night. He ripped the device from its holder on the windshield. Before Dinapoli could get a word out of his mouth, Driscoll shouted at him in frustration.

"Don't say another word! Just drive. And give me your cell phone."

While Dinapoli followed the line of cars ahead of him toward Manhattan, Driscoll removed the phone's SIM card and dropped it out the window as soon as they entered a long left curve. From this angle no one behind them would be able to see something hitting the pavement. Then he did the same with the EZ Pass transponder. He looked menacingly toward Dinapoli, whose forehead was sweating profusely even though the car's interior was still chilly.

"You screw up again, Dinapoli, and I'll turn you into spaghetti sauce."

51.

Nazareth and Gimble were finishing a quick dinner at a burger joint not far from Driscoll's basement hideout when Chief Crawford caught up with them.

"Your guy never showed for the flight to Phoenix. We had nearly a dozen cops and a couple hundred pissed off passengers who didn't like being delayed. But no Driscoll."

"He was just yanking our chains, Chief," Nazareth said, "but I don't think he's been able to run yet. My gut tells me he's still in Queens trying to find a set of wheels. If that happens . . ."

"Then he disappears," Crawford said. "Yeah, I know. We've got every cop on that side of the river looking for him, but time is slipping away. Pete, I do not want to lose this asshole."

"We're doing all the right things, Chief. I can't think of anything else we can throw at this. But if I do," he said, "you'll be the first to know."

He summarized the conversation for Gimble, who obviously was lost in thought many miles away.

"Still with me partner?" he smiled.

She held up one finger, asking for a little more time to process whatever idea had grabbed hold of her. Then she looked at him and grinned.

"Got it!" she said. "Something has been kicking around in the back of my head since we took that call from Officer Polinski out near Laguardia. Listen to this, Pete. In one of my college courses a team of us had to hunt for scorpions at night."

"Scorpions? You had scorpions out there?"

"Absolutely. But not in the dorms."

"Oh, that's good."

"Very good, actually. But here's the thing," she said excitedly. "Do you know how to find them at night?"

"Carefully, I suppose."

"Thanks, wiseass. What you do is you make them glow in the dark by shining a UV flashlight on them."

"And they glow in the dark? Seriously?"

"Yep, they really do. And what does this have to do with Driscoll?"

"I was going to ask you that."

"The woman he tried to carjack nailed him with pepper spray . . ."

"And most pepper sprays have a UV dye in them. Of course. Damn, you're good, Tara," he smiled. "You're definitely a keeper."

"Well thank you, Pete. I'm glad to know that," she laughed.

"Too bad we don't all have UV flashlights, isn't it?"

"We don't all have them, but I do. It's in a dusty box at the bottom of a cluttered closet at my apartment. Let's go get it. Hey, you never know when it might come in handy."

"You never know. In the meantime," he said, "let's ask Officer Polinski to get hold of the woman who nuked Driscoll and find out whether her pepper spray actually had dye in it."

"Most definitely."

By the time they reached Gimble's apartment they had received word from Polinski that the woman had, in fact, covered her attacker's face and hands with invisible UV dye. Whether Driscoll even knew that was somewhat irrelevant, since the dye would most likely be with him for weeks, even if he tried to wash it off.

"We're still looking for one man in nearly nine million," Gimble said as she replaced the flashlight's batteries, "but if we find him, he'll glow like a Christmas tree."

"Wouldn't that be a lovely gift?" he said.

"The second best gift I can think of," she replied.

"And the first would be?"

"Hanging out by the fireplace in that cabin you were fantasizing about recently. I would really love to do that."

"We nail this guy, and then you and I split for a cabin in the woods."

"With a big stone fireplace, Pete."

"The biggest we can find, Tara."

Nazareth's phone rang as he and Gimble were driving back toward Driscoll's hideout, and he put it on speaker.

"Nazareth," he said.

"This is Sergeant Gina Tindall with the 1-1-5 in Queens. Are you the detective who's got the alert out for Ryan Driscoll?"

"You bet I am," he said. "Have you got something?"

"Not sure. Could be totally unrelated," she told him, "but a few minutes ago we took a call from a Gloria Dinapoli, Queens resident. Her husband called her about an hour ago and said he'd be home in a few minutes to meet with the caterer for their daughter's wedding. Now he's not answering his cell phone, and she's freaked because she saw something about the RTS Killer on TV."

"Did she say where he was when he called?" Gimble asked.

"Yeah, he was at some Italian place not far from the Queens Midtown Tunnel having a drink with one of his clients. The husband's an insurance agent."

"Wouldn't be the first time a guy decided to keep on drinking and not answer his wife's phone call," Nazareth said.

"She swears he'd never blow off anything having to do with their daughter. The wedding is in two weeks," she explained, "and that's all the guy can talk about."

"Okay, at this point," Nazareth began, "I'm willing to chase down damn near anything, and this is a coincidence that could mean something. Let's assume Driscoll hijacked the guy's car. What's he driving?"

"Late model Toyota Camry, silver."

"If you were running, Sergeant, which way would you go from the last known location?"

Tindall thought about it then said, "Most likely I'd get on 278 and head for 87, the N.Y. Thruway. I might grab I-95 instead if I were running for New England. But from the Thruway I can head north, then west. It opens up the whole country for me."

"I agree. So we're looking for a silver Toyota Camry, driver and possibly one passenger. If the car was hijacked an hour ago, it might still be within the five boroughs, but to be safe we'll get the word out to the state police. We'll make that call."

"And I'll get the Department on it from my end," Tindall said. "We'll be all over this."

"Many thanks," Nazareth said, then clicked off.

"So it's all happening over there," Gimble said woefully, "while we're stuck here."

"I'm not so sure, Tara," he told her. "This guy has managed to stay invisible for a hell of a long time, and I wouldn't be at all surprised if he did the unexpected."

"Meaning?"

"Sometimes the best place to hide is in plain sight. If everybody's expecting him to be in Queens, maybe he runs back to Manhattan, hides here for a few days, then splits when things settle down."

"Doubtful," she said, shaking her head.

"Unexpected, but not necessarily doubtful. Let's head over toward the tunnel," he said. "You never know."

52.

The tunnel's yellow glow on Dinapoli's face revealed his terror, something Driscoll found appealing. He was once again the man in charge, the RTS Killer, and those he encountered had damn well better be scared. As the tunnel roadway began to rise, so did his spirits. Maybe returning to Manhattan was best after all. No doubt that bitch in the SUV at Laguardia had called the police by now, he thought, and maybe they'd also found the cab driver's body. On both counts he was probably better off in Manhattan, since every available cop would be heading toward Queens.

The Camry broke out of the tunnel into a chilly, overcast Manhattan night, and Driscoll couldn't suppress his smile. In less than an hour Dinapoli would be attracting rats in Central Park while his new car was barreling due west.

"Straight ahead," he ordered. "Follow the *Crosstown, 37th Street* sign." He raised the gun in case Dinapoli had forgotten who was calling all the shots.

"Let me out here, and I swear to God I'll keep my mouth shut. I've got a family at home," Dinapoli pleaded.

"Your family will get you back in a box the next time you open your big mouth," Driscoll replied, placing the gun's muzzle against the side of the guy's head. "You'll be missing some body parts, though. Is that what you want?"

The guy shook his head, not daring to say another word. He prayed that somehow he would live to see another day even though he was certain his captor planned to kill him. He could identify Driscoll, the car, and the last known location. In short, he was the perfect witness. And it was clear that leaving a witness behind wasn't in his captor's playbook.

They cruised 37th Street until Driscoll ordered a right turn onto Madison. Traffic was moderately heavy, and Dinapoli briefly considered jumping from the car when they stopped for a traffic light. But he correctly assumed he'd catch a bullet in the back before

Driscoll jumped from the car and disappeared into the crowds of commuters and shoppers. They might catch the guy eventually, he thought, but I'd still be dead. So he drove on.

Dinapoli had no idea where they were headed. For block after block they passed office towers, restaurants, and pricey retail shops, but Driscoll said nothing. By the time they reached 65th Dinapoli had concluded they were on their way to the G.W. Bridge, but Driscoll unexpectedly ordered him to turn.

"Take a left on 66th," he said, "then go straight."

Dinapoli did as he was told, and one block later they caught a green light, crossed 5th Avenue, and drove between the stone pillars at the entrance of Central Park. They had entered a place that might have been hundreds of miles away from Manhattan, a dark forest where bare branches reached like skeletons in the night, backlit by the dim glow of streetlights from Central Park West a half mile away. They were on the 65th Street Transverse, which spanned the entire breadth of the park, and Dinapoli suddenly knew that this is where his life would end.

The roadway was separated from the park on both sides by high stone walls, and Dinapoli's fear intensified as he nervously guided the car between the walls and passed under the first of several bridges spanning the 65th Street Transverse. His heart was leaping out of his chest as the voice deep inside his brain cried, "Now, do it now!"

As they approached the second bridge, Dinapoli hit the accelerator and swerved toward the stone wall on their right. The car's entire right side slammed into the wall, lighting up the December sky with a shower of sparks, but Dinapoli kept his foot on the gas.

"Turn, turn!" Driscoll screamed as he dropped the gun and braced himself with both hands against the dashboard. But Dinapoli powered on until just before the car's right front end made contact with the stone archway of the second bridge. Then he stomped on the brake, kept the steering wheel turned toward the wall, and jumped from the car before it had come to a full stop. The adrenaline rush helped him move faster than he had in decades as he ran back toward Madison Avenue, waving at cars all the way.

Driscoll fumbled for his gun with one hand and tugged at the seat belt with the other. The passenger side of the car was jammed hard against the stone wall, which meant he had to slide across the front seat and use the driver's door. By the time he had found the gun and worked his way out of the car, he had only one option. Run like hell. As soon as Dinapoli called 911 the police would be all over this place with a vengeance.

Driscoll jogged toward Central Park West. All he had to do was cross the park and disappear among the throngs of Christmas shoppers. He could hang out somewhere -- a bar, a restaurant, maybe even a department store -- until the police moved on. After that he would simply find another vehicle. And, yes, this time he would kill the driver before stealing the car, which is what he should have done with Dinapoli back in Queens.

After 100 yards he had trouble breathing. By one 150 he was finished. Running was out of the question. He bent over and rested his hands on his thighs. How the hell had he gotten so far out of shape? He used to run up and down a basketball court for hours, and now it was impossible to jog from one side of Central Park to the other.

Time for a new plan. He scrambled over the stone wall, pushed his way through a tangle of shrubs whose sharp branches ripped at his face and hands, and headed south. Not even the NYPD had enough people to find one man at night in Central Park.

53.

The detectives were stopped at a red light on 27th Street when the dispatcher reported a possible hostage situation in Central Park. Nazareth hit the gas, and as they blew past Radio City Music Hall, flashing lights and siren parting traffic for them, Chief Crawford called on Gimble's cell phone.

"We're on our way, Chief," she yelled as Nazareth swerved around a Con Ed truck that blocked the right side of 6th Avenue.

"Just wanted you to know that this may be your boy Driscoll," he said. "The 911 call came from Angelo Dinapoli, the guy who went missing in Queens. His description of the kidnapper is a little off, but it's close. If it's Driscoll, he's lost the beard and mustache. No glasses either."

"Did Dinapoli have any idea where Driscoll was headed?" Gimble asked.

"Wherever he's going," the chief told them, "he's on foot. Dinapoli rammed the passenger side of his car into the wall on the 65th Street Transverse, and he's assuming the front end is disabled. Unless Driscoll grabs another ride, he's hoofing it."

"Chief, we need to get as many cops as possible around the lower end of the park," Nazareth said as he and Gimble approached 59th Street and the park's southernmost entrance. "If we keep him inside the park, we'll run him down. But if he gets to the street, we're going to lose him. This may be our last shot."

"Hold on," the chief told him. After 30 seconds he was back. "Okay, we'll be locking down the southern end of the park. Where are you now?"

"We just entered the park from 59th and 6th. I'm going to drive up about 300 yards and park. Unless he's already on the street, Driscoll should be somewhere between the softball fields on the west and the zoo on the east."

"What makes you think he's running south?"

"He needs to make it to the street, Chief, and running north wastes time."

Nazareth hit the brakes and pulled off Center Drive about halfway between 59th Street and the 65th Street Transverse. He left the flashers on as he locked the doors.

"We're going on foot now. Tara and I will begin working the inside of the park, but we need cops on the sidewalk ASAP."

"They're on the way, Pete."

"Sounds good. We're moving."

The two detectives drew their weapons, much to the alarm of pedestrians who had braved the cold on this night. One young guy stepped in front of his girlfriend and raised his hands.

"NYPD," Nazareth shouted. "Turn around and go back to 59th. And tell everyone you see to do the same."

"You got it," the guy said. He and his girlfriend turned and started running instead of walking.

"Which way, Pete?"

"Down here the most heavily wooded sections are over by the ball fields and around the zoo." He looked in all directions, wondering what he'd do in Driscoll's place. "He'd get off the 65th Street Transverse as soon as he could, because you've got cars going through there all the time. And I don't think he'd go near the zoo, because there are too many buildings between him and the street."

"And the skating rink," she said. "Too many people there."

"Excellent point. So my guess is . . . ."

"Someplace near Umpire Rock," Gimble said. "If you draw a straight line between Columbus Circle and the spot where he abandoned the car, Umpire Rock would be right near the center."

"Then that's where we go," he said. "No flashlight unless we catch something moving."

They stepped off the pavement and cautiously entered the woods at the northern edge of the Heckscher Playground. During the day the playground was a place where city kids enjoyed themselves swinging or sliding or climbing with their friends. At night, however -- especially a cold, overcast December night -- it was a forbidding stretch where ominous black trunks and overgrown thickets were overly inviting to a madman with bad intentions. To the untrained eye Nazareth and Gimble might have been mistaken for the hunters, but they knew better. All Driscoll needed to do was sit and wait for them to walk by. They had bullseyes on their chests.

But they didn't expect Driscoll to be lurking in the bushes. His only chance, they reasoned, was to get out of the park as quickly as possible, then either steal a car or maybe grab a bus at the Port Authority Terminal. So they moved steadily toward the landmark Umpire Rock, a half-billion-year-old colossus of bedrock 150 feet across and more than feet high.

When they were about 50 yards away, they both spotted the movement. It seemed to be the silhouette of a man's head and shoulders poking out of a large crevice near the top of the rock. They watched as several times the shape disappeared into the crevice, then reappeared, as though whoever was up there was on the lookout.

"Would he really be dumb enough to climb up there when every cop in New York City is after him?" Gimble whispered.

"If he plans to go out in a blaze of glory," Nazareth replied, "maybe that's how he'd do it. Try to take a few of us with him."

"Well wherever he's going, you can bet your ass he'll be traveling alone."

"Agreed. How about you work your way around to the left," he said, "while I come in from the trees on the right. In precisely two minutes we begin moving toward the rock. When we get there, you go up the left side, and I'll take the right. One of us should have a clear shot if necessary."

"Got it," she said. "Clock begins . . . now."

The overcast night was a mixed blessing. It made it easier for them to sneak up on whoever was atop the rock, but it also provided excellent cover for someone who might be stalking them among the trees. So they kept their eyes open and their fingers on the triggers. Gimble had the simpler approach because there were fewer trees on her side of the rock. But this also meant she would be more exposed during her final sprint and would make the better target if Driscoll saw them coming.

They were both in position with time to spare and waited for the seconds to tick away. Four, three, two, one . . . and they ran toward Umpire Rock, a natural structure so immense that climbers actually came here to practice their skills. Fortunately for the detectives the rock also had a long sloped face that anyone could easily walk up.

Gimble froze when she saw the silhouette appear again. Whoever it was seemed to look right at her, then slowly sank back into the crevice out of sight. All clear. As soon as the two detectives stood across from each other at the base of the rock, Nazareth signalled toward their goal. They crouched low and silently began hiking up the steep incline toward their target. The rock's ragged face made a nighttime ascent extremely hazardous. One misstep could easily produce a broken leg or worse, while a patch of ice might lead to a disastrous fall from this height.

Again the silhouette appeared, seemed to face directly toward Gimble, then turned away. This time as soon as the person turned his back, Nazareth lit up the top of Umpire Rock with a tactical flashlight whose powerful beam was capable of carrying 300 yards. At less than 10 yards the light was blinding, and the young guy who stood in front of them covered his eyes with his hands and began yelling.

"Turn it off, man! Who the hell is that?"

"NYPD," Nazareth called. "Put your hands on top of your head. Do it now!"

Nazareth lowered the light, and the guy opened his eyes.

"We're coming up. Do not move," Nazareth said. "Do you understand?"

"Yeah, I understand. But I wasn't doing anything."

The guy looked to be in his early twenties and went maybe 6-1 and 160 pounds. Nazareth frisked the guy while Gimble scanned the crevice and saw that he had been building himself a nest for the night - - a foot or more of dried leaves topped by a length of canvas most likely pulled from a dumpster.

"What's your name?" Gimble asked.

"Ted Settles," he said.

"Address?"

"This was supposed to be it for tonight," he said. "Now, who knows?"

"Homeless," Nazareth said.

"Yeah, for sure," Settles answered.

"What drugs are you on?" Nazareth asked.

"No drugs, no booze," he answered. "Also no home, no food, and no job."

"Let me see your arms."

Settles pulled up the sleeves of a well-worn U.S. Army camouflage jacket with his name above the right pocket, and Nazareth checked the guy's arms with the flashlight.

"No tracks," he nodded. "That's good."

"Told you, man. No drugs, no booze."

"And no food," Nazareth nodded. "Right?"

"Yeah, and no food."

"You former military?" Nazareth asked.

"Army, two years in the desert," he nodded. "I should have stayed there."

Nazareth searched an inside pocket of his jacket and came out with three items: his NYPD business card, a sheet listing homeless shelters operated by the Department of Homeless Services, and a $10 bill.

"There's a McDonald's on 56th near 8th," he told Settles. "Go there and get something to eat. Then hit one of these shelters for the night. If you're serious about wanting a job, call me tomorrow. I have a friend who's big on hiring vets. If you don't call me, I can't help."

Settles looked from Nazareth to Gimble and back.

"You do this with every homeless guy you meet? If so, you must be about broke."

Nazareth shook his head. "Hardly ever do it. But I also hardly ever run across a street guy who's not stoned and who happens to be former military. Ball's in your court now. You want help, call me."

"I'll take you up on that." Settles smiled for the first time. "And I appreciate this. I really do. God bless you both." He shook their hands, hurried off the rock, and made tracks for Columbus Circle.

"So does he buy hamburgers," Gimble asked, "or does he buy two bottles of Thunderbird?"

"My money's on the burgers, but we'll know better tomorrow."

"If he calls."

"Yeah. And I think he will. But in the meantime," he said, "let's zigzag our way over toward Central Park West. Let's hope the chief has the park sealed off down here so that Driscoll doesn't stroll off among the Christmas shoppers."

"Better idea," she said. "You zigzag left toward Central Park West while I zigzag right toward the 65th Street Transverse. Then we meet where the two roads come together. If he's still down in this area, we corner him."

He nodded, then reached over and squeezed her shoulder. They walked off the rock and went their separate ways in the dark.

54.

With intense interest Driscoll studied Nazareth and Gimble as he crouched behind the softball bleachers less than 200 feet from Umpire Rock, and he couldn't believe his good fortune when they walked off in opposite directions. He had been carefully maneuvering toward Columbus Circle when Nazareth's bright flashlight had stopped him in his tracks, and he had watched quietly as the two detectives hassled some homeless guy. A smile rose to his lips when he got a clear look at the female detective's face.

Thank you God, he thought, for giving me a second chance to get rid of that bitch.

He stayed low to the ground while creeping through the dense woods adjoining Umpire Rock, and his heart began racing when he saw Gimble slowly and blindly move in his direction. He knelt on one knee in a clump of tall shrubs, checked that the Glock's safety was off, and trained the gun on the detective's midsection. Even if she were wearing a Kevlar vest the force of the shot would put her on her back, leaving her helpless as he calmly walked up and took his revenge. She's the one who had put him in this desperate position, and she would now pay for that with her life.

Gimble popped in and out of view as she prowled among the shadows. Driscoll calculated that the next time she moved to her left she would be no more than 15 feet from his position. He was no expert marksman, but at that distance he could put a round in her gut every time.

His gun hand was perfectly steady. Despite the chill and the police who hunted him, he was on top of his game. Not long ago these two detectives had put the fear of God in him, but now he was the one totally in control. How quickly the right man can adapt when the pressure is on, he thought. When you've got the right stuff you grow stronger in battle, and on this night his fear had been miraculously transformed into steel-hard determination.

He was focused. He was ready. He was invincible.

Gimble, he noticed, was making a fatal mistake. Instead of keeping her eyes focused on the darkness ahead of her, she kept looking high and low in all directions. And each time she did so the streetlights that lined the walking paths completely wiped out her night vision. She was walking toward a bullet and couldn't have seen Driscoll if he had stood up and waved to her.

She held her weapon in front of her with both hands, barrel angled downward, as she approached Driscoll's makeshift hunting blind. When she was no more than 20 feet away she unwittingly turned her torso directly toward him. He raised his gun, aimed just north of her hips, and held his breath -- all steady now -- as he slowly began to squeeze the trigger.

"That's lame!" someone yelled from behind him. Driscoll spun and fired blindly, hitting the left thigh of a young woman who had been strolling toward the ice skating rink with two of her friends. All three had been horsing around as they approached, but Driscoll had been so focused on his prey that he hadn't heard anything until one of them had playfully shouted at the others.

The young woman who had taken the bullet collapsed on the pavement screaming while her two girlfriends ran in opposite directions. Driscoll quickly looked back toward Gimble just as she hit the button on her UV flashlight, lighting up his dye-covered face like a neon billboard. Before she could line up a shot, Driscoll bolted toward the 65th Street Transverse, firing two wild shots over his shoulder as he ran. He nearly tripped over the wounded young woman and in his blind rage momentarily considered shooting her again. But the sound of Gimble crashing through the undergrowth drove him off.

As she approached the injured woman Gimble speed-dialed Nazareth's cell phone.

"Is that gunfire, Tara?" he yelled.

"It's him, Pete. Shot a girl on the walkway just opposite Umpire Rock. She needs help, so I can't go after the son of a bitch. He's headed toward the transverse."

"On my way," he said.

Gimble knelt next to the young woman and examined the gunshot wound. The bullet had struck the center of her upper thigh, and she was in bad shape -- a weak, rapid heartbeat along with heavy sweating, two clear signs of shock. Gimble pulled one of the heavy socks from the ice skates that the victim had been carrying and used it to apply pressure to the wound. There was nothing else she could do now. Saving the young woman trumped chasing Driscoll.

By the time Nazareth reached Gimble's position the young woman's two friends had returned. Each of them had called 911 to report the shooting, as had Nazareth, so in a matter of minutes five NYPD cruisers were parked alongside them and two ambulances were rolling up. Gimble quickly told the arriving officers what had gone down.

"I guarantee you he's not hitting the street anywhere around here," Officer Ron Vincent told her. "We've got cops on the sidewalks around the whole southern end of the park."

"Then he'll go north," Nazareth said angrily. "Which means he's got from here to 110th Street to hide out or hit the sidewalk and vanish forever."

"There's no way we can lock down the whole park," Vincent said.

"True enough," Nazareth said. "So we need to run his ass down while he's still inside. I need four of you to come with Detective Gimble and me. We'll cross the 65th Street Transverse, fan out, and work our way north. Officer Vincent, let command know what's going on, and get word to Chief Crawford that we need as many cops as possible on both Fifth Avenue and Central Park West."

"Done."

"Okay," Nazareth said. "Let's move."

55.

Driscoll scrambled north through the woods alongside Center Drive. He didn't know much about Central Park, but he was familiar enough with the southern end that he planned to stay as far as possible from 5th Avenue to the east and the broad open field across from the Tavern on the Green to the west. The best escape route, he reasoned, lay somewhere beyond 100th Street -- roughly 35 blocks away -- since by now the police would surely have the park's southern section sealed off. Traveling the woods under the cover of darkness would be a piece of cake. Besides, he had 12 rounds left in his Glock, more than enough to handle any potential impediments he might encounter along the way.

The hills were punishing. No matter which way he went he found another hill in front of him. When he was no longer able to run he began walking at a brisk, steady pace. The police would follow him, of course, but they would need to move slowly, fearful of an ambush. He was greatly amused by the thought of his pursuers tiptoeing among the shadows, hands shaking, as they pursued the fabled RTS Killer and the massive firepower he commanded. Although things hadn't gone quite the way he had planned, he had learned a great deal about himself on this day. The police had challenged his manhood, provoking his heroic response, and after tonight he would surely fear no man.

Sirens far to his right. The police were speeding up Madison Avenue, no doubt planning to cut over to 5th Avenue via 77th or 79th. They would try to intercept him someplace up there. Naturally. But he knew the police didn't have the manpower to search every square foot of the huge park, and that's what they would need to do if they hoped to capture him. He occupied no more than one square foot of turf in an expanse of nearly 900 acres. One square foot amid 39 million square feet! The odds of finding him were laughably, absurdly low. He could hide for hours, thoroughly concealed by the woods, thickets, and deep shadows of the night. No way the police would devote their entire force to one man until sunrise. When they left, so would he. He would walk out of the park a free man and never return.

For 20 minutes he crept from tree to tree, avoiding the random Christmas-crazed New Yorkers who strolled the park's walkways in the cold, oblivious to the menacing eyes that watched them. When he reached Terrace Drive up near 72nd Street he needed to make an important decision. Should he cross the road and continue heading north? Should he attempt to leave the park on either the east or west side? Or should he hunker down where he was and let the police walk past him in the dark for the next few hours? After weighing his options he decided to cross Terrace Drive, which was closed to traffic at this hour, and travel another 10 blocks or so before seeing whether it was safe to exit his refuge.

Once across Terrace Drive he moved stealthily among the trees until he climbed the long hill toward an enormous circular concourse at whose center stood the ornate Cherry Hill Fountain and its golden spire. The area was far too exposed for his taste, so he double-timed up yet another hill to the right and reached a section of the park filled with large expanses of shrubbery. Shelter in every direction! He would remember this spot. If things got dicey up ahead, he could return here and hide for as long as necessary.

He set off down the hill to resume his journey north but quickly found himself standing dumbstruck at the shoreline of the 20-acre body of water known simply as The Lake. His eyes widened and his pulse quickened. Water everywhere! He had known there were ponds in Central Park, but he had never anticipated anything like this. Now what?

He frantically paced the shoreline until he was just able to make out a large arched shape emerging from the darkness. Driscoll had stumbled upon the Bow Bridge and, beyond it, the 38-acre section of dense woods known as The Ramble. It looked like a place where a man could hide out damn near forever, but first he needed to cross the bridge without being spotted.

He crept closer, crawled into the bushes, and waited. Five minutes. Ten. Fifteen. In all that time only three gangbangers had crossed over from The Ramble, and on a night like this he didn't expect to see many more walkers. Besides, the bridge was no more than 60 or 70 feet long. If he ran all-out he would cover the distance in 15 or 20 strides. Ten seconds or less, he figured. He liked his chances.

And if he encountered someone as he crossed over? That's why God made Glocks, he smiled.

56.

By the time Nazareth, Gimble, and the four patrolmen crossed the 65th Street Transverse to begin their search, nearly 20 minutes had passed since Driscoll had shot the young woman. Even worse, Chief Crawford called Nazareth to say it would be another 15 minutes before he could have officers posted at alternate corners between 65th Street and the 79th Street Transverse on both 5th Avenue and Central Park West. Ten officers would patrol the avenues on each side of the park, but that would leave large gaps in the coverage.

Nazareth was frustrated by the slow deployment. "In 15 minutes this guy could be long gone."

"Tell me something I don't know," Crawford replied. "It is what it is, Pete. I'll have at least 25 or 30 cops in place shortly, but they're driving, not flying. It's Christmas gridlock season."

"What about putting guys in the woods up at the 79th Street Transverse and having them move down toward us? We can squeeze this guy in a vise if he's still in the woods."

"We'll have eight ESU troops in place at 79th within 20 minutes," said Crawford. "The supervisor will call you as soon as they're ready to move out, and he'll stay in touch with you for the duration. Gotta run, Pete. Go get this guy."

Nazareth was delighted to have the search joined by the Emergency Service Unit, whose members always brought a formidable amount of training, tactical expertise, and firepower to the game. None of that would matter, of course, if Driscoll had already slipped out of the park and hit the street. But that wasn't something Nazareth could worry about now. He briefed Gimble and the four patrolmen on the chief's call, then led his team north.

Because Central Park is a half mile across, each member of the group took responsibility for a swath roughly 150 yards wide -- the length of one and a half football fields -- in the dark and against a serial killer armed with one of the most powerful handguns ever made. In the absence of unlimited manpower this was the only tactic available at the moment, but Nazareth realized it held the potential for disaster. Knowing that Gimble was part of this deadly chess game had him on edge and straining to control his emotions as he and the others crisscrossed the park, often mistaking boulders and windblown bushes for a madman with a Glock.

Nineteen minutes after his team had set out Nazareth got a call from the ESU's Sergeant Mike Bianco, who said that he and his partners would shortly begin moving south from the 79th Street Transverse.

"If he's still in here," Bianco said calmly, "we'll sniff him out, Detective."

A bright light suddenly flashed in Nazareth's head, and he cursed himself for not having seen it sooner.

"Sergeant, how fast can you get us a bloodhound? Let's sniff this son of a bitch out for real."

"No problem getting a dog," Bianco answered, "but the dog needs something to work from. Clothing is best. Do you have anything from the perp?"

"Not right this second, but it'll be here by the time you get us a dog." He called Chief Crawford and told him what he needed.

"Done. Just call me back and tell me where to have it delivered, Pete," Crawford told him.

Nazareth called Bianco back and brought him up to speed. Then he gathered his team.

"Okay, change of plans everybody. The six of us and the ESU guys up north are going to spread out and hold our positions. No more searching," he told them. "It's now strictly about containment. We make sure this guy doesn't get past us. In about 20 minutes we'll have a bloodhound joining us, along with one of Driscoll's jackets."

"The jacket that was hanging in his basement on 13th Street," Gimble said excitedly.

"That's the one. I wish to hell I'd thought of it sooner," he told them, "but I didn't. Anyway, we're almost finished with Driscoll."

"Unless," said one of the patrolmen, "he's already out of the park."

"Well, yeah, there's that," Nazareth nodded.

57.

Driscoll scrambled across the Bow Bridge and immediately veered off into the bushes on his left, tripping over a low fence and tumbling into a bed of fallen leaves and twigs, the side of his head missing the trunk of a fallen tree by less than two inches. He lay still and slowly caught his breath while scanning the walkway for any signs of unwelcome guests. Nothing. After brushing himself off he resumed his trek through the heavy woods on the lake's shoreline, now and then catching glimpses of Manhattan's West Side as it reflected on the water of The Lake. The water's edge was thick with vegetation, and it seemed to him that this was another spot where a determined man could stay hidden for as long as he wanted.

He had scarcely entertained that thought when he heard voices. And barking. He crouched in the bushes and readied his weapon.

"Max, dammit, stop! Sit!" some guy yelled.

"What's wrong with him?" a woman said nervously.

"How the hell do I know? He probably hears a frog or something."

"Frogs in December?" she asked, clearly not sold on the idea.

"Sandy, I'm not a Boy Scout. I don't know what he's barking at. Max!" he screamed. "Stop the barking."

Max was still barking when he was dragged away on his leash. As the couple walked off Driscoll heard the woman say, "There was something back there, Tony. I want to go home."

Think, Driscoll told himself. Just stop and think this through.

That's exactly what he did. He sat on a boulder in the shadows, took a long, deep breath, and coached himself to relax. Eyes closed, he thought about the couple and their dog. In that moment he realized why running in the woods had been the wrong move entirely. Good God! He desperately needed to get back onto the streets, even if the police were out there looking for him.

Would they be able to seal off the park's entire perimeter? No, of course not. He would find a way out. He *must* find a way out. Now.

Driscoll jumped to his feet when he saw lights in the woods far ahead of him. Flashlights. How many he couldn't tell, but they were shining back and forth among the trees, and they were all coming his way.

He turned and ran for the Bow Bridge.

58.

The bloodhound and his handler, Officer Larry Roszel, had to wait a few minutes before a patrolman delivered Driscoll's jacket to Nazareth at the corner of 5th Avenue and 68th Street. As soon as K9 "Rocky" had taken a few excited sniffs of the jacket he was ready to run, and Roszel led him back toward the 65th Street Transverse so that he could pick up Driscoll's trail. The dog worked quickly from side to side, oblivious to everything but the scent that had taken up residence within the 200 million olfactory cells of his remarkable nose.

Now that the bloodhound was on the scene Nazareth decided to redeploy his team. Gimble would accompany Officer Roszel, "Rocky," and one of the patrolmen, mainly because Nazareth thought she deserved to be part of the group that took the RTS Killer down. Her split lip and chipped tooth had earned her that right. But he also believed the dog's presence removed the threat of an ambush. This meant she'd be safer as part of the lead group.

Two of the patrolmen would continue searching the 65th Street area just in case Driscoll had decided to hide out there. Then he sent one of the other officers over to patrol the boundary along Central Park West, while he took the 5th Avenue boundary for himself. The more eyes on the sidewalk, he reasoned, the less likely it was that Driscoll could escape the park if -- a big *if* -- the guy hadn't already done so.

The ESU team, meanwhile, would continue working its way south from the 79th Street Transverse. Nazareth expected one of two outcomes. Either Driscoll would be trapped between the ESU group and Gimble's team, or he would bolt to the sidewalk and be spotted by the officers stationed along the two main avenues. Unless the killer had already disappeared into the streets of Manhattan, they would soon take him down.

What bothered Nazareth most was not knowing how Driscoll would choose to go. The guy faced life in prison, so killing a cop while attempting to escape wouldn't bother him in the least. In fact, he might rather die than be captured, since prison life would be especially gruesome for someone who had been slaughtering immigrants. As Nazareth began hiking the woods along 5th Avenue he prayed that he and Gimble would both walk out of the park alive tonight.

Less than five minutes later Gimble called him on his cell phone and said that "Rocky" had jumped all over Driscoll's scent and was leading the team north.

"This is unbelievable to watch," she told him. "The dog picked up his scent not far from where he shot the girl, and now Roszel can hardly hold him back."

"Bloodhounds are amazing creatures, Tara," he said. "If Driscoll is still in here, you're going to nail him. Just keep that UV flashlight ready, and make sure your safety is off."

"Done and done."

The dog was all over Driscoll's trail, and to Gimble this was nothing short of a miracle.

"How can the dog follow Driscoll's footprints after just smelling his jacket?" she asked Roszel as they trotted behind "Rocky."

"What he's mostly picking up is the scent of the perp's skin cells, believe it or not. We each lose about 40,000 skin cells per hour," he explained, "and that's what the bloodhound follows. It can also pick up the scent of breath and sweat, so running is pointless. Your guy might as well sit down and wait for us."

"Actually that's what I'm afraid of," she said soberly. "This guy doesn't care about killing, and I have no idea what he'll do if we come face to face."

"We'll shoot him before he shoots us," said Roszel. "Three guns to one is my kind of math."

The three officers continued to trot behind "Rocky" as they approached Terrace Drive at 72nd Street. It was clear that Driscoll had stuck close to Center Drive, which splits the park from north to south, and to Gimble this was a very good sign indeed. Their guy hadn't gone to the street. At the same time she worried about an ambush.

She didn't want to die just before Christmas.

59.

Driscoll was moving fast and fighting for breath as he bolted across the Bow Bridge, heading south again toward the Cherry Hill Fountain, retracing his steps and praying that he had made the right call. Just before reaching land he stopped, zipped the gun in his jacket, and with both hands hauled himself up and over the railing on the bridge's left side. He landed feet first in 18 inches of frigid water on The Lake's eastern shoreline, then stumbled through a dark maze of rocks, weeds, and muck for nearly 200 feet until he reached a thick stand of low shrubs that had retained much of their foliage despite winter's approach.

He had rolled the dice. Now it was time to sit, wait, and hope that he hadn't screwed up royally.

He tried and failed to focus on something other than his throbbing feet and soaked pants until he heard Gimble's team on Cherry Hill not far from where he crouched in the bushes at the water's edge. They had tracked his original path and, if things went his way, would soon find their way to the Bow Bridge. He waited, gun braced in both hands, shivering in the icy wind that blew hard from the west. And then he saw them: three cops trotting behind a dog, just as he had anticipated. If it hadn't been for that barking mutt earlier, he would never have thought about a bloodhound. But he *had* thought of it. And that, he assured himself, is what separates the men from the boys. The ability to stand tall and think clearly under pressure is ultimately the difference between a winner and a loser.

Despite the cold he felt sweat pouring off him as the dog approached the bridge, stopped to sniff the archway, then scurried toward The Ramble . . . and a major dead end. By the time the dog finished running circles through the woods, Driscoll would be long gone.

His plan now was to work his way carefully back to the trees alongside Terrace Drive, then slip onto 5th Avenue wherever he didn't see a cop. But things needed to happen quickly. He had to be out of the woods long before the dog picked up his trail again.

Ten minutes later, on feet and legs so cold he could barely move them, Driscoll neared the intersection of Terrace Drive and East Drive, less than 100 yards from 5th Avenue. Still hidden by shadows, he pulled out his cell phone, dialed 911, and waited for the dispatcher.

"911," the woman answered.

"I just saw a man with a gun running out of Central Park," he said breathlessly. "He ran across 5th Avenue and down 68th Street." Before the woman was able to respond he added, "Oh, man, he just shot a cop on 68th!" Then he hung up.

In less than two minutes he heard the sirens screaming down 5th Avenue, and he imagined every cop within 10 blocks running toward their fallen comrade on 68th Street. Driscoll shoved the Glock in his pocket and began walking casually toward 5th Avenue.

He was a free man.

60.

Nazareth held his gun in front of him as he deftly moved from tree to tree near 71st Street. Less than 100 feet to his right a succession of squad cars roared down 5th Avenue and turned onto 68th, but he was focused on the woods ahead. He now had this entire section of the park to himself because the officers on the street were keeping everyone else out. This meant that any movement he spotted could be as harmless as leaves blowing in the wind . . . or as deadly as the RTS Killer choosing to kill a cop rather than be captured.

Advantage Driscoll. He could shoot anyone he wanted, while the detective could fire on only one man. A moment of hesitation in the darkness might cost him his life.

Nazareth would have continued walking the park's eastern perimeter if he had known that his fellow officers had abandoned the Terrace Drive/72nd Street intersection to hunt for a nonexistent cop killer on 68th Street. But since he assumed 5th Avenue was covered, he cut to his left and crossed East Drive. While skirting the Rumsey Playfield concert area and moving west he spotted someone strolling along Terrace Drive less than 200 feet away. A heavyset man with his hands thrust in his pockets walked intently toward 5th Avenue, presumably after enjoying a brisk evening walk in Central Park. Had the guy not been warned away by the police?

"Good evening," Nazareth called. "NYPD. Can I speak with you for a moment?"

The guy calmly looked over toward Nazareth, caught his silhouette against the streetlight on East Drive, and pulled the gun from his right pocket. Driscoll fired two rounds as the detective dove for cover behind a boulder. When Nazareth cautiously peered around the rock he saw Driscoll running for the trees near the large outdoor bandshell where New Yorkers assembled for their summer concerts.

Gunfire, not Brahms, is all anyone would hear tonight.

Nazareth raced from tree to tree, trusting that Driscoll would keep moving rather than stop to fire, and grabbed his phone when Gimble called.

"It's him, Tara. Fired two rounds and took off. He's heading toward the bandshell," he yelled.

"I'm on my way south, Pete," she told him. "I just passed the Bethesda Fountain coming up on Terrace."

"Tara, no!" he screamed just as he heard another shot fired.

"Son of a bitch!" Gimble howled. "He just took a chunk out of the tree next to my head."

"Stay the hell down, Tara. He's out to kill someone. Can you see him?"

"He was just in the trees right ahead of me," she said. "Now I don't, wait, he's running."

Nazareth took off in what he hoped was the right direction. No way Driscoll could fire accurately if he was on the move, so this was the time to take him down. Although the detective was no longer a sub-four-minute miler, he still had serious speed and closed the distance in a heartbeat.

"Down, Pete, down!" Gimble screamed into her phone, and he hit the dirt as three more rounds hammered into nearby trees.

"I've got him in sight, Tara," he whispered. "He's crouched behind the base of the war memorial flagpole."

"That's directly in front of me, maybe 50 yards," she told him.

"Where are the guys who were with you?"

"They just got here, Pete. And the ESU team is now on scene."

"Tell them all to hold their positions," he said. "Look over to your left, Tara. I'm going to give you a quick burst with the light on my cell phone. Here goes."

"Got it."

"Okay, make sure they know where the hell I am, and then ask the ESU supervisor leader how he wants to play this."

At that moment she saw Driscoll step from behind the monument and raise his arms.

61.

Driscoll felt nauseous from the cold. His feet were ice blocks. His knees no longer wanted to bend. His fingers ached. His heart pounded out of his chest.

He sat with his back to the war memorial, whose inscription read:

IN COMMEMORATION OF
THE HEROISM AND SACRIFICES
OF THE CITY EMPLOYEES
WHO FOUGHT IN THE VARIOUS WARS
OF THE UNITED STATES

He wondered whether he should laugh or cry. Here he was, a true patriot and soldier in what he believed was the most important war in U.S. history, being hunted like a rat in the night. Cold, aching, tired . . . yet still loyal to the cause. America was being overrun by foreigners. And while others hid behind bolted doors in their fancy brownstones or expensive mahogany desks in their Washington offices, he was out here spilling blood on the battlefield. He had fought this war for them, for his country, for his parents and grandparents. And he had been condemned for it.

The rage seethed deep within him, a supervolcano ready to erupt and obliterate everyone and everything around it. If being hunted in the night was the ultimate injustice, then cowering behind this monument to heroes was the ultimate indignity. Enough! He would cower no longer.

He kissed the fingers of his left hand, touched them to the monument, and stood as he raised both arms in victory. Then he charged Gimble's position, emptying his Glock on the way.

"Tara!" Nazareth screamed when he saw what was happening. He squeezed off only one round before Gimble and her team had come into his line of fire. There was nothing more he could do.

By the time the shooting ended, Driscoll had taken 12 rounds to the body. The ME would later verify that the one bullet placed in Driscoll's head had been fired by Detective Pete Nazareth.

62.

The cardinal on the birdfeeder seemed not to notice that snowflakes were settling gently on its brilliant red feathers as it pecked away at the cache of sunflower seeds. Another eight inches of white stuff so far today, and the forecast called for another two feet by the time the storm ended.

Gimble watched from a large bay window overlooking a frozen lake amid the White Mountains.

"How do you suppose one solitary cardinal can find one solitary birdfeeder in thousands of square miles of wilderness?" she asked.

"You're the detective, Tara," Nazareth said as he tossed another log into the immense stone fireplace. The wood was wonderfully dry and exploded in flame atop the glowing coals that had accumulated throughout the day. Sparks flew in all directions, and the crackling of the log echoed throughout the great room with its 30-foot ceiling.

"Uh, so are you, Pete."

"Yeah, but I'm on vacation," he smiled. "The detective part of my brain never works when I'm on vacation."

"Fair enough. But can you file the question away and answer it when we're back in Manhattan?"

"*When?*" he grinned. "With all this snow maybe it's a question of *whether* we go back to Manhattan. Maybe we'll be here until June."

"I could handle that."

"So could I as a matter of fact."

After spending Christmas Day with friends and family, the detectives had driven off for their fantasy vacation -- a modern log home fit for royalty on 20 mountainous acres in the deep woods of New Hampshire. They had found the rental online and fallen in love with the gorgeous timber interior, the expansive chef-ready kitchen, the staggering view, and the forest -- 20 acres of their own snowy woodlands where the only sound was that of their own footsteps.

That morning they had spent two hours in the woods shooting wildlife. No guns. Just the fancy Canon PowerShot superzoom digital camera that Nazareth had given his fiancee for Christmas. Months back, when they had first met each other on the job, Gimble had mentioned her childhood dream of being a nature photographer. Now she could be, if only as a hobbyist. Like Nazareth, she was hooked on what she did for a living.

Their long fireside conversations never touched on Ryan Driscoll. They had put the RTS Killer case behind them, as they needed to do if they were going to maintain their sanity in this business. Driscoll had been the worst-case scenario: an intelligent misfit who blamed others for everything that was wrong with the world and his own life.

Nazareth and Gimble would never know what had finally lit the fuse in a seemingly normal guy. They also wouldn't waste time speculating. They were cops, not psychologists, psychiatrists, psychotherapists, or philosophers. Only one thing was certain: Ryan Driscoll was not the last mad dog in the pack.

Nazareth fired up the gas grill that the cabin's owner had conveniently placed under an overhang out back and expertly prepared their New Year's Eve main course: grilled Maine lobster tails, large sea scallops, and juicy littleneck clams. Not to be outdone, Gimble served up a classy roasted-vegetable risotto featuring broccoli, asparagus tips, Brussels sprouts, and cremini mushrooms. Dinner lasted nearly two hours and was accompanied by a bottle of 2008 Russian River Valley chardonnay.

They spent the next three hours in front of the fireplace. Nazareth relaxed in a large leather recliner and savored every word of Stephen King's *Mr. Mercedes,* while Gimble curled up on the overstuffed sofa with *At the Edge of the Orchard,* the latest book from her favorite author, Tracy Chevalier. At 11:30 they turned on the huge flat-screen TV for the first time since they had arrived and watched the enormous crowd pretending to enjoy the icy wind that roared across Times Square.

"Did you ever go to Times Square to watch the ball drop, Tara?"

"Thought about it once," she smiled, "but never actually did it. How about you?"

"Yeah, once when I was in college. One of the worst nights of my life. Ten degrees, windy, snowy . . . oh, yeah, and had my wallet stolen," he grimaced. "Wonderful experience."

"This is the best place I've ever watched from," she told him.

"I'll drink to that."

At precisely midnight, as the dazzling ball showered its light over Manhattan, Nazareth popped the cork on a split of fine champagne and poured a glass for each of them.

"To us, and to love," he said softly.

She kissed him. "And to a new year filled with peace."

63.

"This here is one lovely piece," the dealer assured him. He smiled broadly as he handed the rifle over for closer inspection. "Mossberg MVP Patrol, bolt-action, takes 5.56 NATO ammo, and will gladly accept a 30-round magazine."

"The scope comes with it?" the young guy asked.

"Yessir. I outfit all my long guns with scopes," he told him. "But if you don't want it, I can take something off the price."

"No, I definitely need the scope."

Twenty-year-old Stone Jackson lovingly ran his hands over the weapon's smooth, graceful curves, raised the stock to his shoulder, and put the crosshairs on a red- white-and-blue banner that hung from the ceiling at the crowded gun show. *The right of the people to keep and bear arms shall not be infringed*, it read. A treasured line from the state's constitution.

"This is the one," Jackson nodded. And that was that. Buying a weapon in South Carolina was as good as it gets, he thought. See it. Buy it. Lock and load.

He set the rifle gently in the trunk of his 12-year-old Honda and drove off. *Scout-sniper Stone Dross*. Had a nice ring to it.

This was definitely going to be one hell of a happy new year.

CPSIA information can be obtained at www.ICGtesting.com
Printed in the USA
BVOW06s0324070316

439268BV00002B/1/P